ZEROBOXER

ZEROBOXER

FONDA LEE

flux
®
Woodbury, Minnesota

First Edition
First Printing, 2015

Book design by Steffani Sawyer
Cover design by Kevin Brown
Cover illustration: Dominick Finelle/ The July Group

Flux, an imprint of Llewellyn Worldwide Ltd.

Library of Congress Cataloging-in-Publication Data
Lee, Fonda.
  Zeroboxer / Fonda Lee.—First edition.
      pages cm
  Summary: "As seventeen-year-old Carr 'the Raptor' Luka rises to fame in the weightless combat sport of zeroboxing, he learns a devastating secret that jeopardizes not only his future in the sport, but interplanetary relations"—Provided by publisher.
  ISBN 978-0-7387-4338-7
  [1. Boxing—Fiction. 2. Fame—Fiction. 3. Secrets—Fiction. 4. Conduct of life—Fiction. 5. Science fiction.] I. Title.
  PZ7.1.L395Zer 2015
  [Fic]—dc23
                                                              2014045398

Flux
Llewellyn Worldwide Ltd.
2143 Wooddale Drive
Woodbury, MN 55125-2989
www.fluxnow.com

For Nathan.
My cornerman, always.

PART ONE
RISING STAR

ONE

Carr Luka woke from a nap three hours before his fight. He ate two hardboiled eggs, a handful of raw almonds, and a bran muffin, then drank a bottle of water and spent twenty minutes stretching on the floor of his single-room apartment in the inner ring of Valtego Station.

The Moon's desolate, pock-marked dark side loomed large across the upper right corner of his wallscreen. Beyond it, the sunlit blue and white marble of Earth hung suspended in the vast black infinity of space. It wasn't a real view of course—probably not even a live feed, just an old recording. The real views belonged to the expensive premium suites, reserved for Valtego's high rollers. They were betting 3:1 against him, as of yesterday.

He didn't usually follow odds, but Uncle Polly had fake-casually dropped that tidbit on him, angling to amp him up, get the *I'll show those bastards* juice flowing. It had worked all right—not because he cared that some bettors thought he might be a flame-out, but because he hated to think that, after the disaster of his most recent match, Uncle Polly might secretly agree with them. Other promising young fighters had been broken by an early loss; he certainly wouldn't be the first.

Carr stood, shaking out his limbs and reaching for his warm-up clothes. He didn't need to be reminded of the stakes. He'd been on the city space station for a year and a half. This sixth and final fight in his contract would determine whether he landed a new deal or found himself on the next flight back to Earth, relegated to fighting in orbital dives reeking of pot, where the vacuum plumbing regularly gave out and big bubbles of pee floated in the bathrooms.

He made a face; not about to happen. He was no planet rat.

Carr tapped the cuff-link display on his forearm to play something high energy—the neo-urban skid music that was popular earthside these days—as he packed his bag. Gripper gloves and shoes, cup, mouth guard, fight shorts, a towel, a change of clothes for the press conference and after-party. He zipped up the bag and slung it over his shoulder. After a final look around to make sure he hadn't forgotten anything, he stepped out of his room and navigated the halls of the apartment complex up to the main thoroughfare and into Valtego traffic.

The streets were crowded, echoing cavernously with the noise of people and music and cars. Well-dressed couples, families, and packs of young men and women spilled onto the main concourse. When Carr looked up, past the reddish simulated evening light, through the enormous sky windows and into the docking hub, he could see that even more ships had arrived since yesterday. Half a dozen Earth-Mars cargo cyclers, a few private solar-sailing yachts, and plenty of commercial passenger craft. It was one of those times when summer in Earth's northern hemisphere coincided with dust storm season on Mars, inciting residents of both planets to travel. Super high season on Valtego.

He caught the city-station bus as it pulled up with a pneumatic hiss, its silver body flashing the usual promotional banner: *Valtego: It's More Fun on the Dark Side™*. Carr didn't bother to sit down; he was only taking it a few stops. He stood near the door, closed his eyes, and let the burble of voices from the other passengers float around him. He heard English in American, British, and Martian accents, Mandarin, Mars Hindi, Spanish, and German. In his mind, he turned the hum of conversation into a growing swell of cheering, a thunderous crowd calling his name.

His cuff vibrated and a rising chime played in his ear. He glanced down at the display on his forearm, then smiled, shut off the music, and took the call. "Enzo," he said. "Are you going to watch my fight?"

"No, I happen to be hiding in my closet with my screen, under a blanket, for no reason. OF COURSE I'm watching!" Enzo's voice, transmission-delayed by a couple seconds, sounded, in Carr's cochlear receiver, as if the boy was shout-whispering an urgent secret. "My mom is going to go fusion if she finds me." He gave a wheezy, excited cough. There was a pause, and Carr winced, picturing the boy sucking hard on his inhaler.

"Aren't you supposed to be in school?" Carr asked.

"Whatever. School is useless. You barely went."

"Sure I went," he lied. "And I was tutored." Which was true, if you could call Uncle Polly helping him fudge through remote study modules "tutoring." "Besides, *you've* got to make a living using your brain someday."

The boy gave a long sigh. "It's so unfair." He sounded as morose as he had when Carr had first left for Valtego. Carr felt a pang of worry. Now wasn't the time to question the kid, but Enzo was small, he didn't have many friends; who was watching out for him, spending time with him, now that Carr was living in deep orbit on the far side of the Moon? Carr wouldn't trade his place here for anything, but Enzo was one of the few things he missed about Earth.

The bus left behind the rows of densely packed apartment-entrance tubes provided for Valtego's less wealthy residents. It passed shops and restaurants catering to visitors from the planet before turning and sliding to a stop at the gravity zone terminal. The doors opened onto a wide platform bustling with people and lined with colorful holovid ads promising the best deals on theater tickets, spacewalks, hotels.

"I wish you could see this place," Carr said. "It's something else. I'm going to bring you up here someday and show you around." *If I'm still here after today*, came the unwelcome reminder.

"Would you? That would be so stellar," Enzo whispered. "Oh shit, I think my mom is home. Okay, I just called to say good luck! Make him float!"

"Thanks, little man."

The connection clicked out as Carr stepped onto the terminal platform. Uncle Polly and DK were waiting for him, looking comically mismatched standing together—old, pale, and lean, next to young, dark, and muscled. DK clapped Carr on the back. Uncle Polly put his hands on Carr's shoulders and broke into a slow, approving smile that made his left eye squint. "You're a hundred percent ready," he said.

On fight days, Uncle Polly underwent a magical transformation. Every other day, he could chew Carr out in practice, find fault in every detail, cuss at him if he wasn't pushing hard enough, but on fight day, he was optimism incarnate. Carr felt himself grinning, buoyed.

"Where would you rather be right now?" Uncle Polly demanded.

"Nowhere, coach."

"What would you rather be doing?"

"Nothing, coach."

"You ready to fly?"

"Hell yeah."

"Get in the car."

He strapped his duffel bag into the overhead compartment before climbing in. Once everyone was seated, the harness straps tightened and the doors closed. The vehicle shot down the freeway tube—one of several that connected

Valtego's rings with the central zero gravity complex like spokes of a wheel. Carr ran an appreciative hand across the smooth tan upholstery of his seat. He took the commuter bus to the zero-g complex every morning, but the routine trip was far more enjoyable in a private car. Another special fight-day perk.

Streets and buildings shrank as the view of Valtego spread out around them in all its slowly turning immensity, the bright lights and artificial gravity of the city's habitable rings receding as the freeway sailed the car into a breathtaking expanse of space. Carr craned his neck against the mild g-force pressure, looking past the shadow of the Moon and catching, for a few seconds, a glimpse of Earth—a real view, not a projection. The planet always looked smaller in real life than on the wallscreen.

Uncle Polly ran through the game plan once more. "What are you going to do in the first round?"

"Stay out of his grab zone. Wear him out, frustrate him."

"He doesn't like to climb. Make him climb. Second round?"

"Hit him from the corners. Use my fast launches and rebounds."

"Good, good."

"Third round, spin him hard and finish him off."

"You got it. What's your strength against him?"

"My space ear."

"Always fear the better ear! You're ready."

Uncle Polly was not really Carr's uncle. He wasn't even

old, maybe sixty-something, but he was scrawny and bent-backed from a career spent on mining ships and in orbital gyms during a generation when zero gravity alleviation therapy wasn't what it was today and so many years in space took a heavy toll on one's body. He had a full head of short gray hair and a permanently grizzled jaw. But he moved and spoke with the fire of a younger man, and when he slapped his hands on his thighs, he radiated confidence like a solar flare.

The zero gravity complex, recently renamed the Virgin Galactic Center, loomed ahead of them. As the vehicle slowed, the familiar transition to weightlessness tugged at Carr's stomach, pressed his chest against the harness, and drew his limbs upward. They glided past a group of tourists on a beginner-level spacewalk, the suited figures cycling arms and legs slowly and awkwardly as their guide coaxed them along with gentle bursts of his thrusters, like a shepherd leading a herd of nervous farm animals.

The car docked in the parking hold. Carr drifted up to retrieve his bag and pushed it ahead with one hand while unclasping his belt tether and hooking it around the hallway guide-rail with the other. It was an irritating requirement; he could easily climb this place free-floating and blindfolded, but there was a fine if you were caught untethered, even if you were a Valtego resident. Management didn't want anyone setting a bad example for the tourists and seasonal workers, who might hurt themselves crashing into things or get stranded in the middle of a room and create extra work for the maintenance folks who'd have to rescue them.

DK tethered himself and tilted his head to one side, listening. "You hear that?"

Already, the low thrum of a crowd was growing over the steady whoosh of vehicles docking, one after the other. Distant loud music began pulsing through the thick walls of the parking hold. DK smiled, showing small, brilliant white teeth against tropical bronze skin. "Full house tonight, I'll wager. All here to see you, kid."

That wasn't exactly true; the headline fight was between Danyo "Fear Factor" Fukiyama and Jorge "Monster" Rillard, but DK had told Carr that his match had the most hype he'd ever seen for the undercard. Of course, maybe DK was just saying that to pump him up. DK was not a large man—a natural feathermass—and he looked slightly rodent-like with his big ears and fists, large eyes, and small nose, but he exuded a gregarious charisma that was rare in this sport. He was also one of the best young zeroboxers anywhere. His full name was Danilo Kabitain, but no one called him that. He was DK to his flymates, "Captain Pain" to his opponents and the media, and a hell of a man to have in one's corner.

They climbed along the hallway using the evenly spaced rungs, turned right, and passed through the athletes' entrance. The locker room and adjoining warm-up space were empty except for two men. One of them was seated on a bench, feet hooked under the stabilizing rod, elbows on knees, broad shoulders hunched forward. He looked as if the universe had just ended.

"What's the matter, Blake?" Carr asked.

"My fight's canceled." Blake Murphy didn't look up. "The other guy tested positive for endurance-enhancing nanos. Bastard."

"Damn. Sorry to hear it."

Blake's trainer glanced over from where he was furiously shoving his fighter's gear into a bag. "You'll be up early then." He pointed to the small wallscreen that showed the evening's two commentators, Xeth Stone and Jeroan Culver, up on deck. Carr swiped the volume up and Xeth's energetic voice filled the locker room: "…change in lineup, it won't be long now before we see one of the most anticipated matches of the night!"

"That's right, Xeth," Jeroan replied in a straight-man monotone. "Carr Luka is still something of an enigma to this crowd. He burst onto the ZGFA scene last year, gained a strong following when he racked up four impressive wins in a row, and then choked in his last fight against 'Death' Ray Jackson. Now he's going up against the third best zeroboxer in the lowmass division, and the question on everyone's mind is, does he stand a chance of coming back against Ferrano?"

"I think he does, Jeroan," Xeth enthused. "I don't think Luka is a flash-in-the-pan like some people have been saying. I've been doing this a long time, and I tell you, it's been a while since I've seen a guy, born on Earth no less, with the kind of instincts he's shown in the Cube. That kid can *fly*. Did I mention he's still *seventeen*?"

"Sure, he can fly, but Ferrano is an expert grabber. How's he going to do against that?"

Zeroboxing commentators liked to speak of fighters as "grabbers" or "fliers." It was rather artificial, Carr thought, since any good zeroboxer had to be both, but there was some truth to the distinction. To inflict any bare-handed damage to a person in zero gravity, you had to establish a brace or a point of leverage—preferably a vulnerable part of your opponent's body—to keep them from floating away while you hurt them. Or you had to treat space itself as a weapon, using the infinite angles of movement to strike and rebound, strike and rebound, faster and harder than the other guy.

"Luka is an ace flier," Xeth agreed, "but his grabbing game is solid, and it's getting better with every match. I think we're going to see—"

Uncle Polly slashed his hand across the front of the screen to turn it off. "You heard 'em, you're up early! Get changed and warmed up!"

Carr untethered himself, then stripped out of his clothes and handed them to DK, who stuck them to the magnetic locker pegs and passed him his shorts. Uncle Polly hurried off to find the ZGFA official, a dour bulldog of a man who inspected Carr's gripper shoes and gloves and watched as DK wrapped Carr's hands. He flashed a retinal reader across Carr's eyes, checked his vital stats off his cuff—heart rate, blood pressure, and temperature—then gave him the go-ahead. "Forty minutes," he said.

"I need to take a leak," Carr said.

"Make it fast," Uncle Polly warned.

Carr climbed over to the stall and dug his feet under

the toe bar, streaming into the vacuum funnel for what felt like an eternity. Everyone said that for a young zeroboxer he was remarkably composed, never visibly nervous before fights, but his bladder knew better. Maybe that was a good sign; he hadn't been nervous enough before the last match.

The wash dispenser squirted a bubble of soapy water onto his fingers. Blake emerged from one of the other stalls and pulled himself over to the neighboring dispenser.

"Rotten luck," Carr said to him, feeling obligated to put in a few more words of sympathy. "You're bound to get another fight soon. At least they caught him. You wouldn't want a loss on your record because the guy cheated."

Blake looked up, his eyes like two pale blue gas fires. "Who says I would've lost?"

Carr hesitated, wiping off the water with a towel, not sure how he'd somehow given offense. "No one. But even if you won, the guy doesn't deserve to be in the Cube." It made Carr angry that some people tried to fool the system, to take shortcuts around years of time and effort. It was mentally weak.

Blake's mouth sagged a little, his eyes cooling, losing their ferocity. You never could tell with Blake. Most of the time, he was one of the most polite and soft-spoken guys Carr had ever met. But in a fight ... well, he wasn't nick-named "the Destroyer" for nothing. As he turned to leave, he looked back at Carr and said, "Good luck out there. Stay out of those corners, yeah?"

Corners. They had never been a problem for Carr, not until his last fight, when "Death" Ray Jackson had flown him hard for two rounds, then trapped him in a corner in the third and ground it out to win in a split decision. Carr did not take losing well (who did?), especially since he was certain he could have won and had only his own overconfidence and ill-preparedness to blame.

Uncle Polly had given him hell, and he'd deserved it. He could barely look at his coach after the fight. For days, he'd felt so low he couldn't bring himself to leave his apartment. Uncle Polly had shown up on the fifth day. His face had been severe, but his voice had been kind. "It's good for you to know what it feels like on the other side, for once. Now you know. It's shit. So—you planning on whimpering back to Earth for a planet-rat job, or are you going to get off your ass?"

He'd gotten off his ass. It had taken time, though—weeks—to shake off the malaise, and he suspected the loss would stay with him forever, like a benign cyst under the skin.

Carr clambered back out to the warm-up area, shaking his head to clear away the unpleasant memory and refocus on the present. He had another chance—that was what mattered. DK helped him pull on and bind his gripper shoes. Carr wiggled each of his enclosed toes and gave a thumbs-up. He took off his cuff-link and handed it to his friend. Keeping a fighter's cuff for him during a match was an important job for the cornerman and symbolic of trust; DK put it on next to his own. Carr's gloves went on, over his wrapped hands, bound securely several inches up his forearm, leaving the wrists fully mobile. Some zeroboxers opted for the heavier gloves with more wrist support, but Carr didn't think it was worth sacrificing climbing agility.

"Thirty minutes," the official in the hallway called.

"Terran or Martian?" DK retorted, cheeky. Zeroboxing rounds were always measured in the fractionally longer Martian minutes, so it was an ongoing joke that zeroboxers had no sense of standard Terran time.

"Get moving," Uncle Polly said. "You know the drill—five times around the room, then wall-bounces."

Carr swung into the square warm-up room and jogged the walls, up, down, and around, exerting himself just enough to raise his heart rate. There was a lumpy target dummy secured to the center of the room with cable wiring; he launched off a wall, somersaulted to strike the target with both feet, and rebounded to another wall. He worked the dummy from each wall and corner, and in the last five minutes, Uncle Polly called him back down for a brief recovery. Carr was warm now, just beginning to feel a sweat. Uncle Polly drifted in front of him and did a final check on his gloves and shoes. He clapped his fists down over Carr's. "Let's do this."

The official's voice called down the hallway, "Luka, you're up!"

A deep thrill of nervous energy raced through Carr's veins. He faced the hall, drew in a long, uneven breath, then let it hiss out slowly. "We're right behind you," DK reassured him.

Carr gripped the rungs and climbed. At the stadium entrance, the rumble of the crowd suddenly faded as the music and lights dimmed and blue spotlights began sweeping back and forth. The announcer's bass voice bellowed, "Fighting out of the red corner, with a mass of seventy kilograms and a record of four wins, one loss, CAAARRR... 'THE RAPTOR'.... LUKAAA!"

TWO

Carr kicked off the final hallway rung and through the entrance. He somersaulted tightly, then uncoiled, reached, and landed in a dramatic crouch on the deck, gripping it easily with the balls of feet and fingertips. The crowd roared its approval, and as he straightened, Carr saw close-ups of himself on the huge screens hanging around the stadium.

Great stars, there were a lot of people. They filled the tiered stands that stretched in all directions, blurred into shadow beyond the stark, glaring lights. Carr's pulse sped up, beating in his palms and the soles of his feet. Zero-boxing was the sort of thing people watched on screens at home; most planet rats couldn't afford to travel beyond atmosphere very often, and even those that could generally liked their artificial gravity. These spectators were the really hard-core fans, the ones who would rather be strapped into seats, drinking beer from squeeze bottles and brushing away floating globs of spilled orange soda and candy wrappers in order to see the fight live. Tonight, there were thousands of them, some still pulling themselves along the guide-rails to their seats.

Below the deck hung the Cube, empty, like an enormous minimalist ice sculpture. The sweeping spotlight beams distorted on its transparent surface, tingeing its edges and corners with cool blue light. Even experienced zeroboxers got shivers looking at the thing. To willingly enter it was to be completely imprisoned and utterly exposed. It was the prism of truth. There was no hiding in the Cube, no angle from which you could not be seen, and no way out until you had been proven victor or vanquished.

The announcer, Hal Greese, had a thick neck and a gut that, without gravity, migrated upward from the region of his waist to fill out his torso in a kind of general bulbousness. He turned in a slow circle in the center of the deck, one arm raised in anticipation. "Fighting out of the blue corner, with a mass of seventy-one kilograms and a record of nine wins, three losses, JAY … 'DRACULA' … FERRRANNOO!"

Jay Ferrano shot through the entrance, twisting like a corkscrew, and caught the landing deck neatly. A wave of enthusiastic noise vibrated the Cube beneath his feet. Carr looked across at his opponent. He seemed larger than he had in the videos Carr had studied. "Dracula" had gotten his nickname after an early fight when he'd let loose a bellow and accidentally swallowed a floating bubble of his opponent's blood. The fans had loved it and the clip had gone viral. Ferrano had apparently taken to his name, because the suspended screens zoomed in for a close-up of the liquid tattoo stretched across the back of his neck: a bat flapping its wings.

They met in the center of the deck, both of them ignoring the rails and walking steadily on gripper shoes alone. The referee said a bunch of the usual stuff about wanting a good, hard, clean fight and so on. Carr didn't hear any of it. He watched Ferrano. Sometimes you could tell what kind of a fighter a man was by looking at his face in the seconds before a match. Some guys looked cool as ice and fought the same way, patient and technical. Those who didn't even look you in the eyes were either too nervous or, in their hearts, nice fellas who would rather not think of their opponents as human beings they would have to hurt. The ones who growled and glowered as if they wanted to rip your limbs off—they fought because they were angry people.

Ferrano sniffed and cricked his neck from side to side. He looked strong, and mean, and here to play.

The referee told them to touch gloves. They did, and retreated to opposite sides of the deck. Carr was tingling from fingertips to toes. Uncle Polly was murmuring, "You're ready, you're ready. I'll be in your ear the whole time." DK put Carr's mouth guard in, then spread coagulant gel on his face; it lessened the chance he'd get cut, and in the event he did, it would keep most of his blood on him instead of mucking up the air.

The attendant technician held an activation penlight up to his eyes and told Carr to look at a point straight ahead while he fixed the beam on each eye in turn. After a couple of seconds, he said, "Connection's good," and one of the screens above flickered and shifted into the view from Carr's optic cameras, now being fed live to his subscribers.

The deck, which took up one entire outside surface of the Cube, had two entry hatches set into it. The border of Carr's hatch flashed red and slid open. He went to the edge of it and stood like a man with his toes on the lip of a cliff, staring down into two hundred cubic meters of empty space. Then he dove through the opening like a swimmer into water. He piked his body backward and flipped, catching the wall behind him, hands first, feet second, finding spread-fingered purchase on the textured surface, the magnetic pull on his gripper gloves, shoes, and the waistband of his shorts holding him against the wall.

On the other side of the Cube, Jay Ferrano shot through his hatch. Both entrances flashed once more—Ferrano's blue, Carr's red—before sealing off. The bell rang loudly outside the Cube for the benefit of the audience, more quietly in his ear. The fight was on.

Ferrano opened with a straight launch, propelling himself across the Cube with both legs, hands up in a guard. Carr judged the man's path and leapt for an adjacent wall, kicking out at his passing opponent. His foot connected, not with enough power to do damage, but that wasn't the point. It pushed the man in one direction and accelerated Carr's travel in the other, setting up his rebound.

Ferrano turned off the wall and shot straight back. Carr tucked his legs, powered off the surface, and sailed just out of reach. He shot a hand out for the wall, grabbed it, and climbed; for a calculated moment he was directly above Ferrano's head, and he swung down, fists flying for his opponent's face. He nailed a right hook and followed the momentum of his weightless spin with a left elbow, but Ferrano wrapped a leg around his, halting both their rotations and creating a coveted opening to grab and to land punches.

"Cover! Cover and break!" Uncle Polly shouted, his voice tinny in Carr's receiver.

Carr tucked his head between his forearms as Ferrano's right fist started raining down blows. The man's other hand was cupped behind Carr's neck, right leg anchored tight around Carr's thigh. He had to move before Ferrano could lock him up further. He drove his right knee up against his opponent's chest and surged back. They came apart, Carr kicking out to speed up their separation.

"Stick to the plan," Polly urged. "Stay out of his grab zone! Make him fly!"

All planet-born people instinctively had a sense of up and down; it took years of zero gravity training to develop a good space ear, to navigate 360 degrees of movement comfortably without nausea or disorientation. Carr was a natural. He twisted in the air, stretching for the wall with the balls of his feet. His left shoe found a magnetic grip while the rest of him kept traveling; he arched his back and shot his arm out, bracing himself into one of the Cube's right angles. Ferrano was coming after him, but too slowly; he hadn't gotten off a strong push. Carr scrambled across the corner and attacked from behind, punching both heels into his opponent's back, slamming the man into the wall and sending himself flying again.

Ferrano's broad back tensed with frustration and he began chasing the younger fighter around the Cube. They traded blows but Carr kept moving, kept Ferrano coming after him. Uncle Polly's voice was a chant in his ear: "That's it, make him climb, you're good, you're good."

The bell sounded on six Martian minutes. The hatches flashed and slid open; Carr climbed sideways toward the glowing red square outline and pulled himself onto the deck.

He sat, ankles hooked under the stabilizing bar as DK took his mouth guard and squeezed water into his mouth. Uncle Polly appeared in front of him, and for a couple of seconds his voice had a weird double timbre as Carr picked it up from his receiver. Polly stabbed his cuff to mute it and squatted down on his gripper shoes, talking fast and excited. "You're pissing him off and wearing him out. That's exactly what you want. Pick your places. You can fly circles around him; he'll tire long before you do."

Carr felt good—slicked with sweat, but his energy still high. Long before he was given his Cube name "the Raptor," his nickname around the gym had been "Last Man Standing" because of his staying power. Uncle Polly was certain that Carr's cardiovascular endurance and uncanny space ear were the key to him winning against more seasoned fighters.

Carr sloshed water in his mouth and spit it out, the spray breaking into wobbly bubbles that DK swiped away with a towel. "It looks like I'm playing it too safe," he said. "Like I'm not taking it to him enough."

"You look great, kid," DK reassured him, pressing an ice pack to the back of his neck.

Two scantily clad Cube girls drifted above the deck, taut bodies undulating like mermaids as they circled a big, spinning holovid of the number two. Carr bit back down on his mouth guard, unhooked his feet from the bar, and dove back through the hatch just as the bell sounded on the second round.

Ferrano had adjusted his game plan. No immediate power launch and energy-expending chase this time; he wasn't going to be drawn into trying to out-fly Carr. He stuck to the walls, looking for an opening, fighting tight and deliberate. It didn't take long for Carr to start feeling like a crow harassing a porcupine. He was landing hits, but Ferrano had good, swift defense and the blows didn't do a lot of damage.

Carr gritted his teeth, his gut surging with anxiety. He couldn't be sure of winning, not if the rest of the round went like this. The judges might tilt in his favor, but he couldn't count on that. Not for this fight. He needed this fight.

He ran up the corner, bouncing off the right angles

on the balls of his feet, then leapt back down at his opponent, legs scissoring for Ferrano's neck. The man evaded by less than a hand's width and grabbed Carr's leg. They both spun. Ferrano went for a leg lock. Carr twisted out of it, but the move gave Ferrano a brief opening. He threw his legs around Carr's waist, taking rear control and flinging his arm around Carr's neck.

Carr tucked his chin in time to avoid being immediately choked out. Ferrano had him around the jaw instead of the throat; the man's forearm began sawing back and forth.

Uncle Polly was shouting, "You have legs! Legs on a wall!"

He was being ridden and choked piggyback, but in the Cube, up and down were easily reversed. Carr kept his head down, braced his legs and kicked hard off the wall, sending them both shooting backward.

Ferrano's back slammed into the opposite wall, and they bounced. The impact knocked some of the wind out of Ferrano; he didn't let go, but his grip slipped enough for Carr to pull the stranglehold loose, twist his body a little sideways, and start nailing his opponent in the ribs with the tip of his elbow. Ferrano grunted but held on, tried to maneuver back into the choke with his other arm. They turned in space, locked together, everything barrel-rolling by slowly as they fought for advantage. With his free hand, Ferrano started hitting Carr in the head, forcing him to give up his elbow strikes to protect himself. Uncle Polly was yelling something but Carr couldn't hear it; his head was ringing with each blow.

Watching the video of the fight later, Carr would hear Xeth Stone exclaiming at this point, "It looks like Luka is in trouble now—they're drifting and Ferrano is not going to let go! He's just pounding him! This is not looking good for Carr Luka!"

"This is exactly how Ferrano wins," Jeroan said. "He may not look as nimble in the Cube, but you can't underestimate his tenacity."

Everything began to blur and swim. The wall advanced slowly in the column of vision between Carr's raised forearms. Desperate clarity pierced through the roar of blood in his ears and the tinny incomprehensible noise from his implanted receiver. His body began to slacken; Ferrano dug in the choke and started to squeeze.

"Oh … oh, this is it!" Xeth Stone yelled. "Ferrano's got it! He just wore Luka down with those punches."

Jeroan said, "Luka is going to have to tap any second now."

Blood and air were no longer reaching Carr's brain. Pain and blackness closed in. Ferrano growled with effort, completely focused on impending victory. *Just tap and it'll stop,* his meaty, sweaty forearm seemed to promise with each additional millimeter of pressure.

They reached the wall. Carr shot out hands and feet, catching the surface with all four magnetic grippers, and launched himself straight up with every remaining ounce of power in his limbs, as if shooting up the vertical side of a swimming pool toward air. The crown of Ferrano's head, higher than his by a couple inches, slammed into the Cube wall above them.

The impact jarred Carr as well, his tenuous hold on consciousness nearly giving out, darkness scudding across his eyes. But Ferrano's arm fell away and the flood of returning oxygen was like a slap of cold water in Carr's face. His body responded with a wave of sudden energy. He broke free and turned the corner like a spider crouching in its hollow. The walls, though solid, were designed to partially cushion impact; Ferrano was more dazed than injured, his eyes unfocused as he reached out clumsy hands to steady himself. Carr came at him from above, fist connecting square across the chin. Ferrano's head spun first, his body followed, and he went limp as a drifting rag doll.

Peripheral sounds and sensations returned. Outside the Cube, lights strobed and the crowd roared—one giant incoherent mass of noise.

"DID I JUST SEE THAT?" Xeth Stone squealed.

"We have a floater!" Jeroan's usually unflappable voice held a note of awe. "Carr Luka just floated the third best zeroboxer in the lowmass division, in the second round, when it looked like he was done for."

"What a stunning reversal! Ferrano did not see that coming at all! None of us did! I don't know how Luka could take those hits and hang on through that choke, and still have enough left in him to pull that off! What an opener! That might be the fight of the night, Jeroan!"

The referee and a doctor navigated over to Ferrano and examined him, then took hold of his arms and carried him back over to his side of the Cube, propelling themselves with handheld mini-thrusters. Residual adrenaline pulsed through Carr's body with each heartbeat; he felt as jittery as a bug as he jogged, on hands and feet, back to his hatch and out onto the deck. As the referee took his arm, Hal Greese's voice boomed, "At four minutes, thirty-eight seconds in the second round, the winner, by knockout— CARRRRR LUKAAA!"

The sweet high of victory swept over Carr, dizzying him more than any gymnastic feat in the Cube. He saw his own face on the suspended screens—red, puffy, and bruised, shiny with pebbly sweat clinging to a layer of gel—and broke into a grin he felt would never stop. The shadowy tiers of spectators rippled with movement, chanting their approval. He was surrounded by people: DK and Uncle Polly hugging him, the doctor coming to check on him, the technician disconnecting his optic cameras and telling him that his cochlear receiver had been jolted and he'd need to get it fixed—that was why in the last seconds of the match he hadn't heard Polly's voice, only a high, distant whining. Sports journalists materialized out of nowhere, their tethers crowding the rails, raising their cufflinks above each other to catch his words. Carr scrabbled distractedly for what he was supposed to say right now.

"I just want to thank Jay Ferrano and the ZGFA for putting on a great fight. I've got to credit my incredible coach and my cornerman. To my mom and Enzo, back home on Earth—I love you guys." There were more shouted questions, but DK and Uncle Polly ushered him back to the locker room. Carr barely felt the hallway rungs as he floated out of the crush of people.

He looped around the room like a drunken bird, bouncing off the banks of lockers and barreling into DK, who whooped and laughed and threw him into a spin. When he pulled out of it, Carr hooked one foot under a toe bar and leaned back, still grinning stupidly as DK helped him out of his gripper shoes and gloves, toweled him down, and placed a squeeze bottle of electrolyte drink in his hand.

Uncle Polly stood in front of him and leveled a stern finger at his face. "What was that? You were going to stay out of clinch."

"He wasn't falling for it, coach. I couldn't count on being far enough ahead by the end of the third."

"Hell of a risk. He nearly choked you out."

"But he didn't."

"Don't be smart with me. You were impatient to win and you got reckless."

"C'mon, Polly," DK said. "Your boy did good tonight. That knockout is one for the highlight reels."

Uncle Polly huffed. Then his tough demeanor fell away as a slow, crooked smile brightened his stubbly face. "Yeah," he said. "Yeah, it sure was." He put his hands on either side of Carr's face, giving his cheek an approving smack. "Not what I would've done, but damn, it worked."

Carr relaxed. He didn't want Uncle Polly unhappy

with him. He got dressed and no sooner had he put his cuff back on than it vibrated with dozens of messages. Congratulations from friends and teammates, new sub-scriber stats, media hits ... he touched the screen to queue it all, not planning to deal with it until later, but one high priority message flashed insistently. His cochlear receiver was still messed up; when he tried to play the audio tag, it was shrill and jumbled. He saw who the sender was, though, and his stomach did a small, nervous dive, like the final weak aftershock of an earthquake.

Uncle Polly was watching him. "Well?"

Carr looked up and nodded. "The Martian wants to see me."

THREE

The Martian's name was Bax Gant, and he was the co-owner of the Zero Gravity Fighting Association. His business partner, Terran entertainment industry tycoon Bran Merkel, was the money behind the ZGFA but only occasionally seen on Valtego; Gant managed all the day-to-day operations. He was called "the Martian" because he probably *was* the best known Martian on a city-station that was still overwhelmingly Terran, but also because, in zeroboxing circles, he was the sort of singularly influential personality who merited a *the* when spoken about, such as *the* Bossman or *the* Bastard. The Martian.

Carr stood in Gant's office trying not to look uncomfortable. He'd gone to the clinic for an injection of rehab/repair nanos; between the pricey cell-mending molecules and a dose of ibuprofen, post-fight pain wasn't his main problem. He'd had his receiver fixed too, and he wasn't even badly hungover from last night's after-party. It was just that Bax Gant's office felt like a walk-in refrigerator. Comfortable for a man from Mars, but not for someone raised in balmy Toronto. Carr imagined that Gant must feel the reverse; the whole rest of Valtego probably felt like a mild steam bath to him. No wonder he seemed to live in his office.

"Sit down, Luka," Gant said. "Coffee?"

Carr was about to decline, then remembered that he had just finished a fight and could eat and drink whatever he wanted to for a while. "Sure, thanks," he said, sitting down in the chair in front of the desk.

The last time he'd been in Gant's office was the day after his sixteenth birthday. Uncle Polly had sat next to him. The Martian had said, "You're training them from the womb now, are you, Pol?" and then turned a skeptical look on Carr. "The pros aren't like the ammys, kid. You think you're ready?" and Carr had said, "Yes, sir," though he'd been scared. This morning was different. Uncle Polly had cupped Carr's chin in his hand and said, "You're not a kid anymore. You're a pro fighter with a good record, and you're going to get re-signed or I'll eat my towel. Now go in there and talk to that domie, man-to-man."

Gant filled two mugs from the pot on the counter and walked back to the desk. He was the shortest Martian Carr had ever seen, barely six feet tall. Decades spent in Valtego's nearly Earth-level artificial gravity had thickened him, rounded him out a little. The faint hint of red in his hair suggested some European ancestry from way,

way back. The man could almost pass as Terran, though the telltale sheen of his dark, radiation-resistant skin gave him away.

He set one of the mugs in front of Carr, slipping a coaster underneath so as not to mar the surface of the mahogany desk. Real mahogany wood, not synthetic. There was a lot of wood in the room—the desk and chairs, the floor, the shelves that held mementos and photos from big fights Gant had promoted. Precious few non-agricultural trees grew on Mars; the man had a borderline obsession with furniture and objects made from natural materials. Behind his desk was a bamboo-framed watercolor print of Olympus Mons at sunset.

"Nice painting," Carr said. "Have you been there?"

"I'm from Tharsis," Gant said, sitting down across from him. "Never appreciated the view until I left."

"Nice place?"

"Used to be. Crowded now. Too many tourists." Gant snorted at this irony, and Carr wondered what passed for crowded on a planet with a fraction of Earth's population.

The Martian drank from his mug and studied Carr from across the desk. Carr lifted his chin. He could have had his bruised face and swollen jaw fixed up at the clinic, but it was ironclad tradition for zeroboxers to keep their facial wounds for at least a few days—the nastier-looking the better.

"What's your story, Luka?" Gant said finally. "Parents were refugees and shipped off-planet? Father was a drunk and used to beat you?"

Carr shook his head.

"I didn't think so. You're not angry the way some of them are. So why do you fight in the Cube?"

Carr shrugged. "I'm good at it."

"Hmm. After last night, I don't suppose I can disagree. Five-one; not too shabby for a guy born on soil."

"The 'one' got away from me."

"That's what they always say." Gant leaned forward onto his desk with folded arms. "What did you think of the crowd last night?"

"It was big."

Gant nodded, pleased. "Sold-out stadium, and millions more watching on the Systemnet." He jerked his head back toward the painting behind his desk. "I left Mars twenty-five years ago, saying I was going to grow the sport with Terrans. I was practically laughed off the Red Planet. All the best zeroboxers in the Martian system, the top dogs in the Weightless Combat Championship, you know what they said to me? '*Everyone* on the old planet is a planet rat. The most daring and inventive Terrans left generations ago to build Mars and the other settlements. Why would a place with countless gravity-dependent sports want anything different? Zeroboxing'll never catch on.'"

Carr took a swallow of strong coffee. "Guess they were wrong."

"Guess so." Gant jutted his lower jaw slightly forward as he sized Carr up like a buyer considering an item at auction. Carr did his best to wait without fidgeting, without thinking too much about how his future depended on coming down on the good side of this man's ruthless business acumen. Whether you loved or hated the Martian was largely correlated with how useful he thought you were.

Gant picked up his thinscreen and tapped it. "Have you looked at your subscriber stats or media hits?"

"Not yet."

"Good; if your head gets too inflated, you might get the mistaken idea you can weasel a better deal out of me." He handed the screen to Carr. "This is what you've been waiting for."

Carr took the screen, suddenly glad that the meat-locker temperature kept his hands from sweating. He read the new contract quickly, then read it again, his eyes lingering on all the key numbers. His heart began to dance a jig in his chest. Three years and ten more fights guaranteed, his pay starting close to double what he'd made on his first six matches and rising steadily if he won. He'd thought Gant might low-ball and make him negotiate, but this was more than Uncle Polly had told him to expect.

His hand hovered over the fingerprint signature box, not quite believing his fortune.

"Show it to whoever you need to—your coach, your lawyer—but I'm not going to bullshit you: it's a good deal."

Carr pressed his finger to the screen, waited for the confirmation, and handed it back to Gant. "Thank you. Really." His voice had gone a little squeaky; he cleared his throat. "This is what I want to do. What I've always wanted to do."

"Your contract isn't a payout. It's an investment," Gant said. "The ZGFA's investment in you. Don't think for a second this means you've made it, that you don't have to train your ass off harder than ever to keep putting on a good show in the Cube."

"I don't."

"Good. Because there are a hundred guys out there who would eat each other alive to take your place." Gant smiled, not in a cruel way, just *that's the way it is.* "One other thing. You're getting a brandhelm."

Carr's eyebrows furrowed. Marquee athletes had brandhelms, of course, and so did every other famous person from celebrity chefs to CEOs, but Carr was less than a couple of years into a pro career. "I can't afford a brandhelm," he said. "I mean, the deal is fine, but it's not like I've got extra cash right now."

"It's your lucky day then," said the Martian. "Merkel Media Corporation hired heavy on the marketing side and Bran has me convinced we should use the extra manpower up here, promoting our up-and-coming zeroboxers. I'm assigning someone to you." He drummed his blunt-nailed fingers on the desk. "Like I said, an investment. Just to be clear, I don't do this for every hotshot who comes into my office for his first contract renewal."

"No sir."

Gant stood up and Carr stood with him. They shook hands, Carr's fingers numb with cold, Gant's warm and fleshy.

Do it, Carr urged himself. He had somehow, miraculously, made it into the Martian's good books, at least for now. *Go on. Say it.* "Another thing," he said. "Jay Ferrano

35

was the third-ranked lowmass zeroboxer. Now I am." He steeled his gaze. "I want to fight for the title."

The Martian grunted. "Every fighter who's ever been in here has given me that line. They all have the same dream that you do. Some of them I bet big on—the way I just bet on you—and they never lived up to their promise." He eyed Carr, calculating. "You're not special, Luka. Not yet."

FOUR

For the next few days, Carr slept late, indulged in favorite foods (key lime pie from that little café next to the Infinity Grand Hotel—sublime, the best in orbit), returned messages of congratulations, and strode about light with relief that he wasn't going to be shipped back to Earth as a failure.

"Oh man, that fight was STELLAR!" Enzo said when he called. "I've watched it eight times. You know what's funny? Even though I know you won, when I get to that part right near the end, I always feel really worried for a few seconds."

"But just a few."

"Like three or four seconds."

Carr shook his head, awed by the boy's faith. When he'd met Enzo three and a half years ago, the kid had been lying on his back in a weed-choked patch of dirt, his face bruised half purple, shouting and wheezing and swiping for the inhaler that the bigger boy sitting on his chest was waving over his head, just out of reach. After Carr had hauled off the asshole and sent him and his friends home with a promise to make them pee blood the next time he saw them, he squatted down by Enzo and held out the small device, shaking it curiously.

"What is this thing?" he asked.

The boy gasped for breath, high and shrill like a puppy being strangled. He took the inhaler from Carr and sucked on it furiously until he was better. "It's for my asthma," he said, wiping muddy tears from his face.

"Asthma?" Carr made an incredulous face and the boy dropped his puffy eyes to the ground between his toes. Who in this part of the world still had a defunct genetic disease like *asthma?* Only people with parents too poor to afford even the most basic gene therapy but irresponsible enough to have kids anyways. Low, even by the standards of their neighborhood. School boys would go after such a glaring mark of weakness like hyenas after a lame zebra.

"I'd keep that thing hidden if I were you," Carr said, with the sage wisdom of his fourteen years at the time. "And next time a bigger kid starts to knock you down, drop to the ground and roll away from him. If he sits on your chest you're in bad shape, little man. You've got to tuck your chin, keep your hands up, and buck your hips hard, like this, see? When he goes forward, roll on top of him fast and nail him a few good ones in the face. With your fist or your elbow. Got it?"

That was how Carr had picked up a short, talkative, seven-year-old shadow. He didn't mind. He liked it, actually. He didn't have any friends outside of the gym, and in the gym, he was always the youngest at his level. Years ago, he'd begged his mom for a little brother; he'd show him the ropes, look out for him, he promised. Of course, she'd said no. After Carr's gym and tournament expenses, they couldn't afford a pet much less another kid. "You're it for me, darling," she said. "All my eggs in one basket, you could say," and giggled at her own joke. So Enzo was as close as Carr got. And Enzo was funny and clever, even if he had bum lungs.

Most important of all: the kid was a rabid zeroboxing fan. He made Carr recount the entire match against Jay Ferrano, in blow-by-blow detail, twice through before Carr ended the call to let him run off to school.

In a properly good mood, Carr called his mom. "Hi, Mom," he said when she answered. "I won my fight. I have a new contract now, a good one. Three years and ten matches."

"That's super, darling," she said. "Good for you."

Carr didn't ask her if she'd watched the fight. Sometimes she did ("That was a good one," she'd say), sometimes she didn't ("Oh, you've had so *many*, it's hard to keep them all straight—was it the one against that big fellow?"). The truth of it was, he found it excruciating to talk to his mom about zeroboxing. She was always vaguely proud, distantly and unwaveringly supportive, but her interest and knowledge never went much beyond whether he'd won, whether he'd been hurt, and how much money he'd made.

Instead he asked, "How are you doing?"

"Oh, you know me." She laughed. She had a girlish laugh, like bursting soap bubbles. "The same as always." Despite this assertion, she continued, "Ginnie, she was a regular, she moved away to Scarborough so I don't see her anymore. And they're taking down those ugly old buildings by the waterfront, so the route has changed and I have two new stops..."

Sally Luka worked for the Toronto Transit Commission as a bus attendant. It was an utterly superfluous job because the TTC's artificial intelligence system handled all the routing and driving, but the union had managed to preserve the high seniority bus attendant jobs. They argued that people liked to have real humans to greet them, announce their stops, and answer questions if they had any. If they did, Sally would consult the AI, which is what the passenger would simply do themselves if there wasn't a live attendant. Carr's mom had been in her job for twenty-five years. It amazed Carr that she managed to have something inconsequential to say about it every time he spoke to her.

He loved his mom, most of the time, but sometimes he wondered how they could be related.

After he finished talking to her, he sighed in relief and ate a slice of key lime pie. Then he took a look at the money he'd won from the Ferrano fight. He paid overdue rent and bills, stashed away enough to get through the next several months, then transferred the rest to his mom's account. She didn't ask for money, not exactly, but growing up, the lack of it in their lives had been as palpable as a third, ugly family member. So the way it worked now was: she would mention something about the cost of personal data usage going up, he would send money without telling her, she would never acknowledge it, and he never expected her to.

———————

By the fourth day after the fight, Carr was restless. After they'd celebrated the new contract with a trip to Bubbity's all-you-can-eat buffet (where *You're Not Gaining Weight If You're In Space!*), Uncle Polly had told him to take ten days off to let the nanos purge themselves from his body and his bones fully re-mineralize. To Carr, the time felt more like a prison sentence than a vacation. He was most at ease when training hard for an upcoming match. Without one to fixate on, he felt himself sliding into unproductive apathy, which he loathed. He had no interest in or money for the touristy Valtego activities, and while spending a whole day in his apartment playing holovid games or watching Lunar sitcoms (Lunar humor was uniquely, scathingly dark) was a guilty pleasure at first, it made him feel gross, like one of the vacationing planet rats, willingly and constantly trapped in artificial gravity.

Luckily, DK had a fight against Titus "Scorpion" Stockton next month, and Carr had a role as his friend's cornerman to give him something to focus on. DK was all smiles to see him when he showed up at the ZGFA's land-training gym. If DK ever felt nervous against a tough opponent like the Scorpion, it manifested itself as cheerful bravado leading into the final weeks.

"Any of your family coming to see you fight?" Carr asked him. They were working the rubber bands, DK leaping off a trampoline launching pad and hitting targets that Carr threw into the air. Elastic cords clipped to his waist tethered him to the ground, giving him extra resistance. A launch strong enough to propel him a short distance in artificial gravity would explode him across the Cube in a fight.

"One of my brothers, and a cousin," DK said. He grinned his small, pearly toothed grin. "If I got every Kabitain to come to Valtego at once, there wouldn't be enough strippers to entertain them all. They would have to fly in emergency reinforcements."

DK was among the minority of zeroboxers with a family that seemed halfway functional, not to mention one that was so large: two parents, five older siblings (DK claimed to have been driven to fight as a result of being the smallest and ugliest of the lot), and assorted uncles, aunts, and cousins scattered across Earth, Luna, and half a dozen settlements. All Terran, though; DK insisted that none of his blood had turned domie. His grandparents were Catholic, he said, and had been from the region everyone referred to as Asialantis. They had been fortunate enough to have the money and means to leave the submerging islands of Indonesia and use the relocation stipend to buy their way into seasonal work in suborbital transport.

There were other people in the gym, and every few

minutes, someone passing by would say to Carr "Nice fight" or "Hey, congrats." Adri "Assassin" Sansky stopped by to give him a hug and say, "Hey, hot stuff, I hear the Martian jumped higher than a jackrabbit on Luna to sign you again." Carr liked how her words weren't tainted by rivalry. Female zeroboxers held their own grudges, Carr knew; maybe worse ones, since there were fewer of them and they ended up fighting each other repeatedly. Adri, though, despite her ripped physique, still seemed to him like a friendly, plain-pretty girl-next-door. "Better watch this kid, DK," she said, half teasing.

DK punched the final target out of the air and landed, bending his knees to stop his momentum. Carr glanced at him. Though he'd never felt compelled to downplay himself in the Cube before, he said, "It was close. I got lucky."

"Lucky?" DK unhooked himself from the waist harness and hopped off the trampoline, shaking his head. "Lucky is what happens to those who pay their dues. You could have flamed out after that one bad fight, but you didn't. You came back and trained hard, and you delivered." He dropped a hand on Carr's shoulder. "Enjoy the attention. You deserve it."

"Thanks," Carr said, but he didn't feel at ease with DK's praise. He imagined he heard an edge to it, which was probably unfair, a figment of his own mild discomfort. DK was twenty-two years old, had been on Valtego since he was nineteen, and had a strong, though not spectacular, 9-3 record. He'd taken Carr under his wing early on, given him advice, helped him land gym time and a decent apartment, cornered three of his matches, and been, as DK generally was, an all-around helpful guy. Now, Carr was certain, his new contract placed the two of them on par.

Adri was looking past them toward the front entrance. Her eyes narrowed. "Now what's this?"

A woman had walked in. She was dressed like someone from the ZGFA corporate offices upstairs, but she stood at the front of the training floor and turned her head, eyes roaming around the room as if she was looking for someone. Carr hadn't seen her before. He would have remembered her if he had. She was young, head-turningly attractive, and Martian.

Adri's lips straightened into a line as she crossed her arms. "Domies," she grumbled. "You see more of them around here every day."

Carr hadn't really noticed this to be true, but Adri's view of all things Martian had turned bitter ever since her brother had taken the immigration incentives and a quadrupled salary and moved his family to the Red Planet. Now Adri subscribed to *Earth First*, that blatantly pro-Terran protectionism news-feed.

The stranger's searching gaze passed over Carr, then slid back and stopped on him. She strode toward him purposefully. "Carr Luka?" she asked when she reached him.

"Yes," he said.

She extended her right hand, Terran-style. "I'm Risha Ponn. Your new brandhelm."

It took Carr a few beats to recover from his surprise and shake her hand. He'd practically forgotten Gant's mention of a brandhelm; the financial terms of the contract had been far more important at the time.

DK and Adri exchanged a glance of barely concealed astonishment. Carr opened his mouth, fumbling for an explanation about how this wasn't his idea, but DK said, "Looks like you've got business, Carr."

"Yeah," said Adri. "We'll leave you to it then."

"The rest of practice ... " Carr protested, but DK raised a hand in a dismissive, backward wave as he and Adri drew away.

Carr sucked the inside of his cheek. Great. The word around here would be (a) he was conceited, and loaded enough to hire a brandhelm mere days after his contract renewal, or (b) Gant was giving him some unprecedented special treatment. He wasn't sure which was worse. He turned back, unsmiling, to the woman in front of him.

She was a little taller and older than Carr, dark and thin the way Martian women were, with high cheekbones and shapely eyes that suggested she was descended from the Asian colonists who'd founded the domed cities all along the Valles Marineris. He realized he was staring with his mouth slightly agape when she said, a little shortly, "Could we sit down and talk?"

He felt a flash of embarrassed irritation. She'd walked into his gym, disrupted his practice, turned him into a subject of gossip, made him blush, and now presumed that he'd drop everything to meet with her. He held up his arm and pointed to his cuff. "Did you think to call?"

"I wanted to see where you spend your time. I'll need

to learn everything about you, so I may as well start right away." There was an offhanded shrug in her voice, the self-assurance bordering on arrogance that he was familiar with from zeroboxers sizing up each other, not from women when they talked to him. He wasn't sure how he felt about this idea of her learning everything about him.

"There's a noodle place across the street," he said. "I've got an hour. A Terran hour, not a Martian one."

"Fine with me." She walked with him out of the ZGFA building, ignoring the curious looks that followed them. The noodle shop had a dozen tables right beside the street, so diners could gaze up through the sky windows at the stars and the ships in port or get their fill of people-watching, whichever they preferred. Risha wasn't inclined to either, it seemed. She scrolled through the menu for all of five seconds and ordered udon with shrimp. Carr ordered curry udon with a side of edamame, then sat back. He crossed his arms, tucking his hands into his armpits, and looked at her.

"You eat shrimp," he said. Martians, as far as he knew, were all vegetarian. Raising animals for food would be a staggering waste of precious, mined water and terraformed land; he'd heard somewhere that colonists considered the practice immoral.

Risha said, "I'm half-Martian, if you must know."

"I couldn't tell."

"The geneticist made sure I had all the standard Martian traits. My parents didn't want me to be disadvantaged in any way." Risha snorted as she picked up her chopsticks.

"Good thinking at the time. Turns out that when I was twelve, they decided not to renew their marriage contract and I moved with my father to Earth."

"That must have been tough," Carr said. There had been Martian ex-pats in Toronto, but, growing up, he didn't see them on the streets often. They tended to stay in their domed, climate-controlled neighborhoods, uncomfortable with Terran crowds, heat, and open sky.

"The first year was awful. I shrank four inches. Gravity adjustment therapy and bone density treatment made me feel too heavy to get out of bed, and that wasn't even the worst of it. On the bright side, I do eat shrimp." She paused and leveled an impatient look at Carr. "We're supposed to be talking about you, not me."

"I get to learn about you too. Decide if I want you as my brandhelm."

She put down her chopsticks, as if that idea hadn't occurred to her. "I don't think there are other candidates," she said. "Unless you have the money to hire your own?"

Of course he did not. "Maybe I don't need one."

"Everyone needs one. Everyone who wants to be someone. That includes you, I'm sure."

Carr found himself staring again, his initial annoyance blotted out by fascination. Risha had a calm and quick intensity. Everything about her—her steady gaze, the way she leaned slightly forward with her mouth gently pursed, her slender fingers rolling the chopsticks—seemed subtly challenging. Most of the girls Carr met were on vacation, pretty and giggly, ready to have a good time. Risha was different.

She made him want to sit up straight and pay attention. He wasn't used to feeling this way around a woman.

A service droid slid up with their food. As she ate, Risha unfolded a thinscreen and said, while scrolling through her notes without looking at him, "You're trending up strongly. Your subscriber base grew by thirty-nine percent in the forty-eight hours after your match against Jay Ferrano, and your first four fights are the most downloaded of all Terran zeroboxing matches this week. That makes you the fourth most-watched zeroboxer and the fifty-ninth most-watched Terran athlete right now." She nodded to herself at this bit of excellent news. "What's more, your genetic profile should appeal to a very large pool of consumers and sponsors."

Carr was about to ask who the first, second, and third most-watched zeroboxers were, but the question flew from his head. "You looked up my genetic profile?"

She raised her head at his indignant surprise. "Only what's publicly available through an employment check. The point is, you don't have any physical or mental risk factors, off-spec traits, or anything that might be a red flag for sponsors. You're also young, attractive, and advantageously aracial."

Carr had no reply. He was used to being judged on physical characteristics—body mass, reach, speed, strength—but not in the way Risha was laying it out. He'd never considered how being an ethnic mash-up—dark hair, gray eyes, light olive skin—might be useful to him in any way, or imagined sponsors evaluating him on criteria unrelated to his ability to win in the Cube. He supposed he did need a brandhelm after all. He hid this sour thought behind a long drag of salty udon soup.

"It's preliminary," she continued, "but I've written up the outline of a ZGFA brand campaign promoting the rise of the next generation of Terran zeroboxing stars, elevating you as the leading asset."

Carr supposed he ought to feel flattered. Instead, he scratched the back of his neck, confused. "Aren't you getting a little ahead of yourself?"

"How so?"

"I hate to dash your optimism, but I'm still a new guy here. I've got six pro fights under me. You want to look just at the younger fighters? Heck, DK's had nearly a dozen matches. Blake's right up there too."

"Danilo Kabitain?" Risha nodded absently, plucking the tail off a shrimp. "Not as marketable. He's obviously from Asialantis—a weak market, no one with money lives there anymore—plus he was born on a settlement and has never lived on Earth, so he's not even technically Terran. Murphy is polarizing among fans and has a moderate-high risk of asocial behavior that won't sit well with sponsors."

"They're good zeroboxers," Carr said, defensive.

"Broad appeal is what we need, to grow awareness and popularity of the sport." She slid the thinscreen toward him. "We need to start increasing your touchpoints if we're going to retain your new subscribers. You haven't been sending out anything from your optic cameras or broadcasting any exclusive post-fight commentary."

Carr's eyes swam at the blocks of graphs and numbers she'd shoved in front of him. He pushed the thinscreen back across the table. "The only 'touchpoints' on my mind are the ones scored in the Cube. Those are the only important ones."

She tilted her chin down and studied him, mouth pursed. The light had started to soften into simulated evening. The halogen street lanterns came on, and the boulevard began to fill with people hunting for dinner spots, arriving or leaving the gravity zone terminal, wandering past the bright holovid banners that encouraged them to visit *Second Womb: A Weightless Spa Experience.* Risha folded her thinscreen. She said, a little slower and more quietly, "We're on the same team, Carr Luka."

A thought occurred to him as he nudged his empty bowl aside. "How many clients have you had, Risha Ponn?" He articulated her full name, as she had done with his.

She hesitated a moment, her confident mask slipping a little.

"I'm the first one, right?"

"Yes." She held his gaze. "I asked for this job. I've always wanted to work off-planet."

Great stars. An overzealous, way-too-easy-on-the-eyes, half-Martian rookie brandhelm. He didn't know what he'd been expecting, but this wasn't it. In a brief spasm of paranoia, Carr wondered if Gant had dumped her on him just to keep her busy with one of his less valuable fighters.

Then he squinted with satisfaction. He knew who Risha was after all. She was that fighter entering the Cube on Valtego for the first time, aloof and anxious, desperately hungry to prove himself. Carr had met that guy plenty of times; he'd been him, too.

"All right," he said, leaning back and stretching, feeling more relaxed. "We might have started off a bit prickly with each other. Seems like we can agree that I know next to nothing about this marketing stuff, and you're no zero-boxer. I guess I'll have to trust you, and if we're going to be on the same team, like you say, then you've got to do the same with me."

Risha was silent for a moment. Then she crossed her long, glistening legs, tucking a strand of black hair behind her ear in a small movement that made her seem younger and just a touch vulnerable. "You know," she said, "you're quite consistent with what I expected from studying your fights and interviews. Athletically gifted, ambitious, and arrogant, but more intelligent and emotionally stable than is typical for a man who makes a living with his fists." She smiled then, a small but lovely smile. "I like you, Carr. I think we'll work well together after all." She extended her hand to him across the table.

Carr laughed. At least Risha fit one Martian stereotype, speaking her mind as bluntly as a scientist pronouncing results. Her hand, when he took it, was firm and hot, like a smooth, sun-warmed stone. "Okay," he said. "Here we go, then."

FIVE

The tour group, sixteen people in all, floated out to the deck tentatively, tethered to the guide-rails and firmly grasping the hallway rungs. Without the clamor of the crowd and the sharpness of adrenaline, the Cube and its stadium seemed altogether different. Tame, empty, just a large transparent room hanging in space. That didn't stop the tourists from gazing in wonder at the structure and the vacant tiers of seating, oohing and ahhing and madly tapping cuff-links to send their optic feeds to friends.

Idly, Carr wondered who they were: high rollers on a complimentary special excursion, corporate executives on a team-building trip, travel journalists, or just people with the right connections to Valtego brass. These behind-the-scenes tours interrupted training, especially when zeroboxers were asked to come out and act as guides, but it would be stupid to say no to something that helped pay the bills around the gym and kept the ZGFA in the Valtego city council's good graces. Today, everyone else was busy, and since Carr was two weeks post-fight with no word yet about his next match, he'd naturally been tapped to entertain the planet rats.

"How many of you have watched zeroboxing?" he asked, raising his voice over the sound of the janitor droid's vacuum hose as it swept the stands. A sizable show of hands. "Does anyone know how it originated?"

"On mining ships," shouted an overweight man floating in the back.

Carr nodded. "The old ion propulsion ships used to take months to make each leg of the trip from Mars to the Main Belt, over to Earth with their cargo, and back to Mars. The crews would be signed up for voyages that lasted for years. Well, you can imagine these miners were pretty rough guys, on ships with not a lot of room. Remineralization therapy wasn't that great back then, so they also needed to keep exercising and blow off steam. They started using the recycling holds for sport fights, which is why amateur matches are still called 'recyclers.'"

A hand shot up in the back. "Did you plan that move against Ferrano, or did it just happen?"

"Err… sometimes you start with a plan, but then throw it out and make a new plan about two seconds before you do it."

A woman in the front asked, "Do you know who you're going to fight next?"

Carr spread his hands, "Hey, hold on. If you want to ask me questions, let's save them for the end so you don't miss the good part of this tour, okay?" Employing the mid-fight strategy adjustment he'd just described, he decided to skip the rest of his educational spiel. "Who's been on a spacewalk?" Most of them. "Who's been in a Cube?" Only one. "Well this is your chance. Two at a time in there, and if you feel nauseous at any point, just tug the tether and we'll pull you out."

There was a murmur of excitement, and people lined up at the entry hatches. Carr let the first two in, a young woman and a slightly older man, both of whom looked like office workers in their gym clothes. He watched them drift toward the center, the man cycling his arms and legs superfluously, the woman squealing as she started to turn upside down. Instinctively she tried to turn back "right side up" instead of simply stretching her feet out for the wall with her cheap rental grippers. Carr hoped she wouldn't be sick. It happened once in a while, and no one wanted to be responsible for clean-up.

"I love watching your fights. You're so athletic." An impressive bosom appeared in front of him, attached to a smiling woman with color-changing hair dye. "Will you sign my chest?" She held out a black marker.

"Sure." Carr signed the cleavage above the hem of the woman's scooped neck shirt while her friend captured the whole thing with a cuff-link camera. She was short, creamy, doughy—the opposite of Risha Ponn. She gave him a smothering hug that smelled of vanilla, her hair shifting from sandy blond to auburn red. Carr wondered if his new brandhelm would consider this a "touchpoint" and whether she would approve—then wondered why he was wondering that.

He reeled in the two people in the Cube—both of them grinning weakly, having valiantly and successfully held onto their breakfasts—and let in the two women, who began whooping and pushing each other off the walls. The next man in line was the one who had raised his hand and claimed to have been in a Cube before. "Carr, I'm Brock Wheeden. I've followed your fights closely, and it's a real pleasure to meet you." He shook Carr's hand.

"Thanks." The name was vaguely familiar. So was the man's face: a short orange beard darker than his hair and a slightly squashed nose.

"I think the young talent in the ZGFA is why you're seeing the huge growth in viewership. Terran zeroboxing is really taking off. Who knows, maybe the sport will become as popular on Earth as it is on Mars."

The name and the face clicked. Wheeden was a prominent zeroboxing commentator on the Systemnet. He hosted a regular series called *Cube Talk with Brock*. It couldn't be a coincidence that he was here, could it?

"You would know more about that than I would," Carr said. "I like your feed. I've used it to research opponents."

"You just made my day," Brock said. "You mind if I quote you on that?"

Wheeden's friend, next to him, asked, "So do you think you could beat the Reaper?"

Carr raised his eyebrows at the loaded question. Thirty-year-old Henri "the Reaper" Manon was the reigning ZGFA lowmass champion. Wheeden and his friend were looking at Carr expectantly; no doubt a juicy bit of trash-talk from the Raptor would make it onto Brock's feed within minutes.

Carr hesitated; this wasn't a press conference, and he wasn't a title contender, not yet. Gant wasn't fond of fighters going off script and fanning speculation. "Sooner or later," he said simply.

"So you agree with Xeth Stone that the Reaper has slowed down in his last couple matches?" Wheeden pressed.

Carr smiled. Lighting a match was different from igniting plasma fuel. "Looks like it's your turn in the Cube," he said, helping the two women out and motioning the men in.

What a difference, Carr marveled. Last year, no one stopped him for his autograph or tried to extract pithy quotes from him. Last year, he'd been just another broke, nameless kid on Valtego, like lanky, mop-headed Scull over there, manning the other hatch and occasionally glancing over at him in surreptitious awe.

"You're the man of the hour, Carr," said a voice near his shoulder.

The man next in line was older than the rest, but Carr could not tell how much older. His gray-blond hair was combed back over a high forehead. He was pale, as if he'd never seen the sun. Even his eyes were pale, like an overcast sky. Multiple age-reversal treatments had given his face an artificially smooth, unblemished appearance, like a piece of wax fruit. "You're very level-headed about all the attention," he said.

Carr shrugged. "Fighting isn't a popularity contest."

After his first four fights, people had started using words like "phenom" and "prodigy," and he'd let it get to his head. Even with Uncle Polly to keep him in line, there had been new friends, and parties, and girls... heck, he'd only been sixteen. He'd gotten drunk on it all, let himself be lulled into losing a fight he should have won. Then he started hearing words like "flame out" and "one shot." Now he was on the up and up again. Attention could be good or bad, he decided, but it didn't really matter.

The man smiled, as if Carr had said something to make him happy, but there was no real warmth, just a smug rising of the corners of his mouth. "That's a sagacious comment to make, at your age."

Carr gave the stranger a sidelong glance. Something about the man's overly familiar tone, and the way he kept looking at him, made Carr's skin itch. His mind prickled unpleasantly with the suspicion that he'd seen this distinctive, whitish face before. Some time ago. Where? "Have we met?" he asked.

"Not properly." Small creases appeared around the corners of the man's eyes. "But I know quite a lot about you. I'm an enormous fan of yours, Carr. Your mother and I met many years ago. So you could say I'm an old family friend."

"Funny she's never mentioned you." A slimy worry uncurled in Carr's stomach. He decided he did not like the man. He did not like the way his name sounded in the man's mouth, the r's too harsh, and how the man used his name too often, as if he were exercising some right to do so. He helped Wheeden and his friend out of the Cube and said, "Your turn."

"Ah, no," said the stranger, stepping aside politely. "We have much in common, Carr, but your vestibular system is not one of them. I'll remain a spectator."

What an odd thing to say. The curl of worry bulged into mild panic. Carr tamped it down. He had nothing in common with this man; they looked nothing alike. Different eyes and nose and mouth, different build. His eyes narrowed. "I didn't catch your name, mister."

Carr's cuff went off, playing a rising note in his ear. He looked down at the display. Gant.

"Scull, take over for a few minutes, will you?" he called, gesturing to his cuff. Scull nodded, and with a wary, backward glance, Carr grabbed the guide-rail and swung himself just inside the hall that led to the locker room. He hooked an ankle around a hallway rung to check his glide, holding himself in place as he accepted the call.

"What are you doing, Luka? Getting fat and bored out your mind yet?" The Martian sounded like he was walking through a noisy crowd.

"Just about, sir."

"Well, cheer up. I have a headline fight for you. Jaycen Douglas was supposed to go up against BB Dunn, but he just pulled out because of injury. Needs another surgery, the doctor says. You want his spot?"

Depending on who you talked to you, Douglas was either the second best zeroboxer in the division, or Dunn was. Dunn had a better record, and had beaten Jay Ferrano, but then he'd lost to Douglas in a contested judge's decision. A rematch between them had been arranged to settle the matter. Now it wasn't going to happen. "When's the fight?"

"Three weeks."

Three weeks! A ridiculously short amount of time to train for a new opponent. As much as Carr lived for his next match, he'd expected two to three months to prepare, not three weeks. He was supposed to corner DK's match in eighteen days.

He ought to talk to Uncle Polly, think about this, get back to Gant later.

As if he'd read Carr's mind, the Martian's voice slowed, turned measured. "Now look, I'm offering this to you, but it's your choice whether to take it. You have momentum right now, and I get it, you don't want to risk losing that. Don't take on more than you can handle. Play it safe…if you think that's best."

There was a chance Gant's prudent words were sincere. More likely he knew what buttons to push to arrange the fights he wanted. Whichever it was, the words scraped at Carr's insides like wire bristle; he grimaced. He remembered the last conversation they'd had—*I just bet on you*—and imagined the Martian moving chips off Carr's square.

He glanced back down the hall at the tour group. Strange; the pale, smooth-faced man was gone. The rest of

the group was still milling about, most of them as uncoor-
dinated in zero gravity as elephant seals on land.

The idea of turning down a fight, any fight, seemed
wrong. Like a beggar pushing away food, or a plant turning
away from sun. Besides, winning this match would make
him the indisputable contender for the title. "I'll take it," he
said.

SIX

"Go again," Carr insisted.

Blake groaned but complied, tackling Carr and pulling him off the wall, wrapping both legs around his waist. Carr hoped never to be caught by BB Dunn in such a compromised position, but he was determined to train for it until he could break the man's forward control in his sleep. Blake packed a few more kilos than Dunn but had roughly the same proportions and grappling style, which made him a good stand-in.

Uncle Polly followed them as they battled. "Hands up, hands up," he reminded Carr. "You're telegraphing your moves again—he'll see that coming a light year away."

Carr crunched his body and drove the tip of his elbow into Blake's thigh until he had enough room to twist his hips sideways. They bounced lightly into the wall and Carr grabbed it, using it for stability as he shot one knee up between himself and Blake. He pushed off and swiveled his lower body hard, wrapping his legs around Blake's neck in a vise and squeezing until the other man tapped.

"That was good," Blake said as they hung onto the wall, catching their breaths. "You're a lot faster with that now."

"You're still relying on the wall and it won't always be there for you," Polly said. "You need to be able to do it floating. You've got one week to hone your submission game, and if it's not there, you're going to have to count on out-flying Dunn. You ready to do that?"

Carr gritted his teeth. He'd been thinking the exact same thing. Frenzied preparation had thrown him and Uncle Polly into a sort of psychic state, where half the time one of them knew what the other would say before he said it. BB Dunn, they both knew, was no Jay Ferrano. He had grace—that's how people in the business referred to a zero-boxer who made it look easy, who could cripple you in the absence of gravity and made it look like a beautiful thing of nature. The fighter with grace was the man. BB Dunn was so agile in the Cube he was called "the Earless One." The pun came from a rumor that he had some vestibular defect that prevented him from ever being disoriented. It also dangerously understated how good the man's grappling was.

"One more time," Carr said, even though they'd been in the Virgin Galactic Center for hours. The sports doctor had warned him that such prolonged zero gravity exposure was going to render his most recent re-mineralization ineffective, but Carr figured if he won the fight, he'd have the money to redo the treatment.

Blake checked the time on his cuff. "I told DK I'd meet him for land-training and pick up tape and gel for his fight."

"Shit, of course. Sorry I forgot. Get out of here." Carr shook his head. He felt bad enough about having bailed as DK's cornerman without monopolizing Blake as well. He'd said to DK, "I'll still do it if you need me to," but it was only a verbal gesture; they both knew it was ridiculous. DK's fight was three days before his; Carr couldn't possibly focus on his friend's match when he had so little time to train for his own.

DK had been understanding. "Hey, no worries, I get it, it's Dunn. You want this one," he'd said, but Carr knew it was a pain to replace a cornerman on short notice. He still felt guilty.

As Blake climbed his way over to the hatch, Uncle Polly said to Carr, "You need a break? Or more flying drills?"

When he'd told Uncle Polly about the Dunn fight, his trainer had shouted, "Three weeks? Three fucking weeks? Damn Gant's domie hide! What the hell were you thinking when you took it?"

"You think I should've turned it down?"

"No. It's BB Dunn! Of course you should've taken it. But you should've fucking asked me!"

Carr took the towel that Polly handed him and wiped the sweat from his face. The Cube had begun to feel like a sauna. Without gravity, warm air did not rise, it just stayed in place, growing thicker and more stifling. Thankfully, the ventilation fans built into the walls kicked on automatically, forcibly circulating cooler air into the enclosure. "Flying drills," he said.

Uncle Polly lobbed a stuffed bolster the size of a man's torso through the air. Carr scrambled up the wall, bounded off a right corner and launched himself at it, tackling it hard and rotating his body to control the rebound with his feet. They did the drill again, and again, Polly trying to throw him off, Carr snatching the target out of the air like a hawk knocking a sparrow out in mid-flight.

DK's advice had been, "Don't go crazy and overtrain. You don't want to burn yourself out." But Carr didn't really believe in overtraining. Sure, he'd been warned about burn out and injury, but so far he'd been lucky and hadn't suffered anything serious. Even without nanos, he always healed quickly from minor issues and seemed to get by fine with five to six hours of sleep per night. Three weeks was nearly four hundred waking hours, quite a lot of time if he made the most of every one of them. He wasn't going to go in poorly prepared, like he had with Jackson. He wasn't ever going to do that again.

Uncle Polly always drew the line eventually. He'd been a trainer for a long time, and he had an instinctive feel for what Carr needed: when he needed to be encouraged, when he needed to be yelled at, when he needed to be pushed harder or reeled back in. "Calling it a night," he shouted now. "I know you'd keep going if I didn't." Then he pointed at the deck, which seemed, because of where they were in space, to be hanging below them. "Looks like you've got an audience."

Carr tilted his head. Risha Ponn held lightly onto the guide-rail as she walked, seemingly upside down, across the deck. Carr stifled both a smile and a groan. He was in pre-fight monasticism: no alcohol, no caffeine, no junk food, no girls. Risha was distracting as hell: legs that went on and on, chin-length black hair floating in a dark halo around her head, thinscreen tucked under one arm, poised to overwhelm him with information.

"She's a bit old for you," Uncle Polly said, startling Carr out of his thoughts.

"Coach," Carr protested, the tips of his ears starting to burn, "I wasn't going there."

"Sure you were," said Polly. "I was your age once. I'm just saying."

Carr couldn't tell if Uncle Polly intended to be as stern as his voice or as teasing as his eyes. "Even if I was going there, she's not," he said. "Not too old, I mean. I'll bet you she's twenty-one. Twenty-two at the most."

His coach shrugged, lips crooking as if fighting a smile. Carr blew out an exasperated breath and sailed toward the entry hatch, executing a tight flip as he went through. He landed on the deck, facing Risha. "What are you doing here?"

"Looking for you, obviously, in the place you spend ninety percent of your time," she replied. "Nice to see you too."

Heat crept into Carr's face. He backtracked and tried

to get off on a better foot. "I meant, how did you get in here?"

"I work for the ZGFA. Same as you, remember?" Risha smiled at Uncle Polly as he came out of the Cube. "Hello, Pol."

"Risha."

For reasons that Carr could not fathom, Uncle Polly and Risha Ponn had, in a mere two weeks, hit it off rather splendidly. She got away with calling him by his real name, Pol. He, for his part, referred to her as "that domie girl" with a note of grudging affection in his voice.

"May I take Carr for a couple hours?" she said, as if asking to borrow a vehicle.

"Sure can," said Polly before Carr could protest on his own behalf. "We just finished up."

"I have a taxi waiting." Risha led the way back down the hall toward the main docking hold.

Carr followed her, frowning. He stopped to gather his bag from its magnetic locker. "Is this important? My fight is next week."

"I haven't forgotten." She moved comfortably and gracefully, without clinging to guide-rails or tether. He wondered if it came to her naturally. Did she space-dance or play any zero-g sports? When they reached the hold, the waiting car opened when she held her cuff to the reader, and she instructed the vehicle to take them to Mia Terra food plaza in the outer ring. The harnesses tightened, and the car pulled away from the Virgin Galactic Center and sped down the freeway tube. "There will be food at Mia Terra you can eat, I hope?" she said.

"I have my dinner in my bag," Carr replied. "So go wherever you like."

As the pressure of gravity returned, Carr felt it in his body—more blood circulating to his lower torso and legs, a mild sense of queasiness as his stomach and organs settled downward. His clothes flattened damply against his skin, and it occurred to him that he stank of sweat. He always showered back in his apartment (zero gravity showers were truly awful) and now he would have to reek throughout dinner.

He glanced over at Risha, in trim white pants and a matching sleeveless top made of some gauzy, cooling material. It probably kept her Martian metabolism—designed for dry, bitter cold and lower oxygen—from overheating, but it also suggested "tropical vacation" and hugged her body in all the right places. He looked back down at himself, in gym clothes thrown over his training shorts. He pulled at the fastening band of his gloves with his teeth, tugging them off, irritated at himself.

"You're quiet," Risha said.

"Thinking about my fight," he lied.

Mia Terra food plaza bustled at all hours with pre- and post-show theater patrons, shoppers wandering over from the main strip of high-end stores, and the usual crowd of casino and hotel customers. Risha made straight for a place with a short line of two Martians and one Terran, which had a single item on the menu. Carr studied it curiously when she returned. It appeared to be a steaming bowl of deep purple stew.

"*Tzuka* chili," she explained. "Comfort food from the Valles. The most authentic version I've found in Terran orbit so far. You should try it when you're not on a pre-fight deprivation diet."

Carr snorted noncommittally. "Every zeroboxer has had *tzuka* beans." They were a staple superfood, designed by Martian agricultural scientists. Red Planet residents relied on the stuff all winter, but it had never been very popular on Earth.

"You haven't tried them like this," Risha insisted. "Valles cuisine does amazing stuff with *tzuka* beans." They claimed a small table near the light fountain at the edge of the plaza. Carr unpacked his carefully proportioned dinner: brown rice, chicken breast strips, a cup of chopped kale, and a custom-formulated supplement shake that the label told him included Zinc Ultrahigh, Max Vita, Enzyme Pulse, Adrenal Blast, and a dozen other things including chocolate flavoring. Risha looked at his meal and said, "I'll take *tzuka* chili any day."

They tucked into their food. "Do you miss it?" Carr asked. "Mars, that is."

She shook her head. "I left when I was a child. It doesn't feel like home to me anymore." She looked out across the plaza for a quiet moment before turning back to him. "But I don't belong on Earth either. I'm not designed for it; I don't fit in." She gave a helpless shrug. "On Valtego, it's never too hot. Martian and Terran ships come through every day. I can eat shrimp or *tzuka*."

Carr nodded. "Planet life is overrated."

Her lips moved in the beginning of a smile, parting as if she was going to say more. Then she reached for her thinscreen and unfolded it. "We *do* have business to talk about. Aren't you curious as to what your brandhelm has been up to?"

"I was planning on asking you, eight days from now."

"You now have InBevMC and Skinnwear confirmed as sponsors, and two others close to signing. The reason I need to talk to you is ImOptix—I'm positioning them as a tentpole sponsor and they want you broadcasting with their newest, highest-resolution optic implants. So you'll need to go in to upgrade, and you can't be hit in the head for forty-eight hours afterward."

Carr opened his mouth, then closed it again. "I…what? No, I don't have time to go in to upgrade my optics."

"It'll only take an hour. Two max. Can you do it tomorrow morning?"

"No."

"Morning after tomorrow, then. Otherwise we'll run out of time. And no head impact for two days, remember."

"That's crazy. I have a fight in seven days. How do you expect me to—"

"Gant approved my proposed brand campaign. I got your pre-fight interview spot extended from five to ten minutes."

She was like a verbal zeroboxer, throwing moves too fast to counter. Carr let out a slow breath. How had she gotten so much done in such a short amount of time? "I'm impressed," he said finally.

"So you'll do it?"

"Do I have a choice? I promised to trust you on all this stuff." Carr glared. "If I don't win ... "

"Do you think you'll win?"

"I'm not about to jinx myself."

"I think you will."

"Based on what special zeroboxing knowledge that you possess?"

"BB Dunn thought he was going to be fighting Jaycen Douglas. Douglas is nothing like you. Now Dunn has three weeks to train to fight you, just like you have three weeks to train for him. But in his mind, he's taking a step down, fighting a consolation match when what he really wanted was a Douglas rematch." Risha tapped Carr on the bare forearm with her index finger. "You've been training non-stop; he's been trying to salvage the lost hype by trash-talking you. He was just on *Cube Talk with Brock*, saying that he really feels sorry for you, it must be scary for a young fighter pulled in as a replacement, and he looks forward to teaching you a few things."

"He said that?"

Risha took a bite of chili, leaned back, and smiled, as if she'd won some match he didn't know they were having. His thoughts ping-ponged between how he was going to break Dunn's face, and how exotic and beautiful she was. Before he could stop himself, he said, "How old are you?"

Catching her off-guard gave Carr a twinge of satisfaction. He even thought he saw her blush, though he couldn't be sure—it might just have been the pink fountain light reflecting off her skin, like sunset off a wet seal.

"Eleven," she said. "Martian years."

He blinked at her. "So … twenty-one?"

"Twenty. Why are you smiling?"

"No reason. Just a little bet with my coach."

She angled her shoulders away from him and fiddled with the spoon in her bowl. "I skipped two grades when I moved to Earth."

"You're crazy smart, is what you're saying."

"That is not what I said. Martian schools are academically ahead of Terran ones." She gave him a mildly exasperated look. "You seem intent on turning our conversations around on me. Do you enjoy unbalancing me professionally, or are you just sexually attracted to me?"

"Both," he said without hesitation. He could still feel the tingling hot spot on his arm where she'd tapped him with her finger earlier. "Don't take it the wrong way. You're doing a good job as a brandhelm, really."

Risha opened her mouth to reply, but someone began shouting and they both turned toward the sound.

"SINNERS! We have sown the seeds of our destruction. Engineered life is impure life, promised to the devil!" A man had climbed up onto the ledge of the light fountain. He had several days worth of stubble on his unwashed face and a thinning thatch of unkempt hair, which he kept repeatedly running his hands through as his tirade grew louder and more incoherent. A large, scrawled sign hung around his neck:

> Soldier X —Veteran and GUINEA PIG
>
> Renounce Repent Be PURE!!!!
>
> God gives it a body as HE has chosen—
> 1 Corinthians 15:38-39

Most people near the man shifted away hastily, and passersby made wide circles to avoid him. The two men who'd been in the *tzuka* chili line with Risha, the only other Martians in sight, were seated at a nearby table. Their tan uniforms and banded sleeves marked them as crew of Interplanet Freight, one of the three main shipping companies that came through Valtego. One of the crew members scowled in disgust, then touched his thumb to his front upper teeth and flicked it toward the man in a Martian gesture of contempt. "Ah, shut up and eat dust!"

The ranting man's eyes, darting and unfocused, high on bliss bombs or sweet dust, swiveled around. "Abominations!" he shouted at the Martians.

The crewman's eyes slitted and he started up from his seat. "Say that again, earthworm."

His companion waved a hand lazily. "Sit down. That vacck-head's not worth it."

"Unholy and impure!" shrieked the man on the fountain ledge.

Carr stood up. "Let's go," he said to Risha. "You don't need to listen to this."

Risha got to her feet. The man caught sight of her and pointed a rigid finger. "*Abomination,*" he hissed again, dragging the word out into each of its syllables.

Carr put a hand under Risha's elbow and his body between her and the crazy nut as he steered them away from the center of the food plaza. He spared a glance behind, long enough to see two security guards hurrying toward the commotion, one of them talking down the crewmen, the other approaching the man on the fountain with a drawn stun stick. The occasional drifter could show up on Valtego and be largely ignored, but any incident that antagonized one of the big Martian shipping firms would probably land the man in a cell or on the first police transport back to Earth. Keeping his grip on Risha, Carr navigated them past tables and food vendors, away from the crowds and the light.

In a few minutes they were walking down a residential street, apartment complex tubes descending on either side into swanky penthouses with unobstructed views of space. There was high-quality simulated night in this neighborhood—a very natural softness to the dusk, the fragrance of blooming trees in the air. Carr climbed his hand from Risha's elbow to her tense upper arm and stroked it. The sheen of her skin paled a little under the pressure, then came back again when he moved his hand away. The effect made him want to do it again. "Hey," he said, "forget that nut."

She turned toward him, her eyes reflecting the starlight from the expansive sky windows. "He couldn't really be a Soldier X case, could he?"

Carr shook his head. "No way. That scandal happened before he was born." Decades ago. He vaguely recalled learning about it in modern history class. Thousands of private sector soldiers had consented to genetic tampering that was supposed to improve their executive reasoning and reflexes, but instead gave them a degenerative neurological disorder. Criminal charges, lawsuits, and massive settlements ensued. "Maybe he knew someone who was part of it. Or he was just plain delusional and vacuum-headed on bliss."

Risha's mouth was still grim. "Vaccked or not, there actually are Terrans who believe the same as him."

"That we should all join the Purity Movement and reject even basic gene therapy? That Martians aren't human?" Carr wrinkled his nose. "Yeah, sure, there are people who believe all sorts of crap."

They sat down on a bench tucked into a small garden of artificial plants. Even a few live ones grew in hydroponic containers, and there was the gentle, recorded burble of water. Carr tried to think of a way to steer the conversation back in the pleasant, exciting direction it had been going before the whole raving-lunatic incident.

"Where are you living?" he asked, chagrined that he hadn't bothered to check on how she was settling in on Valtego. "Do you have a place?"

Risha smiled a little, her shoulders relaxing. "I think I've found an apartment I like in the inner ring. I've been staying with a friend in the meantime. She lives in the Celestial on Eighth, not far from here."

"I'll walk you back there," Carr offered. He wasn't that familiar with this part of Valtego; he checked his cuff for directions and a red directional arrow appeared in the corner of his vision. They walked in silence for a few minutes. He stole glances at Risha, achingly aware of her nearness, but she seemed lost in thought.

"Martians aren't just different in the way Terran races are different from each other," she said finally. "We did it to ourselves. We turned our backs on the old planet and *chose* to make ourselves different. Maybe even better. That's what the average person on Earth thinks." They reached the entrance tube of the apartment complex and she turned to face him, hugging her own arms though he knew she wasn't cold. Her armor of competence was down; beneath it, he caught a glimpse of something pensive, even anxious. "In school I learned that if it wasn't for genetic designers, the Martian colonies probably wouldn't have survived after Earth stopped supporting them. But when I moved to Earth, I learned that Terrans thought Martians were arrogant, trying to dominate the solar system, acting above God and whatnot. How does that happen? How do people conveniently forget history?"

Carr shook his head, feeling ludicrously compelled to say something in defense of his planet. "Terrans aren't just a bunch of stupid bigots. Earth has so much more history, so many people, there's religion, and poverty…" He ran a hand through his short hair. "I grew up in a poor, shitty neighborhood in Toronto, and the kids I knew, they didn't have big, bright, hopeful futures. I'm lucky, because I made it here. I heard that something like eighty percent of Terrans have never left the planet surface. All those other billions of kids down there, they hear that livable space on Mars is growing while on Earth it's shrinking, that all the major discoveries are being made off-planet, and so are the jobs. No wonder some of them turn out like the guy in the food plaza."

She was silent for a moment, dark eyes roaming over him thoughtfully. "So what makes you special?"

"What do you mean?"

"You said you were lucky because you made it here. How did you do it?"

He wasn't sure what she expected him to say. "Wanting it enough, I suppose. Working my ass off."

She nodded several times, her eyes glistening. "Yes."

He didn't see why his answer was exciting to her, but he decided the slow, breathless way she'd said "yes" might be the sexiest thing he'd ever heard. He hoped she didn't invite him inside, because he would have to accept immediately.

"Risha," he said, "Look. I know I haven't been a great client so far. Or even a friend. After next week, maybe we could, you know, spend a bit more time together..."

"I'm your brandhelm. We'll be spending plenty of time together."

Was that smile a promise?

He watched her slender, white-clad form disappear into the apartment. His mind was acting like an inexperienced zeroboxer in the Cube, bouncing unsteadily from wall to wall: BB Dunn, ImOptix, Terrans, Martians,

Risha. He felt, suddenly, as if Risha was counting on him. Depending on him, even. That when he met his opponent in the Cube next week, he wouldn't just be fighting for himself, or for Uncle Polly, but for her as well. And as smart and driven as she was, she needed someone to fight for her.

The thought settled into him, made him feel warm, and lengthened his strides as he headed for home.

SEVEN

Carr went into the fight with BB Dunn wishing he could have had another three weeks to prepare, but it turned out he didn't need them. The fight went as Risha had foreseen. Dunn came out flying and didn't let up. He attacked fast, from every angle, employing every tactic to spin, throw, and disorient his opponent. Against Jaycen Douglas, it would have been the perfect strategy. Against Carr, it was completely flawed. Unlike Douglas, Carr had a space ear to rival, perhaps even surpass, Dunn's, and he had the staying power to climb, fly, and trade blows for a whole round without getting winded, and without a hint of nausea or dizziness.

By the third round, Dunn realized his error and turned to his submission game, but Carr had spent the previous week drilling his ability to break and counter Dunn's moves. With three minutes left on the clock, he choked Dunn out while floating.

When the two fighters met back on the deck and the referee raised Carr's hand, the packed stands went wild. For the ninety-five percent of humanity living on planets, no sport was as thrillingly superhuman as a zeroboxing match between two spectacular fliers at the top of their game. Dunn v. Luka had been such a match, topped by a rousing underdog victory. The fight lit up on the Systemnet, shared and replayed the second it ended.

Dunn looked to be in shock, as if he didn't yet realize that the match was over and he had lost. "You got me, kid," he muttered as they clasped hands. "You're something else. You got me."

Carr was better prepared for the crush of fans and journalists this time. He had Blake and Scull run interference to keep them at bay until he could get to the locker room to recover and celebrate. Risha came down, yelling with excitement, and she and Uncle Polly hugged each other wildly, spinning around together in the air like an exuberant human caduceus. Carr drank in the sight, letting its sweet flavor infuse his euphoria. Victory was a better high than a hundred bliss bombs. Perfect and real, lasting for days, even weeks, before being polished and stored in its own special nook of his soul, each win unique and everlasting, wanting nothing except more neighbors.

The post-fight press conference was standing room only. Carr wore his new Skinnwear top and jacket. The only thing anyone wanted to talk about was how he was now the youngest-ever contender for the division title and when that fight would happen. How did he explain his success? How had he prepared for this fight on such short notice? Did he have anything to say to Henri "the Reaper" Manon?

"Just be yourself," Risha had counseled him moments before, her words whispered into his ear as soft and close as if she were in his receiver. "People already like you. They think you're tough but gracious. Play to that."

Carr nodded at the journalists. "I'd say the Reaper has to start looking over his shoulder." He said it with a smile, and no nastiness. There was a lot of frenzied cuff-jabbing as the quote went flying out into the ether.

The after-party was held at Aloft, a low-g dance club. Carr was pleased that he had the perfect post-fight face: undamaged around the eyes and mouth but stitched above his left eyebrow, so he could wear his fight prominently without looking like a troll in photos and video clips.

The dance floor throbbed with wanton energy. Sweaty bodies leapt high, rippling in the darkness with liquid tattoos and skin dye and shifting hair color. At the bar and on the couches, where people could mute their receivers and have audible conversations, Carr was plied with drinks. DK, fresh from a narrow victory over Titus Stockton two days earlier, bought a round. Blake and Scull did more than their part to keep the booze flowing, especially after Adri and a bunch of her friends showed up. There was a seemingly endless parade of fellow zeroboxers, sponsors, and ZGFA brass for Carr to accept congratulations from. He could not possibly remember all their names and faces and hoped his new optics were capturing it all so he could figure it out later.

From the corner of his eye, Carr caught a glimpse of someone he'd seen before. At first he thought he must be mistaken, but when he swung his head back around, there he was—the pale, waxen-faced man from the tour group. He was leaning against the bar with a glass in one hand, watching Carr from across the room.

What was *he* doing here? Carr frowned and took a small step forward, angling his head to see through a cloud of artificial mist. Two ImBevMC Keg Girls blocked his view as they sallied past in front of him, handing out drink coupons.

"Another round of splatter shots!" Uncle Polly was being that most awkwardly entertaining of creatures, an old man acting as giddy as a kid, telling stories he'd told before, only louder. Someone pulled Carr back into the circle and pressed a glass into his hand. "One … two … three!" They threw their shots into the air, the liquid flying up in wobbly forms before descending slowly, all of them craning to catch theirs in their mouth and suck it down before it hit the table, the floor, their clothes or face.

Carr looked back toward the bar, but the man was no longer there.

Risha did not get drunk. Carr had done his job in the Cube; now it was her turn. She introduced him to Skinnwear's Director of Sports Marketing, two ImBevMC executives, and a number of zeroboxing commentators, all the while keeping up a witty banter with Brock Wheeden. Carr watched her as she worked the room, smiling and chatting, her cuff flashing continuously with exchanged linkage codes.

Carr realized that he'd suddenly achieved something he had fantasized about since the age of thirteen. When he stood still, he was soon surrounded by attractive women. Soft bodies lined up to press against him for photos and clips, exposed cleavage leaned toward him, coy smiles and scented necks vied for his attention. It was irony beyond all comprehension that he was impatient for them to be gone. He had groupies now; he had to get free of them.

"You've got to help me here," he begged DK. "You and the guys have got to help me with these girls."

DK, still sporting a swollen eye as his own fight scar, saw where Carr's gaze wandered and laughed. "Leave it to us," he promised.

Carr wove through people and caught Risha's wrist. He took her drink from her and set it down on the magnetic bar top. Then he pulled her toward the dance floor, away from the man she'd been speaking to, who opened his mouth as if to protest but didn't.

"Carr," she said, "that was the PR Director for the entire city-station of Valtego."

"Then I'd say tonight he owes me."

On the dance floor, Carr's optics kicked in, overlaying his vision with sparkles and strobing light effects that pulsed in time to the music. His receiver amplified the heavy beat, picked up and added harmonic chords. He drew Risha close. "Could you stop being my brandhelm for just a few hours?"

"A good brandhelm is always looking out for her client's interests," she said.

He slipped his hand into hers, their fingers interlacing. "I could tell you what my one interest is right now, and it doesn't include any PR directors." His face heated in the darkness. He was presuming too much. Perhaps he was just a client to her. Just a kid, just a fighter. But victory made him reckless.

Risha laughed and relaxed, moving to the music, leading him deeper into the crowd. She was taller than every other girl on the floor and danced as enchantingly as he'd imagined, at ease in low gravity, barely touching the ground. She turned heads, drew interested stares and jealous glances. The mist wove around her limbs, the light glinted off her skin.

Carr followed her without speaking, anticipation coiled inside him like a spring. He smiled to himself as people shifted out of his way. No man was going to challenge him tonight. Tomorrow he would feel all the places where bones had been jarred, where fists or feet had done damage, where muscles had been strained and skin bruised. But tonight he was invincible.

Bodies and warm darkness folded in around them. He put an arm around Risha's waist, pressed his palm into the small of her back, his heart thrumming like a bird's. She draped her arms over his shoulders as they danced.

Everything else fell away; everything except the movement of Risha's hips under his hands and the nearness of her body.

He kissed her. Her mouth opening for him, and the heat of her satin skin, thrilled him nearly to the point of pain.

She drew her lips away and whispered into his ear, "I want to take you somewhere."

Anywhere. "Now?"

"Yes." She tugged him off the dance floor. They hurried out the rear entrance of the club before anyone could see them making an escape. The music and pulsing lights fell away. Laughing at their own stealth, they clambered into a waiting taxi. Risha gave it directions, and it slid into motion. Then they were alone in the car, and kissing again, and if the taxi's thrusters had failed and left them stranded, floating indefinitely, Carr would not have minded.

He was disappointed when they reached the inner ring's lively streets after only a few minutes, but when he saw where the taxi had taken them, a grin crawled across his face. "You're brilliant," he said.

"I know." There was a smile in her voice as she led him inside.

The liquid tattoo artist at Living Ink was the best on Valtego and charged more than Carr had ever been able to afford. Carr lay on his stomach, head turned to the side, gazing at Risha, one hand linked with hers as the man worked. It took a long time; he should have felt sleepy given the hour, but sleep was the furthest thing from his mind. Every time the artist was done with one section, Risha ran her fingertips lightly down the raw, tender skin and leaned in to touch it gently with her lips. The mingled pain and pleasure lit every nerve in Carr's body.

When it was finally done, he stood and flexed his shoulders gingerly.

Risha stepped away from him. "It's perfect," she said softly.

Carr studied himself in the double full-length mirrors. He felt as though he were looking not at himself, but the person he would become. A promise he'd signed into his skin. He closed his hand over Risha's wrist and tugged her forward again. He imagined he'd proven himself to her today, that self-deprivation and hard work, physical trial and triumph, had made him worthy. Their lips met and he took flight, inked wings opening wide across his back.

———

"If you think I called you here to offer you a title shot, swallow your disappointment now."

It was three days later, and Carr was in Bax Gant's office, wise enough to be wearing a sweater this time. He'd started to sit down but paused. An older man, a long-faced Terran with bushy eyebrows and a smart suit, was already seated in a chair next to Gant's desk, straightening his cuffs and regarding Carr intently. Carr looked back at the Martian as he sat slowly. "You don't think I've earned a match against Manon?"

"Stars in heaven, Luka, a match between you and the Reaper seems to be the only thing anyone is asking me about these days," Gant grumbled. "Personally, I think it's too early. You took a short-notice fight against Dunn and blew it out of the water. You're in a good place right now. Milk it a little. People have latched onto the romantic idea of 'youngest champion ever,' but there's no need to rush into a title fight. The belt will wait."

Carr was silent, his expression stony.

Gant threw up exasperated hands. "The fight will happen, but I can't just snap my fingers and give it to you. Manon and his people have to agree, and they'll want to pick when. I've got to juggle a lot of considerations."

"So what is this meeting about then?" If all Gant wanted was to tell him he wasn't getting a title fight, he could easily have called or messaged. Carr glanced at the long-faced Terran. "Who are you?"

Gant answered. "Mr. Larsen is a senior brand management specialist from Merkel Media."

Mr. Larsen's thick eyebrows waggled as he reached over to shake Carr's hand, too firmly. "*Please*, call me Dean."

"You're one of the Merkel guys, huh? Maybe you know Risha Ponn, my brandhelm."

My brandhelm. Heat trembled behind Carr's navel. He loved the casually professional way that sounded when he said it out loud, even as his mind wheeled off to decidedly unprofessional places. What had Risha *done* to him? Turned his brain into a dedicated fan-feed that he couldn't turn off. What was she doing for dinner tonight? Let there be some urgent business to discuss with him. How did she learn to dance so damn sexy? What was she wearing *right now*?

He said to Gant, "Is she coming to this meeting?"

As if on cue, Risha stepped into the office and took a seat in the last available chair. A smile lit up inside Carr, starting somewhere in the center of his chest. It petered out unexpectedly before it could reach his face. Risha's expression was tight and downcast, as if something was bothering her and she was trying hard not to show it.

Gant didn't seem to notice. "Now that we're all here, let's get started." He turned to Carr. "I asked you here because we're kicking off a major marketing campaign. It's the right time to do it; zeroboxing viewership is on a steep rise, and marquee fighters are starting to become household names. We can ride the wave of your recent wins, really take the sport to the next level."

Carr tugged his eyes away from Risha and back to Gant. He waited for what the man was getting at.

The Martian leaned forward, gesturing toward Carr expansively. "You're going to be our brand ambassador. The face of the ZGFA. You're Terran, you're young and well-known, you've got grace in the Cube, and you're not a bully or a volatile headcase. In short, you're perfect for the job."

Carr glanced at Risha again, but she didn't meet his gaze, seeming oddly intent on studying the fight memorabilia on Gant's shelves. What was wrong with her? Didn't she think this was good news?

"The plan is still in development," Gant continued, "but there'll be several integrated components." He swiped at his wallscreen, pulling up a diagram of concentric circles like a bull's-eye. In the center was an image of Carr, overlaid with the words *EXPLODE THE SPORT OF ZEROBOX-ING BY LEVERAGING KEY ASSETS.*

"You'll star in a feature documentary, a multi-platform ad campaign, and a global publicity tour. We're also working on how to offer a more premium experience to your subscribers." As Gant spoke, his voice gaining momentum, the outer rings of the bull's-eye filled in with labels matching each of his examples until the small picture of Carr was surrounded by words in all caps. The Martian paused, fixed Carr with a meaningful stare. "We're going to make you big, Luka. Real big."

Carr stared at the screen. His pulse had begun racing alongside his imagination, and he shifted in his seat uneasily. The Martian sure knew how to nudge a man's ego. "What about my matches?" he asked.

"You'll get your fights," Gant reassured him. "Maybe a little less frequently. Naturally, more responsibility will mean more pay. More than what you make in the Cube."

Dumbfounded excitement expanded in Carr's chest and vied against a vague dread in his stomach. Two months ago he wasn't sure he'd have his contract renewed. Now, all this. He would be an idiot not to jump at the opportunity, but the idea of being followed around by a movie crew, or being trekked around Earth on some public relations campaign, sounded an awful lot like giving group tours to planet rats, times a thousand. That wasn't his thing. What he knew was training, and fighting, and winning. Rinse and repeat. He put his elbows down on Gant's desk and bit his thumb knuckle.

Gant exchanged a glance with Dean Larsen. He looked back at Carr. "Listen," he said, more serenely now, as if they were drinking buddies having a heart-to-heart over a beer. "This isn't just about getting more people to watch Cube matches and growing the ZGFA. Though of course we're going to do that. What we're really doing here is selling hope. Hope for all those kids living in Toronto, or Moscow, or Beijing, wondering if they have a future. What would inspire them?"

Enzo sprang to Carr's mind. Enzo, with his asthmatic wheeze and crappy inhaler, whose mom spent her money on lotto tickets instead of the gene therapy he needed. Enzo, who followed his fights religiously, whose personal feed, tracked by nearly no one, was peppered with zero-boxing references.

Gant leveled a finger at Carr. "I'll tell you what those kids need to see. Someone who shows them that not all Terrans are planet rats. Someone who proves that with hard work and grit, an ordinary guy born on Earth can beat the odds."

Carr blinked. Gant's words echoed in his head, oddly familiar. The conversation he'd had with Risha outside Mia Terra food plaza ... this was her doing. She'd seized upon what he'd said and used it to build a campaign, to cement him in the spotlight with the Martian. He swiveled his gaze to her again, his mouth going slack, impressed and grateful and mildly horrified.

She met his gaze, finally, and gave him a strange, forced little smile, as if she was reassuring him.

"Bran Merkel is completely on board with our strategy," Gant continued. "It's such a high priority that he's assigned Mr. Larsen here to lead it."

Dean Larsen smiled at Carr, too widely. "I'm looking forward to *personally* handling your profile from now on."

"Handling it how?"

Gant explained, "Mr. Larsen will be your new brandhelm."

"I already have a brandhelm."

Dean Larsen gestured to Risha without looking at her. "Ms. Ponn has done a commendable job so far, but she is a *junior* brandhelm. Given your *elevated profile*, it would be best if you were managed by someone with a *great deal* more experience from now on." He held up a hand of reassurance. "Don't worry, I'm sure there'll be a job waiting for Ms. Ponn back on Earth."

A miserable shadow passed briefly across Risha's face. She spoke, finally, her voice quieter than normal. "I'll be staying on through next week, to make sure the whole transition goes smoothly." She looked as if she wanted to say something else to him, but she stopped, pressing her lips together tightly.

Carr turned on Gant. "I don't want him. I want Risha to stay on as my brandhelm."

"Now, Luka…" There was a warning note in Gant's voice. Did he think that Carr was being unreasonable? Talking from his cock instead of his head? Carr didn't care. He didn't like Dean Larsen's eyebrows or the way the man emphasized certain words for no particular reason. He liked Risha. He really, really liked her. He liked looking at her. He liked how someone so smart could exist in a body that turned him so stupid. He liked the way she spoke to him, and the way she made him walk a little taller, and the fact that the dull world outside of the Cube seemed sharper when he was with her.

This whole thing was her idea, and she was getting shafted.

"I haven't said yes," Carr said. "You need me to cooperate."

"We are talking about a level of personal branding that *few athletes* achieve," Dean Larsen sniffed, his wide smile gone. "Any of your peers would eagerly take your place."

"Sure they would. But who's going to make your big strategy work? You guys have thought this whole thing through too much to go changing your main ingredient." Hesitation showed on their faces; he was right. He faced Gant and plowed on, feeling out of his depth and compensating the way he knew how, by looking mean: squaring his shoulders, lifting his chin. "I want to do this, and I'll work hard for you, but we have to do it my way."

Gant scowled, but he was listening.

"Risha stays on as my brandhelm. I want my matches, on schedule. We work around my training. For the eight weeks before I fight, I won't leave Valtego." He paused. "And I want my title fight."

Silence. Risha's mouth was soft and slightly open, her astonished gaze like the heat of the sun on the side of Carr's face. Dean Larsen began to sputter something in protest, but Bax Gant held up a hand.

"Damn," he said. A slow grin seeped across his face. "What did I tell you, Larsen? The kid is a born fighter." He pointed a finger at Carr and another at Risha, snapping his scowl back into place. "Get your shit ready. You leave on tour next week."

EIGHT

It was Carr's first trip back since he'd left the planet on a one-way ticket to Valtego, flying economy class with two Lunar stopovers. The return journey, nearly two years later, was an express flight made in VIP seats on a J-class Virgin Galactic super-cruiser. As the green and blue planet loomed up, impossibly large, the cloud-wrapped outline of Western Europe filling the entirety of his window view, Carr struggled to take deep, calm breaths—and not just because of the g-forces from atmospheric reentry. Pulling away from the docking hub of Valtego and watching the city-station recede and then disappear behind the Moon had made his gut roil with anxiety.

The previous night he'd had a nightmare in which he was, for some unknown reason, stranded on Earth. In his dream, he was supposed to be competing in a fight, but instead he was watching a sports news-feed in which some other fighter had taken his place in the Cube. He'd woken in a panic and hadn't been able to get back to sleep.

When he told Risha about the dream, he'd expected her to laugh it off reassuringly. Instead, she said that when she was on Earth, she had nightmares in which the sky was crushing her.

She'd come by his apartment to pick him up and was sitting on his bed, her packed suitcase next to her, watching him cram clothes into a duffel bag. He paused to tackle her to the mattress. She yelped as he rolled on top of her, covering her body with his. "Don't worry," Carr said. He kissed her temple. "I won't let the sky fall on you."

Her shoulders and chest jiggled pleasantly under him in soft laughter. "You would beat it into submission."

"I would. Make it tap." He pressed his hips down over hers. He wanted to have sex with Risha so badly it sometimes made his vision swim.

Her sigh of wonder came out hot against his neck. "You're my client. You're Terran. You're younger than me—you're not even eighteen yet."

"I will be in a couple months. Why does that matter?" He pushed up on his elbows, worried. For the past week, he'd been catching himself wondering if *this*—the two of them—felt as real to her as it did to him. Would her next words be, "So we should keep this relationship professional"? Because it was too late for that. For him it was.

"I don't want to feel like I'm doing something hasty, taking advantage of you somehow." But she smiled, lifting her head to kiss him, and he relaxed a little. "A couple months isn't long," she said.

He disagreed entirely; the idea of her "taking advantage of him" was appealing in the extreme. But he kissed her back silently and laid his head next to hers.

"I didn't plan this, you know," she said softly.

"Really? You're so good at planning everything else."

"Not this."

There were two sides to Risha, Carr decided, which balanced each other like rock and water in a Zen garden. The sexily intimidating, rapid-fire Risha with her thinscreen, who charged him up, and the Risha who feared the sky, who spoke slower and touched gently, who made him want to do anything for her. "My life has changed so much since I've come to Valtego," this Risha said. "There's something about living off-planet. It makes you feel like anything is possible."

Carr understood. "Valtego is more my home than Earth is now." It sounded true as he said it. He'd lived more, accomplished more, in the past two years than in all his years before; his whole childhood had been mere preparation. Going back to Earth now didn't feel like a homecoming, just a thing he had to do.

The captain's voice came on in the cabin to inform them they would soon be landing. Uncle Polly was leaned back in his seat, his eyes closed, but Carr could tell the old man wasn't sleeping. Polly traveled back to the Greater Earth area somewhat regularly to keep up with the business end of Xtreme Xero, the orbital gym he and his brother owned, where he'd brought Carr and practically raised him since the age of seven. Polly always complained about going planetside. "Have to visit the old dirt ball," he'd say.

Carr had told him that he didn't need to come on this trip if he didn't want to. It was going to be nearly three weeks of nonstop publicity events: meeting people, talking into cameras, being flown from city to city, crowd to crowd. Uncle Polly had made a face as he looked at Carr's schedule. "Someone has to keep your head above water, make sure the Merkel Media goons don't let you become a fat piece of waste. I'm going to talk to that domie girl," he'd said. "You need to fit in an hour of land-training every morning, and another hour in the evening, in hotels if we have to. It's not too much to ask that you get to an orbital gym twice a week."

"You're right, coach," Carr admitted. "I need you."

"Damn straight."

The view of Earth sank into impenetrable white mist. When they emerged, Carr could no longer see the outline of the continent, only the land itself rushing up toward them; it was like zooming in on a holovid. The uncomfortable pressure lifted as they descended over Heathrow Aerospaceport. One night in London, to meet with the ImOptix management team, then on to Paris, Munich, and Moscow before heading to Asia, then North America. Fifteen cities in twenty days.

His head felt heavy at the thought. Growing up, Carr had spent little time on other continents—only brief stops here and there on his way around the amateur circuit of

Earth's few orbital arenas, sleeping in cheap motels and traveling on juddering rocket-planes so old they were nearing decommission.

London was warm, gray, and muggy. As soon as they disembarked, they were met by a chartered van and two men who Risha introduced as Eason and Marc from Merkel Media's Events Management department. Carr shook their hands. "I've never done this sort of thing before. You know that, right? Press conferences, sure, but not this."

"Just show up and be the star." Eason sported a British accent and an outlandish, retro sense of style; his cuff had a faux-metal skin and he wore chunky black plastic glasses frames he must have found at an antique store or costume shop. "Leave all the details to us."

A live attendant took their bags and jackets, settled them into the upholstered seats, offered them drinks, and programmed in their destination before sliding the door shut. As the vehicle glided into motion and merged into traffic, Uncle Polly opened the window, letting in a gust of humid air. He breathed in a deep drag. "Smell that, Carr?" he said. "Real planet air. Not much I like about being earth-side, but the air...there's so much more character to it."

Carr leaned his head out of the window. Uncle Polly had a point. City-station air was always the same, always bland and manufactured. Sure, they could flavor it all sorts of ways, and the hydroponic greenhouses and gardens on Valtego came close to smelling like planet air, but not quite. Only Earth had air that changed and moved and could be different from day to day, infused with dirt and salt and rain and smog and all the essences of life and humanity. He pulled in a lungful as he drank in the sight of the passing landscape. So much space, so many buildings and trees; the sky as huge and light as space was dark and endless. He was surprised by how it touched him. He had missed it after all.

The van slowed as it entered central London. As they drove past the Parliament building, Carr pointed to the large crowd of people gathered on the green in front of the Palace of Westminster. They were carrying signs, chanting, marching back and forth. A line of security droids blocked the demonstration from the entrance, and behind them, several uniformed policemen kept a vigilant eye on the situation. "What's going on there?" Carr asked.

"Protesters," Eason huffed. "They've been there for a week. A mishmash coalition of conservatives, Purity Movement, anti-colonization advocates, and marsphobes."

"What are they angry about?"

Marc, a short man who sounded American, said, "There's a bill before the European Congress that would amend the Bremen Accord and broaden what genetic modifications are legal." He touched his neck involuntarily, fiddling with a small gold crucifix that he wore. "If it passes, it could pave the way for resettlement."

"*Pffft*," was Uncle Polly's reply. "Comes up every few years, these resettlement efforts. They'll never happen. Too bloody expensive."

"Not if we follow the Martian example," Eason said. "If we could live in extreme temperatures, on far less water, with resistance to tropical diseases—in a few generations, we could repopulate most of the planet."

Marc was shaking his head. "The Bremen Accord exists for a reason! Sure, gene therapy saves lives, but genetic enhancement? That should *never* be legal, not on this planet. Not so long as, God willing, people remember that racism, wars, and genocide all spring from the idea of certain people being better than others. You can call it 'adaptive modification' like the colonists do, but it's enhancement all the same. It's not right." He looked as though he would say more but snapped his mouth shut instead, darting his eyes over to Risha and away again as he realized he might have caused offense.

But Risha wasn't paying attention to their conversation. She sat stiffly, her legs crossed, her back so straight that with her height, her head nearly reached the roof of the van. She touched the back of her hand to her mouth, dabbing away the sweat on her upper lip. "Do you mind putting the windows back up?" There was a tight note in her voice. Carr remembered the nightmare she'd shared with him, about the sky crushing her. He quickly touched the control to close the windows.

"Sorry," he said. He reached a hand over, placed it on her knee. "You going to be okay?"

"Of course. I lived on Earth for years." She forced a smile, but it was weak around the edges. "It's just... been a while." She leaned her head back and took a slow breath. He kept his hand on her leg, tracing her kneecap with his fingers. By the time they reached ImOptix corporate head-quarters, Risha seemed a little less tense, more herself.

The van glided to a smooth halt in front of a tall old building made of glass and steel, all smooth sides and sharp corners. Nothing nano-assembled, no carbon fiber—a real relic. It seemed an incongruous headquarters for a cutting-edge company like ImOptix, but you couldn't deny that there was something truly awe-inspiring about these old European buildings.

"We'll go ahead to the hotel, get you checked in and a comm link set up," Marc said. "You have an hour here; you need to leave ImOptix at exactly 16:00 if Carr is going to eat and prepare before the evening interview."

"16:30 is probably fine," Risha said. "I already have his notes prepped."

She and Carr entered the ImOptix building, crossed its echoing, light-filled lobby, and took an elevator that whisked them up to the fifty-seventh floor.

Carr watched their reflections in the glass rise up through the sky. "What am I supposed to do here?" he asked.

"Just listen and look interested. Not *too* interested. They were on the verge of finalizing the offer before your BB Dunn fight, and your win has given us a lot more leverage. So I'm working on sweetening the terms."

The elevator door opened onto a large conference room with a long black table in the center and floor-to-ceiling windows filling one wall. Around the table were a dozen people in suits, who turned in their seats to look at Carr.

A flutter of unfamiliar nerves ran through his gut. He

had never been in any place so ... *clean*. It reminded him of some of the five-star hotels on Valtego, whose marble-tiled lobbies he occasionally glimpsed but never went into. Gant's office was like a broom closet compared to this place. Carr felt conscious suddenly that he was wearing the same clothes he'd flown to Earth in—casual pants, a short-sleeved Skinnwear top—and wondered why Risha hadn't thought to have him change into something nicer. She was dressed in a fashionable skirt-suit.

Risha took control. "Carr, let me introduce you to the ImOptix management team." She rattled off the names of each of the people—the VP of this, the General Manager of that, titles that went in one of Carr's ears and out the other. As they each rose to greet him, he shook their hands and fell back on fight instinct: when you feel out of your league, don't show fear. Keep your body relaxed and ready, and look your opponent in the eyes, firmly.

"Congratulations on your recent win," said a tall, dark-skinned man—Raj, the Something-Important-of-Something. "We're very excited to show you what we've been working on." He gestured Carr and Risha toward two seats at the end of the table. The wall of windows instantly darkened into a smooth screen, and the ImOptix logo appeared across it.

"Our motto here at ImOptix is simple," Raj said. "Faster. Stronger. Sharper." The words flashed, one by one, onto the screen. "That's the ethos that powers the design of our latest generation of optical implants, the L series, which has the highest resolution ever achieved in optical camera technology, the fastest transmission speeds, and better-than-ever visual overlay features."

Raj talked at length about the ground-breaking advances that had gone into making the new optics, the size and growth of the market, and the branding strategy. Carr forced himself to be attentive, all the while wondering if he was supposed to be remembering any of this, or saying anything, and what any it had to do with him. At last, Raj said, "Nothing showcases 'Faster, Stronger, Sharper' and resonates with our savvy young target consumers better than zeroboxing."

A video started playing on the screen. Carr's optics picked up the signal and automatically shifted the image into high resolution 3D while darkening the periphery of his vision. He sat up. It was himself, in the Cube, his eyes intense with focus.

A narrator's deep voice said, *"To win, you have to be faster."* Video-Carr exploded off the Cube wall, the camera tracking the launch into slow motion. *"You have to be stronger."* His fist connected with an opponent's face with a sound effect enhanced *crack.* *"You have to be sharper."* A brilliantly high-resolution image appeared of a single droplet of sweat, spinning in zero gravity, before the final low-angle, high-contrast shot: Carr on the deck of the Cube, hands raised in victory, the stands vibrating with roaring spectators. The screen faded back to the ImOptix logo. *"The new L series from ImOptix. See it all."*

The screen lightened and turned back into a wall of windows. Light flooded the room again, and Carr's vision returned to normal. He discovered that his heart was pounding. The sight of himself like that in the Cube, the way the camera had made him look so ... heroic, like a character in a movie ... he felt a shiver run up and down his spine. He leaned back in his seat and crossed his arms, tucking his hands into his armpits so no one would see his jitters.

"Of course, this ad spot is just a mock-up using existing footage," Raj said. "As soon as we get the green light, we would arrange a film shoot to get enough of an asset bank to build a full campaign."

Carr blinked and realized that everyone was looking at him expectantly. His mind felt suddenly blank. All he could think of to say was, "It's not my best fight."

"Pardon me?" said Raj.

"The shot you have in there, of me hitting Ricky Daluma—it wasn't my best fight."

Risha leaned toward him. "For the real ad, they'll use the shot you want. You'll see and approve it before it goes live."

The people around the conference table nodded vigorously in agreement.

Carr nodded slowly. He let out a breath and brought his hands behind his head. "What can I say? It's really good." He pointed at the windows where the screen used to be. "That was amazing."

Smiles broke out. He got the very weird feeling that all these people had been waiting for him to say that, and he'd just released a big happy bomb in the room. He wondered if, as soon as he left, they were going to celebrate, and jump on their cuffs to congratulate their underlings, and start rolling ahead with budgets and film-shoot schedules and marketing plans.

"How are you enjoying your new optics?" asked a curvy middle-aged woman whose name he'd already forgotten but who had something to do with product development.

"They're great," he said. "Except for the part about not getting hit in the head for two days after getting them put in. Sort of hard in my job to go for two days without a shot to the head."

Everyone laughed. Risha stood, and Carr took that as his signal to do the same. "We'll be in touch," she said as they did a parting round of handshakes.

Alone together in the elevator, Carr looked at her questioningly. "Did that go all right?"

"Better than all right," she assured him. "They'll come back with their highest offer yet by tomorrow, I'm sure of it." She turned to him, and her face, which had been as cool as a Martian winter during the meeting, broke into a smile that sent warmth racing up Carr's neck. "You were perfect."

"What do you mean? I didn't do anything."

"You looked confident, you paid attention, you were serious but funny, and you didn't act like a prima donna or a jerk. Do you have any idea how rare that is for a sports celebrity?" She pulled the collar of his shirt toward her and kissed him.

It was a long kiss, one that lasted until the elevator slid to a stop at the bottom floor, and it made Carr think that spending twenty days stuck on a planet wouldn't be so bad after all.

He got the call on day eighteen.

They were at Xtreme Xero, the gym he'd practically grown up in. A few years ago, it had been the largest of only a handful of North American orbital gyms. Now, there were more than a dozen. The last time he'd been here, he was fifteen going on sixteen, the youngest and highest-ranked amateur zeroboxer in the Terran system, shit-scared excited that he'd just landed a spot on Valtego and would be leaving everything he knew behind.

Now a reverent hush fell over the gym as he entered.

The place had grown. Looking around, Carr saw a few familiar faces but a lot more unfamiliar ones. There were two training Cubes now, and the climbing area had been upgraded. Uncle Polly had a hand glued to Carr's shoulder and was grinning from ear to ear, steering him around like the prodigal son on a return tour and introducing him to everyone. Uncle Polly's brother Mor, or Uncle Morrie as Carr had always known him, clapped his hands together sharply, and every trainee in the room pulled themselves over to the small gathering space, gripper shoes clinging to the magnetic flooring.

"Now," said Morrie, "you all know Carr. Some of you

personally, others from watching his fights. He's one of ours, of course, the best, and we're real proud he's come home to visit. How old were you when you started here, Carr?"

"Seven," Carr said.

Morrie clapped a hand to Carr's other shoulder. "Nine years after this kid came up from the surface for the first time, he started fighting on Valtego Station. If you don't know that he just toppled BB Dunn to become the second-ranked lowmass zeroboxer, you got no business being here. When's your title fight, Carr?"

"Don't know yet."

"Well, it's got to be soon. Good luck to you. We're all looking forward to seeing you with that belt. You hear that, you planet rats? You train your asses off, you might be half as good as Carr someday."

"Maybe better," Carr put in with a smile, for the benefit of the awestruck-looking kids in the front row.

"Carr's a busy man now, not like you slackers, so he's only here for the afternoon. Carr, the boys here did a round-robin tourney last weekend to figure out who gets to fly with you. That okay? You got time to fly with a couple of them? It'd mean a lot."

"Sure, let's do it." Carr found himself grinning, itchy with anticipation.

The last seventeen days had been a blur. Frankly, he was exhausted from being ferried from one place to another, from one crowd to the next, from media interview to sponsor meeting to fan reception to gym after gym of aspiring zeroboxers. It was nothing like the deep, purposeful fatigue of training, but an exhaustion altogether different, a nagging weariness from being mentally "on" all the time. The only thing that had helped him stay sane were the twice-daily workouts Uncle Polly kept him on religiously and the few times they'd gotten beyond gravity for some weightless work. Being here, though, he felt rejuvenated. Back in his element.

Risha was sitting out in the shuttle, working through an endless list of calls, but Eason and Marc were in the gym, clearing the way for the camera crew to film unobstructed as Carr stripped down to his shorts and donned his gripper gloves. The footage would go into the documentary film, which Gant had now decided would be released in three parts. Having the cameras follow him around had taken several days to get used to, but he barely noticed them now.

Carr swung himself into the training Cube. A wave of nostalgia swept over him; it was like being back in his childhood bedroom. The particular texture of the walls, the feel of the magnetic microgravity, the way the fans on one side were louder than the other...

A lanky black boy of fourteen or fifteen pulled himself in, to the encouraging cheers and applause of his teammates.

"What's your name?" Carr asked.

"Deryk," said the boy. He looked flush with excitement and slightly terrified.

"Nice to meet you, Deryk. Where are you from?"

"Chicago. I've been taking the lunar bus up here every

afternoon for six years. I want to fight in the ZGFA some-day, just like you."

"You won the tourney here last week, huh? You must be pretty good," Carr said. They touched gloves. "Let's see what you can do."

He didn't have to go easy on the kid. Deryk was solid. He was a good striker, could climb and fly with agility, and played a confident, if somewhat predictable and limited, grabbing game. Carr hit him a lot, but not very hard, and when the buzzer sounded on six Martian minutes, Deryk was still hanging in there. His friends outside of the Cube burst into cheers and clapping.

"Work on not giving up control when you're in clinch," Carr advised him. "And mix up the speed and angle of your rebounds—don't fall into a pattern. But you've got a future in the Cube."

The kid nodded in wordless gratitude as he bent over, catching his breath. Carr wasn't breathing hard yet, had barely broken a sweat. As Deryk made his way back to the hatch, Carr motioned for the next kid to come in. Just then, his cuff vibrated and played a rising note in his ear. He glanced down at it.

His stomach did a small flip. He motioned for a pause and, catching Uncle Polly's eye, mouthed urgently, "It's the Martian."

Polly shooed the watching kids back as Carr took the call.

"You got yourself a title fight, Luka," said Gant's voice into his ear.

Carr pulled in a breath that tingled all the way out to his toes.

"Manon's people said yes. But here's the thing," Gant continued. "They want to hold it this month."

Carr was speechless. "Bastards," he finally exclaimed. "They know I'm down here turning into an out-of-shape gravity bum. How am I supposed to fight this month?" He wasn't even in the Cube with Manon yet and he wanted to punch him in the face. What kind of self-respecting zero-boxer proposed a fight on that kind of a condition? Winning only counted if it was fair, not if you stacked the odds against your opponent.

"Yeah, well, don't be surprised they're trying to work the timing to their advantage. Your tour is getting a lot of buzz. You're hot right now, and the Reaper wants to show you up, fight you as soon as you return so he can take the wind right out of your sails."

"That's crazy," Carr said. "I can't do it. With Dunn, at least I was coming off another fight."

"Relax. They're pulling this stunt because Manon's contract doesn't come up for renewal until next year, and in the meantime you're getting more sponsorship and publicity than he is, even though he's the reigning champion. They're pissed and they want me to know it." Gant sounded unperturbed. Faintly amused, even. "I talked them off the ledge and out to New Year's Day. That's two months from when you get back."

Carr rubbed a hand across his face. "Hang on a second."

He muted his receiver and drifted over to where Uncle Polly was waiting by the Cube hatch. "New Year's," he said. "They want to hold it in two months."

To his surprise, Uncle Polly merely grunted in the back of his throat. "Figures." He looked at Carr with an oddly measured expression. "Well, what are you going to say?"

"You think I can do it? This is it, coach. This is my title shot. You think I can be ready in two months?"

Uncle Polly pulled himself up so they were face to face. "*You* have to know what you're capable of, Carr."

Carr looked his coach in the eye. Uncle Polly had controlled pretty much every aspect of his training until now. Just when Carr expected him to be most opinionated, Polly was leaving the decision up to him? He didn't have time to be confused; he touched his cuff to take his receiver off mute.

"You got an answer for me, Luka?"

"You have to promise me that as soon as I land on Valtego, there won't be anything distracting—none of this brand ambassador stuff—until after the match."

"You got it."

"Then you got yourself a title fight."

Carr could almost hear the man's smile. He wondered just how much of the drama over the timing had really been Manon and how much Gant had engineered it, eager to ride the momentum of the tour, to build up the hype of a match between his champion and his rising star. The fight, now set for Valtego's busiest week of the year, was guaranteed to sell out at premium ticket prices. The Martian was a winner no matter who won in the Cube.

"See you when you get home," Gant said, and the connection went quiet.

Carr floated over to the hatch and hung in its opening. A crowd of faces was gazing at him with held breaths. Uncle Polly and Uncle Morrie were trying to look serious in attempts to hide their smiles.

"It's happening," Carr said. "I fight for the belt on New Year's Day."

The place erupted. Cheering and applause and people beating their fists on the side of the Cube in celebration. Eason and Marc tapped their cuffs frantically, no doubt relaying the news and already making itinerary adjustments for the next three days. The film crew wielded their handheld cameras and head-mounted optic enhancers, trying to capture panning shots of the crowd and close-up shots of Carr, and Uncle Polly, and Morrie, and everything.

Carr let all the noise and excitement wash over him like water running down his back. He was already thinking ahead, his mind starting to whir, laying out a training strategy for a compressed time frame. He had to get his hands on good footage of all the Reaper's matches. And he had to think about who should stand in for Manon in practice bouts, and who would be available to corner for him. Two days. He still had two days on this dirt ball before he could get back to Valtego.

But he couldn't, wouldn't, cut them short, not even for this, because there was still one stop he needed to make.

He had to visit home. See his mother, and Enzo. After two years, he owed them a visit, owed it to them to share the news in person. Then he could get back to where he belonged.

NINE

Taking the shuttle into Toronto Interplanetary Aerospace-port, Carr marveled at how much the city had grown over the past few years. He'd read somewhere that it was a large city even hundreds of years ago, back when winter had gripped it in freezing cold and snow. Large by the standards of the time, that is. The Great Northern Migrations had swelled it to a metropolis of forty million, with buildings and roads stretching out like an enormous amoeba across the banks of the Great Lakes.

After they landed and made their way to the taxi queue, Risha said, "I'm going straight to the hotel with Eason and Marc."

Even though the weather felt perfect to Carr—it was a mild fall day—Risha had on a sleeveless cooling top that wicked away the subtropical heat and humidity and showed off a tantalizing amount of her glistening skin. She looked uncomfortable, eager to get into a climate-controlled building as quickly as possible.

Carr drew her away a little and put his hands on her waist. Her sweat had a certain scent he could only describe as warm and peppery. He said, "Come with me. If you want."

Risha tilted her head coyly, eyebrows raised. "Terran men only introduce their mothers to women they're serious about."

"Yeah."

The taxi pulled up and the queue attendant began loading their bags.

"What would she think of me being Martian?"

"Doesn't matter." To prove his point, Carr pulled her a little closer, so their hips touched. Risha was not the only Martian in sight; there were two businessmen in the line and a family of tourists, but they were the only couple, and they drew stares.

She made a *hmmm* sound and put a hand on his chest. "Unfortunately, I have a staggering load of work to do. Gant won't waste any time making the announcement, which means the whole schedule has to be thrown out. You really need your brandhelm to get to work." She extricated herself from him and held her cuff up to the reader on the next taxi. As the door slid open and Eason and Marc climbed in, she looked back and said, "Don't broadcast anything, and don't answer any questions until you hear from me. I'll see you in the evening." She stepped into the waiting vehicle and the door slid shut.

Carr climbed into the other taxi with Uncle Polly and

was silent as the car's computer calculated the route. They sped into motion, smoothly entering the freeway. Carr stared out the window, lost in thought.

"You're not going to be distracted from a championship belt by that domie girl, are you?" Uncle Polly asked.

Carr looked up sharply, into Uncle Polly's crooked, teasing smile. "You still owe me something for that bet," he said.

"You like her a lot." Half question, half statement.

"Guess so. Yeah." Carr shifted in his seat, worried that Uncle Polly might ask more questions, or want to have a talk about women, even though that was not the sort of thing they usually discussed. There had been the occasional "chat" in Carr's adolescence, mostly cautionary tales about how doing certain stupid things involving girls, drugs, or cops could destroy a zeroboxer's career. But just in case his coach was on the verge of shoehorning in some surrogate parenting, Carr changed the subject. "You didn't have to come with me to see Sally."

Uncle Polly's expression did not change, but his eyes tightened at the corners. "Came all this way already. Might as well."

Uncle Polly always seemed to tense up around Carr's mother. Carr had never understood why, but when he was about nine or ten years old, the two of them had abruptly stopped speaking to each other. They'd patched it up after a few months, but there wasn't a lot of warmth there. It bothered Carr a little because he figured the rift might have something to do with him, but both Polly and Sally pretended not to know what he was talking about if he ever brought it up. ("I've got nothing against your mother." "Your coach knows best, darling.") It wasn't a romantic thing—Carr was dead sure of that. There weren't many people less similar than Uncle Polly and Sally Luka.

The car pulled off the freeway and the bustle of the city engulfed them. Dense streams of people, all ages and races, crowded the streets; giant ads vied for attention on the sides of buildings; old skyscrapers poked up in between the gleam of translucent concrete and the lattice structure of nanobuilt towers. Carr leaned against the window, quiet with nostalgia as he took in the sights, some new, some familiar. Fragments of clear blue sky slid past above them, stark with sunshine.

In a few minutes, they turned into his old neighborhood. It was much the same as he remembered it. Tall palms rose up on either side of the narrow residential streets, and the smell of blooming flowers and ripening fruit mingled with the humid stink of garbage and sweat. The buildings here were small, old, and dirty, and the businesses sketchy: an adult holovid theater, a closed liquid tattoo parlor, a tiny dive of a bar that served gin spiked with sweet dust if you knew how to ask for it.

Sally Luka still lived in the walk-up apartment that Carr had grown up in. As they came to a stop outside, the onboard computer announcing their arrival, he saw the figure of a boy sitting on the front steps. Carr smiled as he stepped out of the taxi. "Enzo," he called.

The boy shot to his feet and ran down the steps toward them. He tackled Carr in a hug and they wrestled, laughing as Carr picked his friend up and mock-slammed him into the tiny brown patch of crabgrass that counted as lawn.

Enzo had grown a lot since Carr had left, from an undersized nine-year-old to an ungainly just-turned-eleven, all elbows and knees, messy hair, and big ears. Carr's grin faded as he pulled the boy back up to standing. "What's this, little man?" He flicked the rim of the glasses on Enzo's face with his finger.

"I need them," Enzo wheezed, "to see straight."

The frames were round, and unlike Eason's retro style accessories, they had real lenses inside. Carr's heart sank. "Why don't you get your eyes fixed, then?"

He guessed the answer before Enzo lowered his face in embarrassment. "My mom doesn't have the money right now. She said maybe in a few months..."

A surge of anger brought heat to Carr's scalp. It was bad enough that the kid had an asthmatic wheeze and carried around an inhaler. Now he was half-blind too? What next, a peg leg? Didn't Enzo's mother care that her son walked around with genetic poverty written all over him?

Carr lowered his voice. "How much money do you need?" If he won the title fight...

Enzo flushed, shifting his feet. "Oh no, I didn't mean to sound like I was asking... I mean, my mom wouldn't like that. And the glasses don't bother me really. She says it won't be for long." He didn't sound convincing.

Carr forced a smile back into place for the boy's sake. "People are wearing those for style now, did you know that?"

"Really?" Enzo brightened a little. He looked past Carr and said, "Hi, coach."

"Hi, kid," Uncle Polly said. Carr wondered if Polly remembered Enzo's name or just recognized him with tolerant amusement as "that little scab"—the kid who always called him "coach" even though the poor boy could never be a zeroboxer himself, never in a million years.

"Why aren't you inside with my mom?" Carr looked up the front steps of the apartment building. "She knows I'm coming, doesn't she? I messaged both of you." He wondered, with sudden worry, if Sally had already gone through the money he'd sent her after his last fight, if her data had been turned off again.

"She knows," Enzo said. "She has some guy visiting right now."

Carr frowned. Some guy visiting? He squatted down on the grass in front of Enzo. "I'm going to go up and see her for a while. I'll come find you afterward, yeah?" He tousled the boy's hair and lowered his voice conspiratorially. "I've got some big news to share with you."

Enzo's eyes widened, comically large behind his glasses, and his mouth dropped open. "Don't shit me, Carr! For real? I've been checking the ZGFA news-feed, like, every five minutes." He sucked in a breath, so excited Carr was afraid he might start to cough. "When? Can you tell me when?"

"Sixty-three days, little man. Start counting."

"STELLAR," Enzo breathed, his face going slack with the transcendence of a religious epiphany.

Carr grinned. "Tell you more later, I promise." He

waved the boy off and climbed the steps to the small foyer and the dim, narrow stairwell. He started up, but had barely made it halfway when Uncle Polly caught him by the arm.

"Carr," he said, and the tone of his coach's voice made Carr stop and turn. There was a strange and anxious look on Polly's face. "Don't go in there yet. There's something I have to talk to you about first. I meant to tell you on this trip; that's one reason I came along. I thought I'd find the right time, but it just hadn't come along yet, and then, with the title fight announcement, well…"

Uncle Polly was talking too fast, even for him. Carr couldn't fathom what on earth could be so important that he needed to bring it up right now, of all times. "What is it, coach? Couldn't it wait?"

"If the man who's in there is who I think—"

Just then, the door on the landing above them swung open. "Carr, is that you? I thought I picked up your signal coming through the front."

"Yeah, it's me, Mom." Carr took the rest of the stairs up to the apartment door. He paused and stood in front of his mother for a second, then stepped in for a hug. She clung to him tight, as if he were a small child who'd been lost at the mall and returned to her, and he hugged her back.

She seemed smaller than he remembered, and his chin could now rest on the top of her head. There was something different about her too; he realized with some displeasure that she'd cut her hair short and dyed it darker, so it was almost as dark as his. But she still smelled like citrus soap and cherry breath mints, and when she pulled back to look at him, the sight of her sun-freckled face, so full of the soft, placid attentiveness he remembered, brought a lump to his throat. She must have been working earlier today because she was still wearing her black and baby-blue bus attendant uniform, unchanged for as long as Carr could remember.

"How are you, Mom?"

"I'm just fine, darling." Her voice caught a tiny bit at the end as she spotted Uncle Polly coming up behind him.

"He's here, isn't he?" Uncle Polly's expression was strung tight as a wire.

Seized by sudden, fearful suspicion, Carr pushed the front door open all the way.

The apartment he'd called home was largely unchanged. Ancient LED lights still ran the length of the small kitchen, beyond which he could see his mother's bedroom and his own room, untouched since he'd left. The living room had the same old sofas and the same light green flooring, and his childhood trophies still cluttered the shelves beside the small flatscreen.

What was different was the man standing in the living room. He was studying the trophies with his hands clasped behind his back. He turned, and his lips moved in his smooth, pale face like the mouth of a mannequin come to life.

"Carr," he said. "Come in. We have a lot to talk about."

TEN

Carr took two steps into the apartment. He turned his shoulders and chin to speak to Sally, but he kept his eyes on the man. "Who the hell *is* this guy, Mom?" Dread scuttled up his back like a spider. "Is he ... he's not my ... " He couldn't get the word "father" out without choking. " ... my *donor*, is he?"

His mother stared at him for a second, then flushed to her ears. "Of course not. Why would you think that?"

Carr started breathing again. "Do you owe him money, then?"

"Carr," she said sharply. "That's not a tone to take. And with a guest here?" Flustered, she wiped her palms on the waist of her black pants and, seemingly at a loss for what else to do with her hands, brought them together. "Mr. R came a long way to see you. Why don't we all sit down?"

"A fine suggestion, Sally," said Mr. R.

Uncle Polly shouldered into the room. "You've got no right, ambushing us like this." His bony fists were clenched, his face reddened to the roots of his gray hair. "You should've let me decide when, instead of just showing up. You've got no right."

Carr's eyes jumped between the two men. "Coach, you know this guy?"

"No *right*, Pol? I don't have the right to see and speak to Carr whenever I wish?" Mr. R's voice was soft, but the gaze he fixed on Polly was as hard as marble.

Uncle Polly seemed to flinch. "It's not the right time. We have a title fight now."

"Yes. Congratulations."

"It's not the right time," Polly repeated.

"It's the perfect time." The stranger turned his back on them and walked over to the lumpy sofa, planting himself in the center of it as if he owned the apartment. He crossed an ankle over his knee and gestured to the seat across from him. "Have a seat, Carr."

Carr didn't move. "Why have you been following me?" Whoever he was, Mr. R had a precise, efficient manner that made his flesh prickle, as if he were being watched by something old and reptilian at the top of the food chain.

"I'm in the … athletic scouting business," the man said. "I have a unique business partnership to discuss with you."

Carr shot a confused, questioning glance at Uncle Polly, who offered a small, wordlessly stricken shake of his head.

He turned back to Mr. R. What kind of person called himself *Mr. R*, anyways? "I'm under contract," Carr said.

"If it's business you want to discuss, then contact my brandhelm. Don't stake out my mom's apartment."

Mr. R said, "This isn't the usual kind of business."

"Come back another time," Uncle Polly said. There was a note of resignation and pleading in his voice that Carr had never heard before. "Let me do it, at least."

Mr. R ignored him and brushed a bit of faded brown sofa lint from his pants, still speaking to Carr. "I'm afraid that surprising you like this might have given you the wrong impression. You see, I want to personally congratulate you on your recent success and your upcoming title fight. I've always been a big supporter of yours. Isn't that right, Sally?"

Carr's mother tried for a smile, as if she were placating an irked bus passenger. She sat down slowly, perching on the very edge of the mismatched armchair, and started choosing her words carefully, as if Carr were six years old and she was preparing him for a trip to the dentist. "You remember, darling, I've told you before. When I was young, well, I didn't have much money. My folks, they were so poor, they had me and my sister without using a geneticist, without even the most basic add-ons." Her voice was speeding up now, as if the pressure on a spigot were being released. "Well, you know, your aunt has had cancer twice, and me with my blood pressure… Well, I was never going to make *their* mistake and have a baby if I couldn't afford to. And I didn't think I *could* afford to, at the time, but then Mr. R—"

"Shit, Mom," Carr said. He knew it. "How much do you owe him?"

"*Language*, Carr," Sally chastised, tinting pink again. "It's not what you think."

"You may not remember, Carr," said Mr. R with an unhurried air, "but I was there for some of your earliest victories." He pointed to one of the biggest trophies on the shelf. "The Western Junior Zero-G Championships— you won it when you were twelve years old, the youngest in your division." He moved his finger over to a dusty championship belt on the wall. "The Junior Terran Cube Royale. You were fourteen—fourteen, was it, Pol?—when you were first scouted by the ZGFA."

A fragment of Carr's memory was coming into focus, like a fuzzy holovid resolving itself. He'd come out of the Cube, having fought and beaten some wiry South American kid in the quarter-finals. Waiting, floating by the screen that would display the draw for the next round, he'd looked for his coach. Uncle Polly was at the edge of the deck talking to someone. The stranger was calm, the balls of his magnetized shoes touching the deck, his hand resting lightly on the guide-rail, but Uncle Polly was agitated, gesturing sharply in time to words that Carr couldn't hear. Later, when he'd asked his coach who the man was, Polly's reply had been tight. "No one you know."

The air in the apartment seemed suddenly very still and heavy. Uncle Polly, still standing near the door, had an awful grimace on his face. Carr made his words come out one at a time. "Coach, what is this all about?" He turned to his mother. "What are you not telling me?"

"Allow me to make it clear." Mr. R patted the chest of

the jacket he wore over his black button-up shirt and withdrew a thinscreen, which he unfolded and placed on the coffee table. His short white fingers slid it across, toward Carr. "You recognize this, I'm sure."

Carr set his jaw and sat down slowly. He picked up the thinscreen and flicked his eyes down to it.

It was an official government document, with the seal of the Nation City of Toronto at the top. The upper third of the page listed his name, gender, and citizen ID, his mother's name and citizen ID, his conception date and place, his birth date and place, the geneticist's license number, and the sequencing date. The rest of the page contained several lines of information:

PATERNITY: Unverified
CHROMOSOMAL SPECIFICATIONS:
    Standard somatic therapy package GENEX v.8.5
    Defect reduction premium suite GENEX v.5.1
    Anti-cancer plus CLT v.6.0
    Anti-obesity and heart health deluxe CLT v.7.2
    Disease resistance upgrade CHROME v.9.2
RISK FACTOR SCORE: 24 (Low)
ENHANCEMENTS: Negative
STATUS: Within acceptable ranges

Carr dropped the screen back on the table. "How did you get this?" A person's genetic profile was private information. An employer could run a check to verify that you were within legally acceptable ranges, but the full profile—

listing which brand and version of chromosomal packages you were born with—could only be obtained with the subject's consent.

Carr's mind spun. How much money was involved here? *It can't be that bad*, he reassured himself. His add-ons were pretty standard. A disease resistance upgrade ... that might be a bit pricey, and he *had* always wondered how his mom had afforded it on top of everything else, but really, how expensive could it be?

Mr. R was watching him carefully. A few translucent blond chest hairs poked over the unfastened top button of his stiff shirt. When he licked his thin lips, Carr pictured an albino rock python.

"Tell me something, Carr," he said. "What do you think your chances are of beating Henri Manon?"

"Answer my question," Carr said.

"Answer mine first. Henri 'the Reaper' is the youngest of the Manon family, the so-called first family of zero gravity combat. Two of his older brothers have worn the championship belt, and his father is the legendary Stace Manon. Henri has been fighting pro for ten years, nearly as long as you've been wearing grippers." The man leaned forward, intent. "What makes you think you'll beat him?"

Carr bared his teeth. "I'll beat him because I'll be better than him. On that day in the Cube, I'll be better than him. That's what I have to believe." He stabbed a finger at the thinscreen. "Now tell me why you have my genetic profile on your thinscreen."

Mr. R said, "It's not your real profile." He swiped the

screen to another document and set it in front of Carr. "This is."

Carr looked down. The top section of the page was the same, but the rest of it was now dense with text.

PATERNITY: Private donor (blocked)
CHROMOSOMAL SPECIFICATIONS:
    Somatic therapy platinum package GENEX v.9.0
    Defect reduction premium suite GENEX v.5.5
    Anti-cancer plus CLT v.6.0
    Anti-obesity and heart health deluxe CLT v.7.2
    Disease resistance ultra CHROME v.12.0
    Custom germline modification—neuromuscular
    Custom germline modification—respiratory
    Custom germline modification—metabolic
    Custom germline modification—immunological
    Custom germline modification—cognitive
    Custom germline modification—temperament
    Custom germline modification—other***
RISK FACTOR SCORE: 9 (Very low)
ENHANCEMENTS: Positive
    Special exemptions: No
    Interplanetary treaty exemption: No
STATUS: Exceeds acceptable ranges

Carr shook his head slowly. The words on the screen seemed to swim. "This is bullshit." His heart was pounding. "You made this up. You're lying."

"You said you were better than Henri Manon. Now

you know why. He may be genetically gifted"—Mr. R sat back calmly—"but not as gifted as you."

Carr spun to stare at his mother. "Mom? It's not true, is it?"

He knew the answer as soon as the words left his mouth. Sally inched a little further toward the edge of her chair and opened her hands to him, in a gentle *ah what can I say* gesture. "I've always wanted the best for you. Always. What you have . . . it's so much more than I could ever have given you on my own." She let out a shaky sigh. "I know, it's a bit of a shock, but when you think about it, you'll realize what this means. How special you are."

Sally had been right: it wasn't what he'd thought. It was worse. "I'm genetically enhanced. Off spec." Carr went cold. "I'm *illegal.*"

Mr. R made a *tsk* sound. "You're acting far more concerned than necessary."

"Concerned? *Concerned*?" Carr half-rose, as if to leap across the low table and seize the man around the neck. "*I'm not allowed to compete.*" The words filmed his throat with acid. In his haze of disbelief, he saw Uncle Polly sag against the door frame. Of course, he knew. Was in on it. They all were.

"You've been competing for years. You will keep doing so." Mr. R lifted his chin to follow Carr but did not shift from his spot. "The only people who have ever seen your real genetic profile are in this room. People you can trust."

"People I can trust," Carr echoed. He felt a derisive laugh start up, then die. "Like you? Who *are* you?"

"As I told you, I'm in the business of discovering and grooming new talent. Only *my* organization is more ... proactive. We don't leave the talent pool up to chance. We create it.

"Your mother is right, Carr. You are special. You're an exceptional athlete, designed off a composite genetic template of naturally occurring top performers. Your reflexes, endurance, and spatial intelligence are all well above normal—though nothing so unusual that it would arouse suspicion. You're less prone to injury, and when you are injured, you heal faster than others. Most important of all, you have the right temperament: aggressive but not impulsive; a disciplined, nearly obsessive mindset; the ability to excel under pressure; and an insatiable competitive drive. It's called 'the warrior gene constellation'—and it's quite a gift."

Carr sat back down heavily. It was surreal, to have things he already mostly knew about himself listed by this stranger as if they were selling features. "What does this mean?" he thought aloud, his voice a monotone.

"Practically speaking? Very little." Mr. R's voice could not be considered warm, but there was a certain practiced, soothing quality to it now. "I provided your potential. But being born gifted doesn't take anything away from you, from all your years of hard work and determination."

"None of that will matter," Carr said. "Not if I'm found out. I'll be banned from the Cube."

"That will not happen. We cover our tracks carefully."

"Athletes are randomly tested."

"The tests screen for performance-enhancing drugs and

nanos, unauthorized implants, and somatic gene procedures—the sort of things unscrupulous athletes will resort to. Your genetic modifications are the most advanced and expensive kind, using Martian technology, and so carefully spliced into your genetic makeup that there are no markers. Only a complete sequencing would reveal what you are."

It seemed to Carr that his head was starting to feel light and his body too heavy, as if he were ascending into orbit on a shaky rocket-plane. Numbly, he said, "What do you want?"

"Simply to share in your success, as a return on my investment in you. Twenty percent of what you earn—your winnings in the Cube, your sponsorship deals, and whatever else Gant pays you. You will receive instructions on how to set up an automatic account transfer. When you go on to accomplish all that you wish for—titles, fame, wealth—you won't even notice the small cut. In fact, if all goes smoothly, you may not even see or hear from me again. You can focus on what you do best—winning in the Cube."

"And if I say no?" But Carr already knew the answer to that too.

"Why would you be so unreasonable?" Mr. R stood up smoothly and casually, like a dinner guest taking his leave. "Every great athlete has others to thank for his success. You owe a great deal to your mother for raising you, and to your coach for training you. You also owe me for designing you. What I ask for is so very little when measured against the gift of your life, your accomplishments, the very fabric of everything you are. Do as I ask, respect the fact that I am your benefactor, and this"—he picked up the thinscreen, folded it with a snap, and pocketed it—"will remain a secret."

Carr rose to his feet, understanding only, through a fog of confusion and anger, that he was being steadily boxed into a corner. "I don't have to stand for this," he said. "I could turn myself in. Blow the top off your whole crooked scheme."

Mr. R lifted his faint eyebrows, as if Carr were a boy throwing a tantrum. "Do you think you're the first success story I've written, Carr? I've protected myself well for decades. Nothing you say or do will be traced back to me. You would only ruin your life, and send your mother and coach to jail. Is that what you want?"

He walked around the coffee table, past Carr, and over to the door. He nodded at Carr's mother. "Sally, you've done a nice job with him." Then he stood in front of Uncle Polly, whose face looked nearly as pale as his, set as it was in a chiseled mask of futile resentment. Mr. R pursed his lips, stretching the skin across his cheeks tight. He lowered his voice, speaking to Polly with a cold, false sympathy. "I know you hoped to delay the inevitable, soften it somehow. Trust me; this is the best way."

He opened the door, then paused and spoke to Carr over his shoulder. "What's the difference between what Henri Manon was given by God or by chance, and what you were given? You will need every one of your enhancements if you hope to win the title. Good luck. I'll be watching."

Mr. R stepped out onto the small landing and closed the door behind him. His footsteps descended the narrow stairs.

ELEVEN

For a long moment Carr stared at the closed door, suspecting the whole thing had not happened, and if it had, it must have been a crazy stunt or scam. Then he sensed Sally and Uncle Polly's wary expressions lying heavy on him, and betrayal rose like bile in his throat.

He lunged at the shelves along the wall and swept his arm across violently, sending dozens of his childhood trophies flying, smashing to the ground in a clattering jumble of gold-plated metal. With a choked sound, he tore the certificates and ribbons off the wall and hurled them across the room. A framed photo—of him winning his first amateur championship at the age of nine—dented the flatscreen, shaking the reflection in it of his own face, contorted with disbelief and rage. When the shelves and walls were bare, he laced his fingers behind his bowed head and paced back and forth down the length of the tiny apart-ment.

Sally and Uncle Polly didn't move, didn't say a word, didn't try to stop him. As a kid, when he got frustrated or angry, he would tear up a room, punch a kid at school, pummel a heavy bag—whatever it took to purge the physi-cal heat of emotion—and then come back down just as fast. He did so now, fire crystallizing into steel, his heart rate falling back to normal. He wondered if this ability to rapidly regain composure was part of his design, and decided it almost certainly was.

Was that how he would always see himself now? As manufactured?

Carr stopped pacing and faced his mother. "You've been lying to me for my whole life."

"I never lied to you, *never*." Sally hadn't moved from her spot on the armchair. Her shoulders were curled, her hands wrapped around her knees. She gave him a beseech-ing, slightly reproachful look: *Can't you try to appreciate all that your mother has done for you?* "I always said that I got the best donor and the best genetics I could afford for you. Haven't I always said that? Haven't I?"

"You could never afford a custom job," Carr said. He felt suddenly that this woman who'd raised him was a stranger he'd never known. "How did you get mixed up with a splice dealer like that?" Because at the end of the day, that was what Mr. R was, wasn't he? A step up from the criminals that traded in people's illegal and ill-considered genetic fantasies to have night vision, or wings, or kids who were clones of famous people.

"I was broke, Carr. Broke, and thirty-six, and my boyfriend had just left me. So I figured that was it—I was going to leave my fertility turned off for good. I got depressed, so depressed I went to this support group. And someone there told me about a medical study you could audition for, and get all your conception and genetics fees paid for. So that's how I met him, and he picked me to make an offer to." There was a strange note of pride in her voice, the way a person might be proud of something they had no control over, like winning the lottery. "He picked me out of everyone else."

Of course he did, Carr thought cruelly. A poor, simple, reasonably stable, hopelessly gullible woman in good genetic health who wanted a child and was used to doing what she was told. His words came out like ice. "Am I even yours?"

Sally pulled back as if he'd slapped her. "Of course you're mine. You're every bit mine, but so much better." Her soft face trembled and she blinked back sudden tears. "I'm nothing special, Carr, you know that. I'll never amount to much. But you … you're going to have a better life. What wouldn't a mother do to give her baby boy a better life? You'll lift us both up, like he promised. I … I'm proud of you, Carr."

A sharp ache pierced Carr's chest and he turned his face away. He was not going to go to her to be held like a little boy. "Why now?" he managed to say. "Why didn't you tell me earlier?"

"Oh, what good would that have been, darling?" Sally

scolded gently. "You didn't need to be bothered by that when you were younger, being so busy training up for the pros and all. You shouldn't burden a boy with decisions and expectations, or take anything away from him at that age. That's how Mr. R always explained it. Besides, what would you have done? Zeroboxing was our golden ticket. Better to live up to your full potential, and pay your debts later, than to sell yourself short, wouldn't you say?" She sounded as if she'd memorized that line, been waiting for years to use it.

"You knew it was illegal, didn't you?" Carr's words were leaden. "You could have gone to jail. You still could."

"He promised me that wouldn't happen," she insisted. "Genetic standards always seem to be changing anyways, and I thought about what an advantage I'd be giving you. It was worth the risk. Wasn't it?"

How could she possibly expect him to answer that? But her voice rose anyways, and she shifted to look at Uncle Polly, as if expecting his support. "Wasn't it?"

Uncle Polly had been silent the whole time. For once, he looked old, his usual youthful energy missing. He was leaning against the wall, his arms crossed, his hands tucked into his armpits. It occurred to Carr that he did the same thing when he was nervous and must have picked up the habit from his coach.

"I don't like that man," Polly said, his voice low and resigned. "He's rotten and self-serving to the core. But he's right about some things, Carr. Nature turns out plenty of its own outliers. You measure the stats of the very best athletes and they're off the charts, sure as if they'd been spliced that way." He glanced at Sally with a bitter solidarity that Carr finally understood. "We're not exactly following the rule book, it's true. But sometimes an opportunity comes along for you to level the field, to stand a chance, you know what I'm saying? And you have to take it."

Carr no longer knew what to believe. "You knew? From the beginning?"

"Not at first." Polly sighed. "Maybe I suspected at some point but pretended I didn't. Look, I was down on coaching. Real down. I'd had two fighters flame out. Good fighters. One kept getting injured, and the other trained up just fine but couldn't handle the pressure of the Cube on fight day. Cracked every time. Then I get an anonymous tip, telling me I've got to see this kid, this seven-year-old living on the planet. I was coming down for something or other anyways, so I look up the name of the land gym I was given, walk in, and see you. It happened just like you remember."

Carr remembered all right. At seven, he'd been taking kickboxing and gymnastics when he wasn't playing basketball or getting into fights at school. He never wondered, at the time, how Sally found the money to indulge every sport he felt the whim to try, but now he had his suspicions. Uncle Polly had walked in on a kids' kickboxing tournament, watched him handily beat ten- and twelve-year-olds, and a month later, Carr had taken his first shuttle bus trip up to Xtreme Xero.

"I trained you for two years, and then I got a call," Uncle Polly continued. "That man brings your mom and me into a room and lays it all out to me. He says, here's the deal. This kid is going to be something. There are about a dozen sports where he could make it big. Zeroboxing fits him like a glove. It's always been big on Mars, and is going to be big on Earth too. Even then, top fighters like the Manons were making serious cash per fight. So he asks me, 'Are you in or out?'"

Carr's words crept out of a throat that had shrunk by two sizes. "So it was all about the money. For you too."

Uncle Polly's demeanor changed instantly. He lurched up, stabbing an indignant finger at Carr. "You watch your mouth, you hear? It was never just about the money. Sure, money was involved, but it wasn't the reason." He was the coach again, in full tirade mode, and Carr shut up reflexively, as if he'd run a drill too slowly or come off a poor sparring round. "By then, I'd seen what you could do, what kind of kid you were. I liked you, not just as a coach, but as a person, you know, kind of like—"

Like a father.

"Like family," Uncle Polly said. "You loved to train, loved to fight. What was I supposed to do? Kick you out? Turn you over to Genepol? It would wreck you. It would wreck me to do it, because you were what I'd always hoped to find. The kind of fighter that comes along once in a lifetime if you're lucky, the champ I'd dreamed of building from the ground up. Everything I gave you, you gave back. You were the best I ever trained. Still are."

Uncle Polly turned his fierce gaze aside, composing himself. "I didn't want it to come out like this, not now, with you so pumped up about the title fight. I wanted to be the one to do it, later, but his share of the purse was too big for that bastard to leave off. I'm sorry it went down like this. I'm real sorry." And Polly did look really sorry, the lines in his face deepening into crevices. "But it's true—this doesn't change who you are, doesn't take anything away from you. Every fight you've won has been on account of you working your ass off and wanting it badly enough."

But even the working, and the wanting, weren't his doing; not exactly. They were part of that one line in his secret genetic profile: *Custom germline modification—temperament.* Such a blunt, technical explanation for his personality.

Carr turned away. He couldn't be here right now. He was too confused. He needed to be alone, to think. He pulled open the apartment door and went down the narrow steps two at a time. He expected one of them to call after him, but they didn't. He banged through the entrance without looking back.

TWELVE

Outside, the sun was shining down on the withered grass and cracked sidewalks, warming the moist air that rolled in from the south off the surface of Lake Ontario and over the tall, honeycomb-stacked waterfront condo buildings. It didn't seem proper for everything to look so bright when his life had just had a black-hole-heavy pallor dropped over it.

Carr started walking, to nowhere in particular. His cuff flashed a silent alert message—he was near his personal daily data capacity. Too many messages, posts, and Systemnet hits streaming in all at once. While he'd been inside his mother's apartment, discovering the criminality of his existence, Bax Gant had announced that the Raptor would be challenging the Reaper in a New Year's Day showdown to determine the ZGFA Lowmass Champion of the Universe.

He walked faster, as if he could escape the vaguely sick feeling settling in his gut.

Fighting Henri Manon for the belt would be breaking the law. If his enhancements were discovered, he'd lose any title he ever won and be banned from ever participating in another sanctioned competition. It was illegal in almost all countries on Earth to knowingly hire someone with non-therapeutic genetic modifications, so career options were limited. Not that there was any other job he could imagine wanting. He would have to leave Greater Earth orbit, exile himself to one of the outer stations, maybe ship out to the asteroid belt.

His breaths were growing fast and shallow. He forced his feet to stop for a minute so he could pull himself together—*it wasn't going to happen*. No one had found out so far, and no one ever would. Mr. R had been confident.

Picturing the man with the smooth face and silver tongue made Carr grind his teeth. He was *not* a tool. He was more than just a ripening cash cow for his unscrupulous creator. He was—what the hell *was* he?

His cuff brought up a priority incoming call and his receiver played its familiar rising chime. He glanced down at the display. Risha. Suddenly, his knees felt weak. If only he could magically pull her through his cuff, bring her to him right now. She was always so quick and competent, able to think her way around anything. He accepted the call.

Before he could say a word, she said, "Prepare to be impressed. The fact that the fight was announced while we're still on Earth is *perfect*. I have your first interview lined up for tonight, in public, right on the Harborfront. Eason is getting the word out on the Systemnet and we're going to have a massive crowd of fans. It wasn't easy, but I managed to rush-order pop-up holovid ads to go up all over the city tomorrow. Still working on your schedule. How was the visit with your mother?"

Carr closed his eyes, mentally reeling. *Disastrous, actually. About that…* "Err, fine. It was fine."

"You're not going to believe this." Risha was breathless with excitement. "Bran Merkel called me directly to say that he's assigning more people to our team. At least one for on-planet promotions and another for Systemnet marketing." She paused. "Your cuff signal is moving around slowly. Are you walking somewhere?"

"I'm just… checking out my old neighborhood."

"When can you be back at the hotel? I have a long list of things to run you through."

"Risha…" He didn't even know how to begin. *Hey, guess what, of all the shitty luck…* No.

"Have to go; the city venue coordinator is calling me. Can you be back in ninety minutes?"

He swallowed. "Yeah, okay."

"Carr." His name on her tongue was rounded and full. "See you soon." She ended the call. A tight band of tenderness and panic squeezed down around his chest.

He realized that his aimless walking had carried him several blocks, to a familiar corner. Enzo's apartment building. He'd forgotten his promise to catch up with his friend.

Carr crossed the street. A small crowd was gathered on

the sidewalk in front of the plain, three-story brick building: a handful of neighborhood children of varying ages, a few curious adults, and a camera crew. With surprise, he recognized the back of Marc's head and lengthened his strides to reach him.

"What's going on here?" he asked.

The man startled and whirled around. "Carr, you're here," he exclaimed. "Perfect. We're getting the local media to precede the event tonight with personal testimonials."

Carr saw, then, that Enzo was in the center of the crowd, talking to a reporter and a cameraman. "Yeah, I've known Carr since I was seven years old. Basically, he's my hero. I've watched every one of his matches about a hundred times. He's the best zeroboxer ever, but he's not stuck up at all. He's a really nice guy and super down-to-earth." Enzo's clothes looked too big on him, and he blinked too much behind his cringe-inducing glasses, but he glowed like a dwarf star. "In fact, he's an even better friend than he is a fighter."

A lump lodged in Carr's throat.

Enzo's mom was standing on the steps of the apartment building, watching. Her face looked different, too thin and taut for her age and body—she'd had some nanosculpting done. She leaned her hips on the railing, her arms crossed, her jaw working over a piece of gum. Her eyes were heavy-lidded with a languid mixture of curiosity and disdain.

Carr regarded her as a man might regard a large rat sharing his dungeon cell. She had nothing to do with his problems, but he could loathe her anyways. He took several steps forward before the kids at the edge of the crowd noticed him.

"He's here," someone called, and the next thing Carr knew, he was surrounded by people all talking at once, taking pictures, jabbing their cuffs to record and transmit optic feeds, asking him for autographs. Marc helped position the cameraman as the reporter pushed to the front.

"Carr," the reporter shouted, "how does it feel to be here in your home neighborhood on the day your championship fight is announced?"

He looked at the crowd, the cameras. Unreal. The whole day was unreal. "Words can't describe it."

"Your mother still lives right here, where you grew up, doesn't she? She must be very proud of you."

"I owe everything to her." Painfully true.

"In just this past year, you've been credited with exploding the popularity of zeroboxing," the reporter continued relentlessly. "What do you think about that?"

"I don't know if it's me so much as more Terrans discovering just what zeroboxing is. I'm glad if I've helped make that happen."

The reporter started to blurt another question, but Carr shook his head and broke free. Enzo's mother straightened away from the railing, her eyes widening as he took the front steps in a couple of bounds and stopped directly in front of her.

"Ms. Loggins," he said. The overly sweet smell of her perfume filled his mouth with a nasty taste. He lowered his voice so he couldn't be overheard. "You have to take Enzo to get his eyes fixed. And his lungs too—they have gene therapy for that. Look at him, will you? He shouldn't have to be like that."

She looked him up and down, one side of her mouth curling in affront. "You think you can come right up and lecture me, do you? Just 'cause you're famous now? You're still the same neighborhood brat to me, Carr Luka. In case you don't know, those things cost money."

"If you *saved* up the money, instead of—" He bit down.

She wagged a painted purple nail at him. "You want to talk about money? I just bet my last two paychecks on you." She sniffed loudly, as if this was his fault. "So you better win now, you hear? You want to do us favors, you win that fight."

Carr had never hit a woman, but he would have liked to give Ms. Loggins a smack to send that piece of chewing gum flying out from between her scornful lips, right in front of the camera. Wouldn't *that* be a publicity stunt to end all. He spun around and went back through the crowd, ignoring the reporter and making for Enzo, who was bouncing on the balls of his feet, still yammering into the camera. He put a hand on the boy's shoulder. "Come on, let's get out of here. You want some ice cream?"

———

Carr ordered double-scoop sundaes for both of them, then kicked himself. What was he thinking? The biggest fight

of his life was in two months and he had to cut mass—
he couldn't eat ice cream. The cold, sweet spheres of mint
chocolate chip sat in the bowl, taunting him, promising
relief from heat and emotional turmoil. For a mad second,
he thought *Screw it.* Screw the fight, screw everything. He
jammed a spoon into the top scoop. Then he pushed the
bowl toward Enzo and got himself a glass of ice water from
the dispenser.

Enzo nudged his glasses up the bridge of his nose and
dove into his sundae. "You can't stay long, huh?" he said,
glum.

Carr shook his head. "I've got two days full of whatever the marketing gurus tell me to do, and then it's back
to Valtego."

Enzo sighed. "I wish you could stay longer. It would
be amazing if I could bring you to school."

"For show and tell?" Carr scoffed, then turned serious.
"How is school?"

"S'okay." Enzo studied his reflection in the spoon.

Carr didn't believe him; a kid with an inhaler and
glasses was begging to be tormented. "You remember what
I told you about kids giving you trouble, right?"

"Never look scared, and keep fighting even if you're
getting thrashed. Hit them hard when their guard is down,
and keep hitting even after you think you've won."

"And go for the face. You bloody someone's face, half
the time the fight goes out of them."

Enzo brightened. "Last month, Ronny Briskus pushed
me into a wall and said my mom was a nutty bliss addict

whore, and I cracked him in the mouth, just like *whack*. We were both sent home, but I gave him a bloody lip."

Carr was inclined to agree with Ronny Briskus, but he reached across the table and shoved Enzo's head affectionately. "Good for you, little man."

The boy grinned over a big spoonful of ice cream. "So have you checked the net chatter yet? The Reaper is already trash-talking you."

"Yeah? What's he saying?"

"Here, let me see if I can find it." Enzo scrolled quickly through his cuff display. "He says, 'I never heard of the kid until last month. Zeroboxing has gotten so popular, I guess they're looking for underwear models to put in the Cube.'"

Carr nearly choked on a swallow of water. "That's a good one. What else?"

"He goes, 'I'm gonna start the new year nice and easy, by taking out the garbage.' Oh wait, here's one more: 'Do you think this poor sucker knows what my last name is?'"

Listening to trash-talk about oneself was a weirdly satisfying sort of masochistic foreplay, Carr decided. Like asking someone to poke you with a twig, over and over again, so you could ride the anticipation, the buildup toward the climactic moment when your fist finally met his mouth. *Ahhh* . . . .a persistent problem suddenly solved. If only all things were so simple.

"Manon is a jerk." Enzo finished one sundae and started in on the second. "I saw this old clip of him totally cussing and shoving some fan around in a bar just for talking to his girlfriend. Then his girlfriend tries to stop him, and Manon starts cussing her out in public too. He's the guy people love to hate. It's going to be so awesome when you lay the smackdown on him."

Carr was silent for a moment. "You know, things don't always go the way you plan. Sometimes, when you least expect it, they get screwed up."

Enzo looked up with as much solemnity as Carr could imagine on the freckled face of an eleven-year-old with glasses. Then he set his spoon down. With utmost seriousness, he said, "I *know* you can do it. I believe in you, Carr."

"I know you do."

Enzo squinted, as if to say *you don't get it*. "You know, my personal feed, it used to have barely any followers, not even my own mom. Now it's totally lit up. People I don't know, from places like Russia and Luna and Pax Lagrange Station, are like...well, look." He tapped his cuff display and turned it around so Carr could see a long comments stream:

> *ur feed rocks*
>
> *hey I am so addicted to zeroboxing too. Luka is my fave*
>
> *omg you are as big a fan of Carr Luka as me*
>
> *holy shit I cannot wait for this title fight. Reaper is mean but Raptor's got so much grace it'll make your dick hard*

And on and on.

"See?" Enzo said. "It's not just me. I know it's your dream to win the title. It's sort of embarrassing to say this, but it's my dream too. Only you're the one doing it." He nodded gravely. "It's called 'living vicariously.'"

Carr saw his future split in two like a cracking mirror. In one version, he did his best to pretend today never happened. He went on to fight for the championship. Win or lose, he returned to the Cube, again and again. He woke up next to Risha in the mornings, and when Enzo was old enough, he found him work on Valtego. He made peace with his mother and Uncle Polly and didn't think about or speak of the twenty percent of his earnings that regularly disappeared from his bank account. Every night before he slept, he thanked the stars for a day in which Mr. R, a police officer, or a ZGFA testing official didn't show up—and he asked for another.

Or... he could refuse to be played by that bastard splice dealer in nice clothes. He could, in Future Version B, take Mr. R's "business" straight to Genepol, the law enforcement arm of the International Commission on Genetics. The man had been running his scheme since before Carr was born; who knew how far and wide it extended. If Carr turned himself in, maybe there was a chance Genepol would go easy on Sally and Uncle Polly. Maybe they would even let him work near Earth, if not on it. He could no longer compete of course; that would violate Terran law and principles of fairness.

This second Carr—someone he didn't recognize— gave up the title fight, gave up everything, let down Risha,

Enzo, Uncle Polly, Gant, and all the fans he'd met and those he hadn't, and never set foot in a Cube again. Unless it was with a tour group.

Carr's jaws snapped down on an ice cube. It shattered under his teeth.

Enzo was saying something. "Carr, did you hear me?"

"What?"

"Don't you have to go? You said you had to leave in an hour."

"Yeah. Yeah, I really do." He stood up. "Hey, why don't you come with me?"

Enzo jumped to his feet. "Really?"

"Sure. My first big interview is at the Harborfront tonight, so you ought to be in the front row, right? You can hang out with me until then, and I'll send you home afterward. I'll even introduce you to my girlfriend."

"Holy crap, you have a girlfriend?" Enzo's eyes widened like an owl's. "Is she, like, super hot? She is, isn't she?" He looked down at himself, smoothing the front of his rumpled shirt, and his voice took an uncertain turn. "She'll think I'm just some annoying kid."

Part of Carr still writhed under a heavy weight that he suspected was there to stay, but he smiled. "No way. You two would totally get each other. You're both hyperenergetic, opinionated know-it-alls who say exactly what's on your mind."

"Well, what are we waiting for? This day keeps getting better!"

THIRTEEN

The last two days on Earth passed in a bright and frenetic blur of interviews and media events and fan gatherings. Carr moved through it all as if he were outside his own body. He watched himself smile for cameras and reporters, spout witty comments, and sign countless autographs. He obligingly threw a few choice barbs at the Reaper, chosen from a list Risha and her marketing team had brainstormed for him. His ironic favorite was in response to the recurring question of how he felt about going up against a member of the legendary Manon family: "Watching his last few matches, I'd say good genes is all Henri's got going for him."

What had happened in his mother's apartment was like a bit of shrapnel embedded inside him, something his immune system kept trying to dislodge. He couldn't get rid of it, but he could, with effort, keep it from creeping to the forefront of his mind. *You can manage this* he told himself over and over, in the same way he handled anxiety before a match, or set aside a bad round, or recovered from a loss: by putting the thoughts and emotions he didn't need into a mental box, shutting the lid, and compressing it, smaller and smaller, until they had no control over him. Then it was easy to let himself get carried away by all the hype and excitement, by Risha and Enzo's enthusiasm, by unflattering thoughts about Henri Manon.

The hardest thing had been going to see his mother by himself one last time before he left Earth. It had been awkward. He bought a holovid projector to replace the old flatscreen he'd dented. After helping to set it up, he stood in the center of the apartment, looking around once more. His trophies were all back in place, a little scuffed. The place looked different to him now. No longer his home—just a cramped old apartment in a low-rent part of town.

"Do you hate me?" Sally whispered. It was such a child-like question that Carr winced. "I thought I was doing the right thing for you," she said sadly. "I thought you would understand, you would appreciate what you are. You would like your life."

"Mom...I do."

That was the thing: could he honestly blame her? He could have been born like any poor planet rat. Like Enzo. Did that make what she had done *right*? He didn't know. He'd always thought of his mother as predictable—the same apartment, the same job, the same rotation of simple meals. Safe and comforting. Dull and unimaginative. He didn't want to think of her as criminally selfish or recklessly self-less—which one it was, that was another thing he didn't know.

"I don't hate you," he said wearily. "But...we're not going to talk about it."

His mother nodded in a paroxysm of relief and moved to hug him. After a moment he hugged her back, stiffly.

"I understand," she said. "I can't regret anything, Carr. Not when it gave me you."

He swallowed a hot and salty lump, said "I'll call you after the fight," and left before she could say anything else.

With Uncle Polly, he didn't bring it up, and his coach didn't either. It was fine. The days were too busy anyways.

As they stood in line in the aerospaceport to board the super-cruiser back to Valtego, Carr finally said, "The second round. Manon always loses speed in the second round, but comes back strong in the third. He saves his biggest moves for the final thirty seconds."

Uncle Polly nodded. "He wins by knockout or submission in the first round, or points at the end of the third."

"Most people give everything they've got to keep up with him in the first, and don't have enough in the tank by the end." Carr chewed his lip. "We need to work on finishing, tacking an extra thirty seconds onto training rounds and taking it up twenty percent in the last minute."

And that was it. By unspoken agreement, they pushed away the ugly stuff that didn't fit and returned to what was really important. They talked non-stop through the entire boarding process. They laid out a training schedule and

Carr made calls to set up appointments with the sports doctor and the nutritionist back on Valtego. He didn't have long to build his body back into peak shape.

"How do you even have enough energy to think right now?" said Risha, settling into the seat next to him when they'd boarded and the *engage harness* sign had come on.

"You're one to talk," he said. After a moment, he leaned in and wound his hand behind her neck. "I don't know how you did it. This whole trip, I don't know how you managed."

"On very little sleep," she said. And indeed she looked exhausted, her dark eyes slightly bloodshot and sunken.

"I don't just mean all the work." The first day in London had been the worst for her, but Carr had noticed the anti-anxiety medication in her traveling bag, had seen the nervous twitch and stiffness in her usually graceful body whenever they were under the open sky, which was often. And she dragged badly in the mornings, waking up in constantly changing hotel rooms with too little rest spent under too much gravity.

She smiled up at him tiredly. Even travel-worn like this, she was beautiful. Alien, in an irresistibly alluring way. "A person can push through anything when she's working for something she believes in," she said. "Or some*one*."

He kissed her. Her lips were sweet and warm, always warmer than his, as if she were slightly and permanently feverish. Or aroused. As the kiss ended, he pulled her in again, moving his mouth over hers possessively.

He couldn't tell her what he'd learned about himself,

he decided. It was better that she didn't know. It would've been better if *he* didn't know. He couldn't ask Risha to share his burden. He was her first client and she was staking her career on him, rising past people far more senior in the Merkel Media Corporation because of him. It was even more than that; they had something special together. A magic, like the kind Uncle Polly said might happen once in a lifetime between a trainer and a fighter, only this was between a man and a woman. He knew she felt it too. He couldn't let her down.

Carr was exhausted after all. He fell asleep as soon as they got above the atmosphere and slept through the entire flight. He didn't see the spectacular view of Earth receding, nor the pockmarked and barren surface of the Moon as they swung past it, passing over the white superstructures of Luna Alpha and Luna Neuvo, or even the sight of Valtego in all its lit and slowly turning glory as the ship docked. He slept as deeply as someone recovering from illness. When he woke up, the disembark lights had come on and he felt better. Purged. Reset.

———————

He threw himself into training. He thought about nothing else. He went to sleep thinking about zeroboxing and woke up from dreams about it. Anything that was not fight preparation (or fight promotion, as per Risha's unstinting directions about maintaining his feed, engaging with fans, and so on) got blown off. He studied videos of Manon like an archaeologist examining the Dead Sea Scrolls, trying to glean meaning that might translate into advantage. He obsessed over his caloric intake, his muscle mass, and the technical details of every move. On his eighteenth birthday, he allowed himself one slice of key lime pie and was back in his grippers an hour later. He was the first one in the gym or the Cube every morning and the last to leave.

"Another thirty seconds," he said on the third evening before the fight. He adjusted the timer and heart rate monitor on his cuff. "I should try to keep my heart rate that high for another thirty."

It was nearly midnight. "We're done in here, Carr," Uncle Polly said from the opposite corner of the Cube. The old man was breathing hard from eating so many of Carr's shots on the pads. He stuck one of them to the Cube wall by its magnetic backing and wiped a thin film of sweat from his forehead. "We've been here for five hours. Not including this morning." He looked around almost nervously, even though they were the only ones here. "Even *you* can't keep this up."

Carr swung around, launched himself through the air, and somersaulted to grip the wall and face his coach. "Can't I?" His voice took on a bitter edge. "You must be curious about what genetic technology is capable of."

The weightless air chilled. Carr felt a spasm of instant regret. He must be too tired after all, to so carelessly reopen this wound after they'd bandaged it up. It wasn't what Uncle Polly had said; it wasn't even the upcoming fight. *He* was the one who was curious, almost scientifically so, about what he was capable of, how hard he could drive his custom-designed body.

Uncle Polly's mouth twitched. In a low voice, he said, "You're right. I don't know what your limits are. But I don't want to slam into them at fusion-speed right before your fight. You need to take the next few days easy. You hear?"

Several seconds passed. Finally, Carr sighed. "All right, coach." He only needed to beat Manon, not punish himself. He headed for the hatch, Uncle Polly's eyes drilling into his back.

He changed, drank some water, and took the late-night bus back to the gravity zone terminal, then a taxi back to his apartment. When he opened the door, he found Risha waiting for him.

That was unexpected. This match was hers too; she worked as many hours as he trained. After being together nearly constantly while touring Earth, they'd barely seen each other since returning to Valtego, except over hasty lunches where she sampled different dishes from the food stands and he ate his specially proportioned heavy-protein meal and supplement-laden shake.

She was sitting up in his bed, her thinscreen and stylus on her lap, her shoes kicked off. Her slender feet were crossed at the ankles. She said, "I spent all day reviewing ads with your face on them, without once seeing your face in real life."

"That's terrible," he said. "I wouldn't want to look at myself all day either."

She favored him with a *ha ha* roll of the eyes. Setting her screen down on the rumpled bedspread, she swung her long legs over the side of the bed, stood up, and came to him, stepping around the accumulating dirty laundry, smelly fight gear, and holovid game console. "Photos don't compare to the real thing." She put her arms around his neck and pressed her lips to his.

He kissed her back, harder. She folded into his embrace. They staggered to the bed, their movements turning needy. When he came up for air, Carr groaned. His hand was under her shirt, his legs twined around hers. "If I wasn't so close to the fight ... " It was tempting to push the match from his mind, to imagine closeting himself with Risha for the next thirty-six hours, ordering in food when they got hungry.

She smoothed back his damp hair, tracing behind his ears. "I know. I want it badly too," she whispered. "Let's just get through the next few days."

He held her close for a minute. As impatient as he was, he was anxious too. Maybe it was because she was older than him, but he didn't want to disappoint her. In more ways than one, he wanted to be worth her while. "Okay," he said. He rolled onto his back.

She propped herself up on her elbows, gazing at him questioningly. "What's going on?"

"What do you mean?"

"You seem tense. It's not like you."

"I've got a championship fight in three days, remember?"

"You don't get nervous before fights."

He stared up at the ceiling and didn't answer for a long

moment. "Feels like I'm not really fighting the Reaper," he said softly. "Just myself."

She rested her head on his chest. "Then you can't lose."

———————

Carr passed New Year's Eve without parties or booze, just a glass of sparkling cider raised with Risha and Uncle Polly. While the rest of Valtego was still sleeping off hangovers, he woke and went for a long walk, sipping from a three-liter jug of electrolyte water and looking up at morning stars twinkling over near-empty streets. Valtego was synchronized to Earth Universal Coordinated Time; the fight was being held mid-afternoon so as many people as possible on the planet could watch it live. He had a few hours still. He returned to his apartment, ate a meal—an egg-white omelet with potatoes, a banana, plain oatmeal mixed with protein powder—and packed his bag.

The adrenaline dump had already started. Carr figured himself a pro at the mental game by now—hell, he'd been competing years before he could shave; he really had no excuse—but these felt almost like first-fight jitters. It'd been a struggle to force himself to eat. He couldn't keep his hands still. He checked his cuff every fifteen minutes and was surprised in every instance to find that only thirty seconds had passed. Finally, he made himself lie down on his back, flat on the floor of his apartment.

Yesterday, he'd gone in for testing and measurement. The doctor had checked his vitals, looked into his eyes and mouth and ears. He'd stripped down to his shorts when told. He'd peed into a little container, given a drop of blood from his thumb, and stood still inside the body scanner. As he'd waited for the results, sweat had gathered in his palms. It was ridiculous. He'd been pre-fight tested before and never had a problem. But he started imagining that maybe the testing had gotten more sophisticated, maybe they sequenced DNA for title fights. He envisioned the technician over by the console pausing, frowning, then turning and whispering to the ZGFA official with the large misshapen nose standing a few feet away in a white shirt and dark pants. The official would turn and squint at him with cold accusation, then walk up and say, "Carr Luka, will you come with me please?"

"Clean," said the technician, and that one word seemed to Carr to fall in a special class of perfect, wonderful words, like "champion" and "love" and his own name. The official drew a signal pen over Carr's cuff to discharge him and he'd walked out casually, relief draining into his feet.

Carr stared up at the featureless ceiling of his apartment. *Admit it. You're afraid.*

Fear could be good. Harnessed and under control, it kept him in the gym that extra hour. In those infinite seconds before he dropped into the Cube, the right kind of fear sharpened his senses to a razor's edge, heightened his instincts. But this was different. He wasn't afraid of being hurt, and he wasn't afraid of losing. Or, if he was, it wasn't the reason he was lying on the floor feeling like a chickenshit amateur.

He was about to fulfill a criminal pact made when he was nothing more than a bundle of cells in a petri dish. If he lost, he would be a failure. If he won, he would be a fraud. Tomorrow, he would have to live either with the knowledge that he'd been designed with every advantage and still blown it, or with the reality that he'd broken the law and was going to keep breaking it. It was so, so warped. He was afraid, deeply afraid, that knowing this was fatal. It would mess up his head in the Cube today, and maybe forever. He might be ruined already.

Carr closed his eyes. He made himself pull in a long breath, pressing the air down to his abdomen and holding it until his arms began to prickle. He let it out, emptying his lungs completely until they burned with need, then drew in another breath. In, hold. Out, hold.

After testing, his mass had been calibrated and officially recorded. Then he'd stepped up to the low platform with the ZGFA logo behind it and faced Henri Manon. The Reaper was broad-shouldered, long-armed, a little soft around his perpetually smirking thick-lipped mouth, and chiseled like an anatomy model. Attached to thick, veined forearms, his fists looked surprisingly small as he raised them for the traditional face-off shot that the cameras were waiting to capture. "C'mon pretty boy, put 'em up," he said, sounding amused and faintly bored. "You get to be in a photo with a Manon. Show it to your kids someday."

In, hold. Out, hold. *There is no someday. There's only today. There's only the next hour, the next minute, the next second.*

Carr believed this every time he went into the Cube. Why should things be any different now? He hadn't changed. Exposing the guts of a machine, seeing how it worked and how it was made, didn't actually change what it was or what it did. And he knew what to do. He could run it through his mind like a holovid that had already been filmed. He began to do so now, seeing every step—from getting into the car that would take him to the Cube, to his warm-up routine, to his entrance on the deck, to the fight itself, to the victory that seemed so close and sweet he could taste it on his tongue. He played the day out again and again, pausing and lingering in some spots, speeding up through others. The fight changed; sometimes he knocked Manon out in thirty seconds, sometimes he battled him to a bitter and exhausted split decision. But every version felt right. Not wrong. Not unfair. Not immoral. Utterly, inarguably *right*.

If he could hold that rightness in his mind, he would be just fine. Better than fine.

His cuff vibrated a reminder. He stood up, stretched, and grabbed his bag. It was time to go.

FOURTEEN

It seemed as if the population of Valtego had doubled from the influx of fans who came to kick off the new year with *ZGFA Spectacle 93: Supernova*, the highest-billed sporting event being played in Greater Earth. Carr had heard that hotels were sold out, charging double the usual rate. There was no way he could walk out into the street, catch the bus, and ride over to the Virgin Galactic Center without being mobbed. Instead, a private limo whisked him from the front of his apartment complex, through the streets, and down the restricted-traffic VIP tube toward the Center.

Uncle Polly usually kept up a steady stream of instructions all the way through the ride. Today, he was silent for the whole first minute, then said, "You need to run through anything, or you know what you're going to do?"

"I know, coach."

"What day is it today?"

"New Year's Day. Fight day."

"I know you missed some good parties last night. I sure did. So I'm telling you now, as your trainer, you better make up for it celebrating tonight. I don't want to see your face tomorrow morning. You better be immobile."

"You got it, coach."

"That's all I've got to say. Well, actually, that's not true. I do have a few more words." Uncle Polly cleared his throat and looked around the inside of the limo. He and Risha were sharing the seat on one side while Carr sat harnessed on the other, Blake and Scull on either side of him. Carr had asked DK to corner for him but DK had begged off, said he was busy, had to visit family.

That was fine, but there was more to it than that. Ever since Carr had returned from Earth, it was as if there was something standing between him and his old friend. He hadn't seen DK much, but he felt it. They hadn't met up to train together like they usually did, DK hadn't called him up to hang out with the guys, and it was Blake who'd invited him to the Kabitain v. Tully after-party last month, not the victor himself. Not that he'd had time to go anyways (Skinnwear product-fitting and title fight ad shoot), but still. He pushed the thought aside. Not important right now.

"I want to thank all of you for being here to support Carr today," Uncle Polly announced. "In some ways, it's been a long road. In other ways, it's been like the blink of an eye. Eleven years ago, I walked into a two-bit gym on Earth and saw this kid. I got this feeling right then—I can't describe it. I said to myself, 'Pol, he's the one.' Well, before I knew it, that kid grew up, and now we're here, and…" Uncle Polly's voice took on an uncharacteristic hitch. "And I wouldn't have it any other way."

Carr thought, not without pain, *I love you too, you old fart, even after everything.* But he said, in a jesting tone, "Coach, if you're going to cry, save it for after the fight, yeah?"

"You little snot," Polly said, and everyone else hid their smiles.

The Virgin Galactic Center loomed up ahead of them. A giant holovid moved across the top of the structure: titan versions of Carr and Henri Manon flying in from opposite directions and colliding in a spinning clinch before disappearing, then materializing and enacting the same thing again. The clip looked realistic; they must have created the ad using footage from each man's prior fights.

The maw of the docking hold engulfed them and the limo slid up to the athletes' entrance. It took a few short minutes to unharness, tether themselves, collect Carr's gear, and float up through the hallway. At the fork in the hall, the group paused.

"Good luck," Risha said. She pulled herself close and kissed Carr lightly. His mouth tingled. He watched her for a second as she turned left, down the hall that led to the stadium seating. He pulled himself right, to the locker room.

Blake helped him through the ritual of getting his gear on. An official came in to do the inspection and give him the all clear. Carr stretched and warmed up, jogging the walls and practicing launches. The title fight was the last one; he had to wait for the undercard matches to finish. He ran through his warm-up routine, then kept doing easy wall bounces so he wouldn't cool down. He felt calm now, all his earlier nervousness purified into a state of alert readiness.

"They're running a little late," Uncle Polly said. He swiped up the volume on the wallscreen. Xeth Stone and Jeroan Culver had their heads together in the commentator's box, the bluish shape of the Cube hanging behind them.

" … are minutes away now from what everyone has been waiting for, the headline fight between Henri 'the Reaper' Manon and Carr 'the Raptor' Luka, to determine who will hold the title of lowmass champion," said Jeroan. "I tell you, this crowd cannot wait. The stands are sold out for what promises to be a spectacular show."

"The viewership numbers are *insane*!" Xeth shouted. "The pre-fight hype has been massive—"

Uncle Polly made a move to shut the screen off, but Carr motioned for him to keep it on.

"—because this truly is a fascinating match-up, between a champion fighter in the prime of his career and a young phenom that has completely taken the sport by storm."

As the two men talked, the camera tracked across the VIP cubeside seats, pausing on the faces of various A-list celebrities including the mayor of Valtego and Stace Manon, the Reaper's aging and legendary father. "The odds certainly favor Manon," Jeroan said. "Some have argued that he's the most talented of his five siblings, and that's saying an awful lot right there. But the Reaper would be making a mistake to dismiss Luka, who seems to be touched by the gods of zeroboxing or something, because—"

"Five minutes!" came the call, and this time Uncle Polly cut off the commentary and Carr pulled himself over to the bench, sliding his feet under the toe bar. Blake checked the bindings of his gripper gloves and shoes and gave him a squirt of water.

"Go get him," Blake said, but there was something about the way the man's ice blue eyes didn't quite meet his that made Carr want to ask, "Something you want to say to me, Murphy? Like why DK isn't here?" Later. He pulled himself up the hallway rungs.

At the end of the hall, the lights went down, and the blue spotlights began sweeping back and forth. Carr reached the stadium entrance and waited. He closed his eyes, holding this moment in his mind like a fragile glass ornament. It thrummed inside him, electric with potential.

Hal Greese's deep voice bellowed, "And the challenger, fighting out of the blue corner, at seventy and a half kilograms, with a record of six wins and one loss, CARR... 'THE RAPTOR'... LUKKKAAA!"

He opened his eyes, saw the perfect prism of the Cube fill his vision. He pushed himself toward it, arms spread in weightless glory like a true bird of prey. His huge ink wings, sparked by movement and adrenaline, raced open across his shoulder blades and biceps.

He piked his body and caught the deck with his feet.

Across from him, Henri Manon curled back a thick upper lip and pointed a finger at Carr's chest. "You," he mouthed, then jabbed his thumb back toward himself, "are mine." He bared teeth, as if he might use them to rend Carr's flesh.

He ought to thank the Reaper. It was easy to get amped up for a fight when you had a genuine dislike for your opponent. Carr matched Manon's stare as the referee motioned them both to the center and said all the usual stuff. A small part of Carr's brain vaguely processed the referee's voice, the cameras, the noise, the crowd, his coach and cornermen behind him, but his perception was telescoping down, to only himself and the man in front of him. The ref asked them to touch gloves. Manon shoved his face a breath away from Carr's. "Last chance to back out and save yourself from hurt, kid. You might have a marketing budget, but you don't have a chance."

Everything about Manon's unpleasant face was super-high resolution; every mole and scar stood out like natural features on a landscape viewed from a plane. Carr narrowed his eyes and the scenery resolved itself back into a person. "You have my belt," he thought aloud.

The Reaper registered his words and fury raced across his eyes like wildfire. "You're dead, pretty boy. No one is going to put your face on an ad again after I'm done with it."

Back in his corner, Carr held still for his optics connection, his mouth guard, the gel. The hatch in his corner flashed blue. He dove through it and the world shrank into the dimensions of the Cube. "I'm with you," Uncle Polly said into his ear. The bell sounded.

Manon shot under and behind him, found his footing,

and opened with a strong barrage of strikes, eager to establish an early advantage. The man had two unparalleled weapons: a lethal left hand and an ability to throw like no one's business. He'd ended fights by flinging opponents into walls and corners until they were too battered to continue. When Carr tidily repositioned and defended himself, Manon braced his grippers, lifted Carr around the waist, and hurled him toward the wall.

Carr went with it. He snapped his arms and legs in, rotating like a ball in flight, then kicked back out and off the wall like a swimmer at the end of a lane. Manon's eyes widened in surprise as Carr sped back toward him and tackled him across the midsection. As they sailed across the Cube, Carr tucked his chin and brought his legs up, fighting to take forward control. Manon twisted and brought his own knees up in defense, and the two of them struggled, grappling wildly in space, seeking and countering locks and holds.

They hit the surface. Both of them reached for a brace, scrambled to their feet, and started trading close-in strikes—fists, elbows, knees. Carr had one arm tucked to the side of his head to ward off the blows raining down on him. With his free hand, he punched Manon in the body, aiming for the space between the last two, smallest ribs. He ignored the burst of white light from the overhand shot connecting with his head and kept his foothold on the wall. He nailed the same spot again. Manon dropped his elbow and Carr lunged into a combination: two clean jabs through the guard, a left to the face, sinking low to the wall as he connected two big shots to the liver. Manon's body buckled away from him with a grunt and the man broke free, kicking Carr hard in the chest as he did so.

The breath went out of Carr. He tracked Manon taking two long strides up the wall and around the corner, launching back down at him like a lethal hamster running around a wheel. Carr threw himself to the side and rolled, sucking air. He dug both his gloved hands into the wall for support and flung his body around as if he were hanging onto a pole or a door frame, legs scissoring for Manon's hips.

The move sent the Reaper spinning head over heels backward. Carr checked his own momentum by driving his hips toward the wall and riding the pull of the Cube's magnetic microgravity around his waist. Uncle Polly's voice said, "He'll be open after that spin!" Carr chased after his opponent, scrambling fast. The Reaper was twisting, reaching, trying to stop his weightless rotation. He found a grip and brought himself to a halt, but Uncle Polly was right; even a man with a good space ear would be dizzy and disoriented for a couple seconds. Carr leapt at Manon with a flying knee strike, hands reaching for the back of the man's head. At the last second, Manon brought his hands up to deflect the knee, but Carr had ahold of him and the impact sent them both airborne again.

"Twenty seconds. Clinch and go for the choke!" Uncle Polly yelled, but Carr was already moving, climbing Manon's body, arm wrapping around the back of the Reaper's neck as if the man's head were a ball tucked in a reverse grip under his armpit. Manon snapped back to his fighting senses and managed to get his fingers between his neck and Carr's forearm, twisting frantically to take the pressure off. Carr squeezed, pulling back with his shoulders, pushing with his hips. The choke was compromised but he was strong; stronger than any man his size. It would work.

"Five seconds," Polly said, and Carr gritted his teeth, felt every muscle in his arm swell as Manon's body writhed, flailing for an out. Carr's shoulder bumped the wall. The bell blared, harsh in his ear. The first round was over.

He let go with a snarl of frustration, pushing Manon away from him. The man's gloved hands scrabbled for the wall, weak and clumsy like a drunk's. He pulled himself away, face red as a solar flare, eyes bulging and seeming to roll independently of each other. They focused on Carr with venom, his face a picture of relief, fury, and shock. Carr choked down his plunging sense of disappointment and pushed off toward his hatch. He'd been mere seconds away from the belt, and both he and the Reaper knew it.

"You were close, so damn close," Uncle Polly said when Carr was seated, feet hooked under the stabilizing bar. "Now forget it, put it aside, don't let it mess you up. You scared him all right—you can see it in his eyes. He's never come close to losing in the first. He's going to come out hard in the second, like a trapped bear."

"Keep on him," Blake said, holding a blissfully cool ice pack to the back of Carr's neck. "He's not used to someone taking it to him for all three rounds."

Uncle Polly said, "Play it smart, now. He's going to brawl. Hitting and throwing—that's what he does best. That's what he's going to fall back on."

Scull took his mouth guard and gave him a squeeze of water. Carr swallowed a little, then sloshed the rest in his mouth and spat into the towel. "He wants to brawl, I'll brawl." He bit back down on his mouth guard and swung himself back into the Cube. Just before the bell sounded, he saw Manon's face—no longer smirking with bravado and confidence, but tenacious and hateful, the expression of a king desperate and determined to ward off the specter of his dethroning. A dangerous man.

Uncle Polly was right; Manon came out full force, not easing back as Carr had seen him do in previous fights. Perhaps he understood that Carr was something different, not someone easily outlasted and pummeled late in the third round. After the way the first round had almost ended, the Reaper wasn't keen to go airborne or grapple, and he gave up on throwing when he saw that Carr seemed immune to disorientation and could twist his body nimbly enough to turn the momentum of most throws to his advantage. The round quickly became what was called in zeroboxing parlance "a wall brawl." The two men exchanged rapid and brutal strikes, each aiming to do damage and wear the other down, then broke apart to climb, and leap, and scramble for superior angles before warring again.

Carr bent his knees, anchoring his feet and waist firmly so he could throw power into a flurry of attacks—face jabs, body shots, uppercuts. A couple of them broke through, but then Manon was not there—he leaped to the adjoining wall, his body suddenly perpendicular to Carr's, his fist delivering a roundhouse punch that connected as an uppercut.

Carr's head snapped back. He imagined his teeth had gone through the roof of his mouth and into his sinuses. Eyes watering fiercely, he dropped his hands to the wall he was standing on, pulling his head out of range, and shot his legs out sideways in a double kick aimed at Manon's head. The man slid aside neatly and caught Carr's ankle, pulling him down and smashing him into the other wall as if he were swinging a large log into the ground.

Carr's body connected and rebounded with shuddering force. He reached over his head, scrambling for purchase; he found it, his fingers tensing, suctioning to the pebbly texture of the Cube's wall. He tucked his body and rolled backward, coming to a crouch that straddled a right angle, his ankles and knees tilted awkwardly as he fought to keep his shoes gripped to the surface.

Uncle Polly shouted, "Get out of the corner!" just as Manon sailed at him.

It happened very fast. Carr ducked a blow and came back up with a high-low jab and a cross punch that smashed into Manon's face above his left eye. The man reeled, and Carr stepped in for another punch. The sharp angle of the wall threw him off; it was like fighting on a steep scree, and he misjudged the placement of his foot by a fraction. The magnetic pull of his grippers slid him down too far and his punch grazed the tip of Manon's chin instead of connecting with the side of his head. The Reaper's notorious left fist fired into the split-second opening and smashed into Carr's jaw with a crack.

Everything went dark.

No. No no no no no

Carr fought the darkness even as it sucked him in like a rocket-plane intake valve. He willed himself to move, but his body was lost to him. He heard, as if from a very great distance, Uncle Polly's voice, calling his name. It sounded very urgent but faint, as if it were being ripped away by a great wind.

For some strange and awful reason, it wasn't Uncle Polly's face that suddenly became clear in his mind, nor was it Risha's, or his mother's, or Enzo's. It was Mr. R, his pale waxen skin and cold eyes. The specter opened his mouth and his lips moved, saying, "I'll be watching," but the words were not audible. They were drowned out by a building roar of noise, a cacophony like the entire Virgin Galactic Center screaming.

Carr's vision came back all of sudden, like a light switch being turned on. His head was rolled back on his neck. He hadn't fallen, of course—there was no gravity to pull him down; he was still anchored by his gripper shoes and his body was floating, limp, like a stalk of seaweed attached to the bottom of the sea. He was watching the upside-down figure of Henri Manon running along the inside walls of the Cube, hands raised in triumph. The noise he'd heard was indeed the roaring of the packed stands, mixed with the far more unpleasant sound of Manon screaming in exultation. Carr blinked; a referee was coming toward him with the aid of mini-thrusters.

The referee hadn't declared a knockout yet. The fight wasn't over. It wasn't over.

Move! he screamed to himself. Feeling flooded back into him like an electric current. He reached out and grabbed the wall. He swayed, nauseous for the first time in he couldn't remember how long, but straightened himself and held a hand up to the referee, who paused, stunned to see him up.

"Reaper!" Carr shouted. "You didn't finish the job!"

Henri Manon whirled around so fast, he almost spun himself off the surface. His jaw dropped, as if Carr were indeed a dead man come back to life. He pointed a trembling finger and shouted to the referee, "He was out! I fucking knocked him out. It's over, the fight is over!"

Carr shook his head and was rewarded with a stab of pain through his skull. "It wasn't called."

The referee hesitated, then tapped his cuff and seemed to be consulting with the other officials.

Manon did not bother to wait. He charged at Carr, who sprang off the wall to evade him. Carr felt slow, rattled, but he could fight; he just needed a few seconds. At the sight of him conscious and moving, the tiers of the stadium erupted in a tsunami of sound that vibrated through the Cube.

Manon chased him from wall to wall, barking curses like an enraged baboon. Carr felt his body kicking into some sort of secondary reserve, his balance returning, his vision focusing again, the pain in his face no longer noticeable.

Uncle Polly's voice, back at normal volume, said in a stunned monotone, "Hang in there, hang in there. Ten seconds."

Carr leaped off a right angle and launched himself at

Manon's back. They clinched and spun off the surface, and the bell sounded.

Back on the deck, Uncle Polly took Carr's face in his hands. "Stars almighty," he said. "What happened?"

"He nailed me with a left," Carr said. He only felt bad pain in his jaw when he tried to talk.

"I could see that," Polly said. "A clean left, right on the button. How were you not knocked out?"

"I think I was, but the ref hadn't called it yet." Over Uncle Polly's shoulder, Carr could see Manon on the other side of the deck, gesturing and shouting furiously, and a trio of officials speaking together, their heads bent over a thinscreen.

"They're reviewing the footage," Blake said.

Scull looked at Carr in undisguised awe. "No one has ever gotten back up after taking the Reaper's killer left."

One of the officials walked over to their corner and spoke to Uncle Polly. "Under ZGFA rules, a knockout is declared when a referee judges a competitor to have been incapacitated for six or more Martian seconds. According to the footage, your fighter got back up after 4.8 seconds, so technically the fight is still on." He indicated Carr with a jerk of his head. "You need to decide if you want to continue or pull him."

"Continue," Carr said immediately.

Uncle Polly squatted down next to him on the balls of his gripper shoes and spoke in a low voice only the two of them could hear. "I know how much this means to you. But you took a bad hit. You're not going to be the same if you go back in there."

"I'm not done. The hit didn't finish me."

"This isn't your only title fight. You're young, you've got time. You'll get more chances."

"Don't pull me, coach." Carr took off the ice pack he'd been pressing to his jaw and met Uncle Polly's eyes. "Please don't pull me. I can keep going, I know I can."

Polly searched Carr's face with a grim, set mouth, making some fast and silent decision based on what he saw there. Then he stood and nodded to the official. "We're still in."

"He needs to be cleared by the doctor," said the official.

The doctor checked Carr's vital signs. "Just because you aren't showing signs of it yet doesn't mean you don't have a concussion," he said, shining a scanning light into Carr's eyes. He whistled. "You've got damn good optics," he said. "They're still intact and online, after all that."

Carr chuckled. He could already envision the ad that his sponsor would get out of this fight, making use of the image of Manon's fist flying toward the screen. He could even imagine the ad copy they would come up with, something like *No other optical implant can take a beating like the new L series from ImOptix.*

The doctor declared him able to fight, adding a caveat about the risk of aggravating possible head trauma. When Carr stood up and made his way back to the hatch, the crowd, which had been shifting and muttering in a rising and falling wave of impatience, roared its unstinting approval. The enormous screens around the stadium closed in on signs being waved in the stands: *CARR-Y ME AWAY!*

RAPTOR-OUS! REAPER=DEAD and *I WANT TO HAVE CARR LUKA'S BABIES.*

During the break, the ventilation fans in the walls of the Cube had been whirring, circulating out the hot, motionless air. The inside of the Cube was charged with the harsh scent of mingled ozone, sweat, and testosterone. The disbelief on Henri Manon's face was matched only by the intensity of his malice. Carr returned the stare without expression. He figured they were even now. He'd nearly won in the first round, and he'd nearly lost in the second. The fight would be decided in these final six minutes. The bull-faced man across from Carr had stopped being Henri Manon, had stopped even being a person, was now only an obstacle to be overcome.

The bell sounded.

They came together like dragons battling atop rocky crags, climbing and launching and hitting, smashing into each other and grappling in flight, exchanging punishing blows while clinging to the cliffside, heaving with effort and moving at superhuman speed through angles impossible in gravity. They were no longer fighting for the title, or for the money, or for the crowd, or even for pride. They were battling out of primal need, because only one of them could be dominant, and dominance was survival. Dominance was meaning.

In the final thirty seconds, Henri Manon did what Carr expected and pulled out all the stops, executing flurry after flurry of attack, of acrobatic moves and striking combinations meant to overwhelm his opponent in the final stretch.

His cardiovascular endurance was astounding, but Carr's was even better, and he'd been training extra long rounds for precisely this. If it was going to come down to a judges' decision, he would put on a hell of a show.

Manon kicked off the wall and swung for his face. Carr went sideways, up and over, and landed behind the Reaper, who had already repositioned. He grabbed Carr's kick as it flew toward him and threw the leg sideways, aiming to send Carr into an uncontrolled spin. Carr pushed his whole body into the momentum, every muscle straining with the effort of creating force without the aid of gravity. He threw his standing leg up to follow the first in a blinding spin kick, his body laid nearly horizontal.

Manon's reflexes were a little slow. It had been a grueling first and second round, and he wasn't accustomed to an opponent who was still this fast at the end of the third. Carr's heel connected solidly with the side of the man's head.

They went flying apart, propelled in opposite directions. Carr caught the Cube wall with the ball of one foot, then fingertips. When he righted himself, he saw Manon floating, motionless. The force of the kick had even hurled the man's feet free of magnetic contact with the surface.

It took a second for the realization to sink in. He'd won. With nineteen seconds left on the clock in the third round, he had won.

He made himself count six slow seconds in his head.

One. Two, three, four. Five. Six.

Manon did not move. He wasn't going to snap back to consciousness after a knockout blow. He wasn't like Carr.

The referee, the same one who'd nearly declared a very different outcome earlier, reached Manon and checked him. He gestured, declaring a knockout.

A wave of emotion broke over Carr's head and engulfed him like an ocean. A shout exploded from the pit of his stomach and burst forth from his lungs. He launched himself off the side of the Cube, somersaulting wildly in the air. He kicked off another wall, then another, then ran a full circle up and around the whole inside surface, whooping and screaming. His jaw hurt, and his head hurt, and everything hurt, and he didn't care—it was all wonderful and ecstatic. He felt as though he might burst into flames at the subatomic level. He couldn't contain everything he felt inside the limited space of his own body.

The blue outline of the hatch flashed open and he shot through like a hawk in a dive, grabbing onto the deck and clinging to it with hands and feet, pressing his forehead to the surface, dizzy with exhilaration. He heard Uncle Polly's wild hollering, his cochlear receiver automatically turning the volume way down so his coach's shouts didn't rupture his eardrums. Then the hollering was live, right over him, and Uncle Polly's arms were lifting him and locking him in a tight embrace. Scull and Blake were clapping him on the back and shouting as well, and the stadium had turned into one giant pulse of motion and indistinguishable noise.

The referee brought him to the center of the deck. He was alone; Manon was still unconscious, being checked now by the doctor. Hal Greese filled his ample frame with air; his voice boomed out across the Virgin Galactic Center, to be carried through Valtego and across space to every city on Earth and beyond, to the settlements of the asteroid belt and the colonies of Mars: "The winner, by knockout, and the new Lowmass Champion of the Universe, the Raptor...CARR LUKA!"

Carr saw, at the edge of the deck, emerging from the shadow of the hall, Risha's tall, slim figure. Trembling hands pressed to her mouth, she went to stand beside Uncle Polly, who put his arm around her shoulders and pulled her close. Risha's eyes, fixed on Carr, were bright with pride, and tears streamed down her cheeks.

Every camera came to rest on Carr's bruised and battered face. The referee brought over the thick belt, emblazoned with the ZGFA logo and the carved shape of the Cube in metallic relief. He held it up and released it, and it floated, weightless, like an object from the heavens. Carr began to cry. The referee pulled the belt out of the air and placed it around his waist, and Carr tried to say something in thanks, but he had no voice.

All his life, he'd wanted this moment. Now he had it, and it was even better than he'd imagined. It was as glorious as a thousand stars being born. It was worth every minute of training, every hurt, every moment of fear or self-doubt, every drop of sweat and blood. It was worth his mother's fateful, misguided choices. With grateful certainty, he knew it was worth being what he was. It was perfect.

PART TWO
OUT OF ORBIT

FIFTEEN

Carr set his cuff against the entry reader and the door opened. His hand around Risha's wrist, he tugged her along after him. "Don't look yet," he said. "Not yet. Okay, now."

She opened her eyes and gasped. He grinned, and wound an arm around her waist. "What do you think?"

"The view... it's incredible." She walked slowly toward the floor-to-ceiling windows that filled one side of the apartment's living room. The sun was shining across the side of the Moon, illuminating a beautiful, barren white landscape of snaking canyons and vast craters. Where the sunlight faded into darkness, there were twinkling clusters of light—the lunar stations at night. Beyond the vista, Earth shone distant in all her slowly rotating blue, green, and white magnificence.

"You can see Mars too, sometimes," he said.

She turned in a circle to take in the rest of the apartment.

It was orders of magnitude bigger and nicer than his old place, but he hadn't gone crazy. A good chunk of his title winnings had gone toward settling bills, including some pricey nanos and brain scans (good news: no sign of chronic traumatic encephalopathy yet), as well as a payment to the best pediatric doctor in Toronto on behalf of the Loggins family. Then, with decidedly mixed feelings, he'd sent the rest to Sally.

He'd called her after the fight, like he'd promised. "My darling, my baby boy," she'd said, sniffling with proud tears, and Carr, with the belt around his waist and flying high on endorphins, had said, "We did it, Mom. It's okay, we did it," and only later questioned what he'd meant. He'd only called Sally twice in the four months since then, and they'd talked about nothing important. He couldn't figure out whether he wanted to be angry, grateful, or forgiving toward her, and trying to reconcile all three was confusing.

The influx of sponsorship money, luckily, had given him more than enough cash to play with when searching for a new place. This two-story unit in the Palisio One (*Leave Earth, Come Home*) was the second place he'd seen. Fantastic view, prime location, and express bus service to the Virgin Galactic Center, meaning fifteen minutes door-to-Cube. He was sold.

He tried not to think about how he could have gotten the place next door, an even larger suite with a jacuzzi, if it weren't for the twenty percent of his earnings that disappeared whenever he made a deposit to his account. As Mr. R had promised, he'd received a message with no return coding, just simple instructions for setting up a direct transfer. He'd ignored it for a few days, and it had shown up again. The third time, it came attached to a copy of his damning genetic profile. A week before the title fight, he'd swallowed the vile taste in his mouth and done as Mr. R demanded.

Carr shoved aside the unpleasant memory. Risha was wandering through the rooms, running her fingers across the built-ins, checking out the kitchen appliances and the entertainment room, clucking with approval at the artificial intelligence upgrades. He followed her with hungry eyes. "There's plenty of closet space in the bedroom," he reminded her. "And an extra key, so you can always stay the night. … Or, you know … *every* night."

She paused and glanced over at him. "You're suggesting I move in with you?"

Carr shrugged, smiling. "It's a big place for one person."

The corners of her lips rose in a sly expression. "You're a bit young to be settling down."

She was obviously teasing him, but he couldn't help wrinkling his nose. "People said I was a bit young to be a title contender too."

Risha closed the pantry door and came back to him. "No one is saying that now."

He gave up resisting and kissed her, working his hands under her shirt and over her breasts. "This is definitely not *settling*," he said. He was still faintly amazed she let him handle her so wantonly. An extremely vivid and deliciously explicit memory from the previous night made his insides shiver.

Sex with Risha ... it was the most amazing, most wonderful part of being champion. Not that those two things were connected; they weren't. But they *felt* like they belonged together. Risha was too devastatingly sexy for anyone *but* a champion, Carr decided. He admitted he'd started out as overeager as a kid standing on the deck before his first fight, but, as was the case with any physical skill he tried, he got better fast. It was all a matter of practice. A lot of practice. There was no such thing as too much practice, after all. Risha had opened up a part of his brain and lit it on molten fire.

"Hmmm." She pulled back from him slightly. "I have a surprise for you too."

"Yeah?" Carr hoped it was something she was wearing. Flimsy and made of lace.

No such luck. She checked her cuff. The schedule it displayed was color-coded according to some scheme mysterious to him. "First we have to go to HQ for an event. We're supposed to be there in ten minutes."

Carr looked longingly back at the bedroom but let himself be tugged out the door.

Several minutes later, they were hopping off the bus in front of ZGFA headquarters. It was located within easy walking distance of the gravity zone terminal, where vehicles queued in and out of the freeway tubes that led to the Virgin Galactic Center. The building was designed, fittingly, in the shape of a perfect cube and constructed with thin, translucent fiber-optic concrete so that under the artificial daylight of Valtego's inner ring business district, it had a sheen that mimicked that of the real Cube.

"What is this event again?" Carr asked as they approached the entrance.

Risha glanced at him sideways from under her lashes. "Don't you look at the itinerary I send to you every morning?"

"I was too tired this morning. You wore me out." He slid a hand down to squeeze her bottom, still nursing his disappointment at having to leave the apartment.

She gave him a mock-stern look. "Behave yourself. It's a school group. And a lot of Terran press."

Carr groaned. "I thought we agreed to cut back on the school groups. This is the third one this month."

"They're important," Risha said. "Did you know you're the second-most-popular athlete among Terran boys aged eight to fourteen, and trending up week after week?" The doors slid open to admit them into a room packed with people. "Besides," she whispered, "this group is special."

Cameras and reporters swung around to track their entrance. Carr barely noticed the cameras anymore, they followed him around so often. He did notice Bax Gant standing in front of a group of about thirty kids who looked to be about ten to twelve years old. Gant was welcoming them and talking about the history of zeroboxing, gesturing around at the ZGFA's land-training gym, which took up the entire first floor of the building.

As soon as they caught sight of Carr, the kids burst into excited shouts and ran toward him, forgetting Gant completely. In the midst of his name being called over and over, and the pleas for autographs and photos, and the crush of small bodies reaching out to touch his arms, Carr's eyes fell immediately upon one familiar figure.

"Enzo!" He grabbed the boy by the shoulders and held him at arm's length, bewildered. "You're here?"

Enzo's face split in a grin of delight. "My feed was named one of the top ten zeroboxing fan-feeds on Earth by ZGFA contest judges, and when they found out that I knew you, my school won a trip to Valtego."

"That's ... fantastic," Carr sputtered. Enzo looked different; gone were his thick, owlish glasses. "You look great," Carr said. "Are your eyes ... ?"

"Yeah. They're fixed. New optics put in too—can you believe it? My first ones. And gene therapy for my asthma. Doctor says I won't need my inhaler anymore."

A lump formed in Carr's throat. He pulled the boy to him and wrapped him in a tight hug. Dozens of cameras inched closer to capture the moment.

"I'm glad to see you, little man," he whispered. He didn't think that winning the championship belt could get any sweeter than it had been on that day, but finally seeing Enzo healthy, knowing that the boy wouldn't have to go through the rest of his life carrying his genetic deficiencies like a public mark of shame ... it made his victory even more worthwhile.

When they pulled apart, Enzo's eyes were fixed on the ground. "I know what you did, paying for everything for me out of your title fight winnings. I don't know what I've done to deserve it or how I could ever thank…" His voice hitched. He swiped his new eyes with the back of his hand, embarrassed to meet Carr's gaze.

"Are you kidding me?" Carr made himself laugh so he wouldn't start getting emotional. "You were my first real fan."

Bax Gant cleared his throat. He'd somehow migrated to stand directly beside Carr and was beaming at him and Enzo as if he were so very proud of both of them. Addressing the entire crowd, he said, "This is a special day, and a special moment, because for every one incredible success story like Carr Luka, there are thousands of kids who can't realize their dreams because they were born without basic genetic care. The fact that Carr"—Gant put a hand on Carr's shoulder—"cares so much about this issue proves that he's a true champion, not just inside the Cube but outside of it too."

Gant put his other arm around Enzo so the cameras could capture all three of them together. "That's why I'm proud to announce that the Zero Gravity Fighting Association is a founding member of the Luka Foundation, whose mission will be to provide basic genetic screening and therapy to Earth's most at-risk and low-income communities."

Reporters started talking all at once, shouting out questions that Carr didn't register. He was glad that fighting in the Cube had taught him how to stay cool, to keep any sign of vulnerability off his face. The Luka Foundation? Where had this come from? He sought out Risha, standing at the edge of the crowd. She smiled at him, but he felt annoyance well up and didn't return her smile. Why hadn't she told him? Relentless brandhelm that she was, she and savvy old Gant had sprung Enzo's school visit on him and timed the whole thing for maximum publicity.

Gant was waving off more questions. "A press release will be out shortly," he assured everyone with a smile. "These lucky kids have a schedule to stick to, and I don't want to take away any more of their time with Carr."

The whole time he signed his name and pressed his thumbprint to cuff displays, posed for photos and clips, and answered random questions ranging from "If you could fight any famous person in history, who would it be?" to "What's your favorite flavor of ice cream?" Carr kept glancing between Enzo, so happy and normal-looking now, Risha and Gant standing together with satisfied glows, the reporters and cameramen, and the handful of zeroboxers in the background who were using the land-training equipment but had paused to watch the goings-on. It was hard to reconcile how genuinely happy he was about helping Enzo and seeing him here, with the staged veneer of it all.

He had a lot to learn and get used to when it came to the celebrity of being a champion.

Finally, teachers began to usher the kids toward the exit and Risha and Gant drew Carr all-too-willingly in the other direction.

"Message me and I'll find you again before you leave, all right?" he made Enzo promise, then hugged him again while half a dozen boys stood around in an awestruck and jealous semi-circle. As they followed their school group, the other kids surrounded Enzo eagerly, vying to talk to him and walk closest to him.

"Come up to my office, both of you," Gant said, striding ahead of them.

Carr started to follow, then paused and turned back. "You go ahead. I'll be there in a few minutes."

He'd spotted DK coming off of the gyroscopic trainer, a machine that developed a zeroboxer's space ear while working cardio and flexibility in 360 degrees of motion. It would make most Terrans ill after about eight seconds, but DK stepped off it casually, threw a towel around his neck, and was crossing the floor filled with machines and trampolines when he spotted Carr coming toward him. His step slowed.

"DK," Carr called. "Haven't seen you for a while. Where've you been hiding?"

The man smiled, but it was small and forced, not the flashy white grin Carr was used to. "I guess we're on different schedules now."

"Yeah, well, I'm all over the map. I barely know my own schedule." He stopped just short of DK, but the man didn't extend his hand or clap him on the shoulder, and Carr felt awkwardly unable to make the first gesture. "So," he said, "you got your next fight lined up?"

DK was silent for a couple seconds, then said stiffly, "I just came off my last fight."

"Aw, hell, of course. I forgot."

"I lost in a split decision," DK said, "in case you forgot that too. Or if you didn't know, being real busy and all." He started walking past Carr toward the locker room.

"C'mon, man, I didn't mean to ... " Carr called after

him. "Look, sorry to hear about your fight. Let's at least fly together sometime, yeah?" But DK was already disappearing through the door.

Carr ground his teeth, then shot a glower around the gym, furious that others had just witnessed his humiliation. He caught sight of Blake watching the exchange impassively from over by the water dispenser. Carr strode up to him, fuming. The man didn't make a move forward or backward, just watched Carr's approach with his pale eyes.

"What's with him?" Carr demanded.

Blake blinked as if it ought to be obvious. "He just ate a loss."

"I know it's not just that. Ever since I got back from Earth, months ago, he's been acting like I fucked his mother."

Blake raised the cup of water to his lips and drank it in one long swallow. When he was done, he tossed the cup into the dematerializing bin. "What do you think?" he said. "He's the Captain. He was here before you. He took you under his wing, showed you the ropes. Can't blame him for figuring he ought to be the one popping up on holovid ads, getting dedicated Systemnet feeds, racking up sponsors and fans. Instead, it's you. And you haven't looked back, not once."

Carr felt a rush of anger turn his stomach. Fine. So it was true—he hadn't been keeping up with his flymates. He'd been obsessed with the title fight, and now, well, there were a lot more things demanding his attention. Blake's words, as blunt and hurtful as a hammer, showed he just didn't understand, any more than DK did.

"Jealous, huh?" Carr said. "Didn't think Captain Pain would be so petty."

Blake shrugged. "He's trained his whole life for something he's watching you walk away with. How would you feel?"

I'd hate it. I'd be jealous as hell. "The Cube doesn't work that way," he said. "It doesn't matter who you are or how long you've trained. It only matters if you win."

"Doesn't hurt to have a pretty face and a good Cinderella story, does it?"

Carr snarled. "Those things are just noise. *I won the belt.* That's what matters here."

"You don't think he knows that? Everyone knows that."

"I would've thought friends would be happy for each other," Carr said, but it sounded pathetic even to him.

"I'm happy for you," Blake said. "Doesn't mean I don't want to kill you sometimes." He smiled his slow, slack smile, but the reckless twin blue fires of the Destroyer's eyes flared for an instant. He could have been teasing, or he could have been dead serious; likely both. Gathering his towel and practice gloves, Blake turned away. "See you around, Carr."

———————

Carr was still in a foul mood when he got to Gant's office. Although the ZGFA offices filled two entire floors of the building, the only one he'd ever been in was Gant's. He wondered what all the other people did—they worked away so anonymously. No one ever paid attention to them, never trained a camera on them. They probably did the same sort of thing every day, their lives as smooth as a slow solar yacht cruise, never feeling ecstatic highs or crippling lows. It was hard to imagine.

Risha was alone in Gant's office, having a conversation with the invisible person on the other end of her call. "The press release goes out today," she was saying, "but we hold on revealing the Luka Foundation logo until Carr has approved it. I have to go. Send me the trending stats once you have them." She touched her cuff to end the call and said to him, "Gant just stepped out. He'll be back in a minute."

"Why didn't you tell me?" Carr demanded. "Why didn't you tell me Enzo was going to be here? Or about this whole Luka Foundation business? Don't you think I ought to know if I'm getting a foundation named after me?"

Risha looked surprised and hurt by his tone. "Weren't you glad to see Enzo? And to learn about the Foundation? I think it's brilliant. And a worthy cause."

"It…it is, but I should have been told it was coming, don't you think?"

"If you'd known beforehand, the moment wouldn't have been genuine. That's what you are: genuine. It's why people love you. People are too savvy and skeptical these days; they would know if it was rehearsed. Everyone there could tell how you really felt when you first saw Enzo without his glasses. And they'll understand why the Luka Foundation is important."

Carr dropped into the chair next to her, scowling. She reached over and rubbed his leg soothingly. He felt the heat of her fingers through his pants. As usual, he was freezing in Gant's office, and she was in a printed, asymmetrical tank top. She'd grown her dark hair long, and it hung over her bare shoulders. Try as he might, it was really hard to stay mad at her.

"When I told you I paid for Enzo's treatments," he said, "I wasn't offering it up for my brandhelm to use as a media stunt. I was telling *you*—Risha—because … " He spread his hands in exasperation. "Because I trust you. I thought … I mean … isn't what we have special? I don't want to think that everything I tell you might show up on a news-feed."

She drew her hand back but leaned in, her delicate features set solemnly. "You *can* trust me. I'm your brandhelm and it's my job to show the world who you are. But I love you, Carr. I would never do anything I thought you wouldn't approve of. I would never hurt you."

He sighed and reached up to run his hand down her smooth, toned arm. "Why do you do what you do?" he asked quietly. "Why a brandhelm, always promoting someone else?"

She considered for a moment. "Because I'm good at it."

"I've heard that line before," Gant said, stepping into his office and dabbing the sweat off his forehead. "I don't know what's more vicious—zeroboxing or marketing. It's got to say something unflattering about me that I'm eyeball-deep in both." He poured himself coffee and glanced at the two of them with a smirk. "I didn't interrupt anything, did I?"

"No," Risha said. "We were just talking about the Foundation and what a worthy cause it is."

Gant sat down and shook his head. "I don't get Terrans. They ban anything resembling enhancement, but they let poor, uneducated parents mess up their kids lives with bad genetics. You did a really charitable thing, Carr, helping that boy out. But who knows what other problems he has, that he might not even know about yet? He might need therapy his whole life for things that could easily have been prevented before he was born." He made a sad noise of disgust and pointed an accusing finger at Carr. "This sort of thing doesn't happen on Mars."

"Why are you pointing at me?" Carr said. "I represent the Terran people now?"

"In this room, I guess you do." He took a sip of coffee.

"To be fair," Risha said, "Earth didn't have the luxury of being founded by scientists and engineers. Humans there evolved over millions of years, not a few generations. They never needed genetic technology just to survive on their planet. So there are millions of people who still think it's okay for a person's fate to be determined by some random combining of sperm and ova." She looked at Carr thoughtfully. "I guess I can see why leaving things up to chance has a certain romantic appeal. Sometimes the results are surprising, and just as beautiful."

Gant snorted. "You've been off Mars too long if you're starting to see things from their point of view. Though I'm not one to talk. My friends back on the Red Planet think I've gone native out here." He gestured at all his wood furniture, his mug of coffee.

Carr felt his insides squirming at the conversation's direction. "Can we get back on topic? Who've you got lined up for me?"

"Single-minded, aren't you?" Gant said. "Every time you're in my office, it's 'who am I fighting next?' You just got off a fight and it's all you want to talk about."

"Living on a city-station," replied Carr dryly, "kind of eliminates the weather as a subject of conversation."

"Look, I don't know yet. It's getting hard to find opponents for you."

Carr had had two other fights since winning the title. They'd come on fast, from guys eager to take first crack at the new champion. Carlos "Berserker" Diaz's coach had pulled his battered and exhausted fighter after two rounds. Jaycen "Sandman" Douglas had come back from post-surgery rehab raring to prove he was the division contender who should have fought Manon to begin with. He'd challenged Carr against his trainer's advice. Carr had put him back in rehab.

"Jackson," Carr said. "I told you I want Ray Jackson."

Gant made a face. "Jackson doesn't want to fight you. Why would he? He beat you before."

"He doesn't think he can do it again?"

"I'd say he likes his record as it stands."

"Offer him more money."

"Why the hell would I do that?"

Carr rubbed a hand across his face. "Then take it out of mine. I'll do the fight for half."

"Are you crazy? That's a ridiculous amount to offer a mid-ranked zeroboxer like Death Ray. Save your money. Move on."

Carr didn't say anything, just gazed at Gant steadily. That one loss was a glaring blemish on his record, unsightly as a hairy, puckered mole. Every time he saw his stats on a screen, or heard them announced, it was there. He wasn't going to give in.

Seeing this, Gant sighed. "Have it your way. I'll see if the man will jump for a big-enough carrot. But after that, I don't know. If you're ready to move up a mass division and fight welter, I could put you up against Blake Murphy."

Carr had been a lowmass since he was sixteen, and he'd grown since then; it *was* time he moved up. But fighting his own cornerman in the Cube? He hesitated for a second; then the whole encounter in the gym downstairs sped through his mind and a bitter taste rose to his mouth. *You want to kill me sometimes, do you, Blake? I'd like to see you try. Just try.* "Fine. After Jackson, I'll move up."

Gant leaned back in his chair and let out a breath that fogged slightly in the cold. "Let's step back and look at the big picture. You're the youngest champion in the history of zeroboxing. What have you got left to prove? Sure, you're going to defend that belt. Maybe you can make it as a weltermass, we'll see. But what else?"

What else was there? Carr furrowed his brow, not sure

what the man was getting at. "I'm not going to take up golf, if that's what you're thinking."

The Martian turned an impatient glare on him. "You're not just a fighter now, Luka. You're a brand. You represent the ZGFA. You're the face of Terran zeroboxing. The marketing campaign and the publicity tour of Earth turned out to be wildly successful, and it sure didn't hurt that you won the title two months later. More Terrans watched that match than have watched zeroboxing in the past two years *combined*. Risha, show him."

Risha unfolded the thinscreen she practically slept with and scrolled through a series of charts with steeply rising lines. "These are the trending numbers for zeroboxing-related feed hits, viewership, and sponsorship dollars."

Carr rubbed his temples in a slow, circular motion. "You want me to do another tour? Another movie? What is it?"

"We're taking the campaign in a new direction," Gant said. "We're thinking of it as Phase Two. Phase One was growing awareness and popularity of the sport. Phase Two is strengthening zeroboxing's emotional relevance for all Terrans. Here's what we've got mocked up so far. It's all preliminary, of course."

He activated his wallscreen and it came to life with an image of Carr captured in mid-flight, arms spread, poised in the moment before an airborne turn, his tattoo wings stretched across a full shot of his muscled back. The tag line read: *Earth Born, Not Earthbound.* The screen shifted to a new image, of Carr launching straight up, unhindered by gravity. *Super Natural* was the copy on that one. Another one was a close-up shot of his taut torso: *Some works of nature can't be improved by science.*

"What do you think?" Risha asked.

"Those cameras are amazing," Carr said. "Do I really look like that?" He noted the light tone in his voice, how it didn't betray the queasy feeling growing in his gut. He read the words on the last ad again and felt the carefully sealed and compressed box stored away inside him tremble under hairline cracks.

"Terran pride is what we're after," Gant said. "The message you stand for is that Terrans can and should be proud to be what they are. Because that crowded, disorderly, messed-up stew that is the cradle of humanity produces true greatness. Natural greatness, bubbling up to rival anything that comes from the labs of Mars or the other colonies."

Except that there's nothing natural about me. Carr watched the flattering ads cycle through again, an awful mix of pleasure and dismay swirling together inside him like oil and vinegar. Only if Mr. R were sitting in this room with him could the irony be more complete. "You sure changed your tune," he said to Gant. "What happened to 'I don't get Terrans' and 'This sort of thing doesn't happen on Mars'?"

Gant waved a dismissive hand. "This is business, Carr. Whatever else I say about Terrans, they're damned good consumers. You know Risha and I are terraphiles at heart." He swiped the repeating ads off of the wallscreen and scrolled around the interface menu, trying to pull up something else. "I need the two of you to come up with a tactical plan for how you're going to support the new marketing direction with Carr's subscribers and fans."

"Already working on it," Risha said at once, tossing her hair behind her shoulders and taking rapid notes on her thinscreen.

"Good," said Gant, finally finding what he was looking for and flicking his fingers to expand it. "Because next year, this is going to be the biggest thing in zeroboxing."

Carr startled at the dramatic sound effect of fusion thrusters firing. Words flew out from the center of the screen and stopped with a crashing, colliding sound:

ZGFA and WCC co-present
WAR OF THE WORLDS

"PREPARE ... for the most epic interplanetary sporting event in history," proclaimed a deep masculine voice. A rousing, theatrical music score began playing as a swift montage of zeroboxers flew across the screen: Terran fighters on one side, Martians—only a few of whom Carr recognized—on the other. The music soared to a rousing climax. Carr and Martian zeroboxer Kye Soard appeared, moving in slow motion, Carr's body and leg coiled for a kick, Soard's fist cocked back. The second before the fake collision happened, the screen went to black and the ZGFA and WCC logos faded back in.

Carr stared at Gant, stunned. "A Terran-Martian tournament?"

"I've been negotiating with the WCC for months, but I'm sure we're close to an agreement. Once they see the latest revenue projections, they'll come on board."

The apprehensive curdling in Carr's stomach worsened, but along with it came a surge of excitement. His hard-earned division title, ZGFA Champion of the Universe, was the highest he could get in Greater Earth orbit. But the premier Martian zeroboxing promotion company, the Weightless Combat Championship, was bigger and more established than even the ZGFA, widely followed and considered to have the best zeroboxers in the whole solar system.

"You think we can go up against the Martians?" he asked.

"If you'd asked me five years ago, I would have said no. But things have changed. Our talent pool is broader and deeper now." Gant puckered his mouth slightly and lifted one eyebrow at Carr, his expression an open challenge.

Carr leaned back, arms crossed, hands tucked into his armpits. Risha and Gant were both looking at him with such expectant enthusiasm and conviction that he felt the uncomfortable urge to laugh. They really believed in what they were selling, in natural-born Terran greatness … in *him*. He hid a shiver of guilty apprehension. He was the only one here who knew that he was as deliberately engineered as any Martian.

Hypocrisy aside, though, it would be a stellar tournament. All the best zeroboxers, Martian and Terran, finally together in one event? Who *wouldn't* watch it? Winning it would be as big as winning the division title. No, bigger. Carr's blood began to sing with anticipation just thinking about it. His skepticism evaporated.

"Do you know who you're going to field yet?" he asked.

"Not yet," Gant said slowly, holding a smug smile in check. "If you have any ideas…"

"Who are the top Martian fighters?" he asked, already on his cuff. "Have you got names, and videos?"

SIXTEEN

It was the third restaurant they'd passed and Carr was beginning to get hungry. "This place looks fine," he said. "I like Indian." His receiver picked up the bistro's audio-engagement tag and started whispering the day's lunch specials to him, which only served to make him hungrier. It also told him the place had won a Best of Valtego rating last year.

Risha made a noncommittal sound and started wandering further down the street. "A post-fight day when you can eat anything? As in, *real food*? We can't waste it on any old place." She glanced over her shoulder, beckoning him with a little motion of her chin. "I know where we should go. The Café Eclipse in the Regency Lagrange. They have the best egg salad."

Carr and his stomach both grumbled, but he acquiesced. There were worse ways to spend an afternoon than wandering in search of the perfect meal. As they walked, Risha reached up to touch the purplish lump surrounding his left eye. "You still have this?"

"I've already spent too much money at the clinic this month," Carr said with a smile. "Besides, I kind of want to keep this one for a while. Maybe I'll let it heal on its own."

It was the one really good hit Ray Jackson had landed on him during their rematch. Carr had to hand it to him; even though Jackson had to be lured into the Cube by the fattest paycheck he'd ever seen, come fight day he sure hadn't acted reluctant to defend his distinction as the only man who'd ever beaten the Raptor. He'd put on a good, hard fight, but Brock Wheeden, on *Cube Talk With Brock*, later commented that Carr had executed the match like a craftsman methodically fixing an earlier, shoddy piece of work. He swarmed his opponent from the start, outflying him, working the corners masterfully, and he broke Death Ray's nose for the insolence of marring his record. Win, by unanimous decision.

It had been a good night all around. Gant had billed the Luka v. Jackson rematch as a superfight, and DK's fight (and win by submission) against Jacoby "the Devil" Bryson had punched up the draw of the undercard. Largest attendance and viewership for a non-title fight to date.

"That bruise will look good for the interview tonight," Risha said, "but there's no way you can have it for the ad shoot this weekend." She looked about to say something else, but just then, they turned onto the next street and saw the large crowd gathered at the entrance of the Regency Lagrange Hotel.

People were chanting, shoving signs into the air, butting up as close as they could to the line of security droids blocking the hotel entrance. Carr was instantly reminded of the scene in front of the Parliament building in London during his publicity tour of Earth last year. But this was Valtego, not Earth. What could there possibly be to protest? Overpriced drinks? Sub-par room service?

"What is going on over there?" he asked. The visual overlay of his optics flashed an information alert into the upper right corner of his vision and he glanced down at his cuff display. *The Valtego Hourly* had posted, five minutes ago, news of an organized demonstration outside the hotel where a large Martian business delegation was holding its trade conference. Carr looked up and scanned the crowd. He could make out what they were shouting now. A man was leading the protest, yelling questions through a microphone.

"Who drains jobs and resources from Earth?" he demanded. "Who lures away our children, turns them into *freaks*?"

"DOMIES!" came the response, in unison.

"Who bullies our rights to mine the asteroid belt? Who wants Earth to be weak and poor?"

"DOMIES!"

"And do Terran governments do anything about it?"

"NO!"

Fabulous egg salad be damned. Carr grabbed Risha

by the hand and started walking calmly but swiftly in the opposite direction. He didn't need to coax her; her face had gone stiff and she kept her head down, her long legs easily matching his pace.

Too late. Half a dozen people were coming straight toward them. By the excitable look on their faces, and the signs they were holding, he guessed they'd just arrived to join the protest, and he and Risha were caught between them and the main crowd. Carr turned and started to cross the street.

"There's one of them right there!" yelled a woman holding a sign that read GOD MADE TERRANS.

"Hey, where're you going?" The man next to her drew his arm back and hurled something at Risha. It hit her in the shoulder and she cried out. He shouted, "Go back to Mars, domie bitch!"

Carr didn't think. He closed the distance in three strides and drove his fist into the man's bearded face with a solid *crack*. The man crumpled at once, and two people screamed. One of the man's companions stared at his unconscious buddy, then closed his fists and took a wild swing at Carr.

Carr stepped out of range. Instinct screamed at him to fight, though he felt strange and heavy. He didn't usually trade blows under so much gravity, with so few directions of movement available to him. No matter. He was going to hand out hurt just fine with any of these assholes.

Sure, but not *all* of them, whispered a small, rational part of his brain. The commotion was attracting more people.

Already this was on dozens of cameras. Carr backed up. "Your buddy deserved it," he yelled. "Now leave off!"

"Domie-loving prick!" the man snarled, and advanced, throwing another swing. Carr slid his face out of the way, punched the man hard in the stomach and shoved him backward.

Several things happened at once. Risha grabbed his arm. The noisy crowd surrounded them. The man caught his balance, gasping, and came back toward Carr, fists raised. A voice yelled, "Hey, that's Carr Luka!"

Several pairs of hands caught the man before he could reach Carr. "That's Carr Luka, the zeroboxer," someone else repeated, and the refrain swept through the crowd, stilling them into uncertainty.

"I don't care who he is," shouted the man, red-faced and struggling.

"You're a moron," someone else said. "He'll kick your ass."

"I'll sue him!"

Carr eyed the crowd warily. With one arm, he kept Risha behind him, though everyone could see her. A weird, pregnant silence descended. Then one person in the crowd took a small step forward. "Hey man," he said, "can I get your autograph? My son is a huge fan. He'd think it was the best thing in the world."

Carr shot him a look of disbelief. "Someone just went apeshit on my girlfriend, you all look like a lynch mob, and you want an autograph? What is wrong with you people? Back the hell away!"

To his immense relief and annoyance, two Valtego city policemen appeared with a handful of security droids and shouted, "Clear off! Get off the street!" and started moving through, dispersing the crowd. Those who didn't immediately obey stumbled back with hands clapped over ears, reacting to the painful warning alarms sent to their cochlear receivers.

One of the policemen came up to Carr and Risha. He flipped his visor up, revealing himself to be a young man with a still-boyish face. "Are you two all right?"

"Yes," Risha answered for them. She looked pale.

"Were you injured, miss?"

"I was hit by a spray-paint bottle," she said, her voice steadying. "It left a bruise, but I'm okay."

The policeman pointed at the man Carr had knocked out, who was now sitting up on the ground, cupping his jaw. He and his angry friend glared in Carr's direction. The officer said, "He's not sure if he'll press charges or sue you, but there were plenty of witnesses as to what happened, so he doesn't have much of a case. I don't see a reason to detain you. I'd stay clear of this area though." He indicated the mass of protesters still in front of the hotel.

Carr nodded, too bothered and angry to say anything.

"Say," the policeman said. He shuffled his feet a little. "Can I get your autograph?"

The interview that night was on a Lunar talk show, and it was supposed to be fluffy, segueing off his decisive win over Jackson into background on his childhood growing up on Earth, his career as a zeroboxer, his plans for the future, that sort of stuff. At the end of it, Carr was going to hint that he hoped to see Terran and Martian zeroboxers in the same Cube soon. That would set the Systemnet buzzing for a few weeks, priming it for Gant's announcement of *War of the Worlds*.

The incident outside the Regency Lagrange changed all that. Carr had said little during the shuttle trip to the Moon's surface and the complimentary limo ride to the studio. Prepped and waiting backstage, he was still in no mood to chat with anyone. He muttered to Risha, "I told you we should have canceled this."

"Definitely not," she said. "Clips of what happened are already out there. You need to control the story before anyone else does. It's a lucky thing we already had this interview lined up." She smoothed Carr's shirt: the top two buttons undone, cuffed sleeves rolled halfway up his forearms for a deliberately careless appearance. Sporting his still-prominent facial bruise, he looked casual, handsome, respectable, and badass all at the same time. "Your feed has been updated with what happened," she added, "and all your subscribers have been messaged to watch the interview. You can't possibly back out now."

Carr took her face in his hands. Given what had happened, he felt anxious about letting her out of his sight. "How can you be so okay? After those guys came after you like that? We can screw this interview and go home. You don't have to be here for my sake."

She shook her head. "You keep fighting after you've been hit." A studio person flashed them the two minute signal. She took his hands from her face but held on to them. "You asked me once why I'm a brandhelm."

"Because you're good at it," he said, remembering.

"Maybe. But I thought about it, and I think it's more than that." Her usual confident smile had been replaced by the vulnerability he knew she allowed only him to see, when they were alone together. The other Risha, the one that made him feel weak and strong at the same time. "I'm half-Terran, designed and born on Mars but raised on Earth. I don't fit in anywhere, I never have. So the idea that a person can shape their own identity, that you can show yourself to the world in a certain way and stand for what you want to . . . I guess it fascinates me."

She looked into his eyes. "That mob today, all they saw was a Martian. I could have been anyone, no one. That's the way it is for most people. We pass dozens of people every day without a single thought, without feeling anything as their faces go by. But it's different for you. You mean something to people. They hear your name, or see your face, and they *feel* something, even if they've never met you."

"I'm just a guy who fights inside a giant box for a living," Carr said. "Just a person."

"Then why did they stop? Why did they go from wanting to hurt us to wanting your autograph?"

"Ten seconds," the studio person called.

"Go on." Risha gave him a gentle but firm push, and Carr walked onto the set and sat down in the comfortable chair opposite Jo Nesta, the host of *Off World*. He shook hands with her as the melodramatic theme music played and the voiceover declared, "We cover the issues worth spending oxygen on!" The *ON AIR* light blinked.

Jo Nesta flashed a winning smile at the camera. She was in her early forties, he guessed. Her blond hair was swept up in the Lunar style, and her face had the arch, sardonic haughtiness that he associated with all Lunar media personalities.

"I have a very special guest with me tonight," Jo Nesta said. "As special as the one I had last night, and even more special than the one from the night before last. If you don't know who Carr Luka is, you're either living under a rock on Ceres or you're Ms. Carson, the preschool teacher who misguidedly taught me that 'hands are not for hitting.' For your benefit, then: Carr, who goes by 'the Raptor' in the Cube, beats the bloody piss out of willing victims for a living, and at age eighteen, he's the youngest-ever ZGFA champion, so he's very good at it. Carr, the first question on my mind, and on the mind of everyone who's just had a bad day at work, is: how can I have your job?"

Carr chuckled. Something about living on the Moon—a place best suited to be a penal colony—must be what gave Moon residents their dark, cynical sense of humor. Although Luna was a self-governing body within the Terran system, the barren hunk of rock was completely dependent on Earth to support the people who worked in its scientific, mining, and transportation sectors.

"Well, in my case, I got into enough fights as a kid that it made sense for me to try making a living out of it," he said. "I was lucky that my coach found me and brought me up to be trained in orbit. When I turned sixteen, I landed my first contract on Valtego and started fighting pro."

"It's not as easy as you make it look though, is it?" Jo Nesta asked. "The other fellows tend to hit back."

"Yeah, they sure do."

"But it doesn't work out so well for them—you have a near-perfect record of wins. What's your secret? Why are you so good? Vitamins?"

Carr smiled, though a small, raw nerve twinged uncomfortably. "I train really hard. I love what I do, so I try to be the best I can for every fight."

"Some of your fans refer to you as the 'boy god of zero-boxing.' How do you feel about being deified?"

"I think 'boy god' sounds prissy."

Jo Nesta laughed, a surprisingly pleasant sound, then dropped her voice, feigning a conspiratorial tone. "Shockingly, not everyone seems to be a fan. Some of your fellow zeroboxers have suggested that your popular success is as much about your crack marketing team and the media campaign that the ZGFA has put behind you as it is about your athletic ability."

Carr's eyes narrowed, his veins growing hot even as he kept an unconcerned smile plastered to his face. He knew who "some of your fellow zeroboxers" referred to. Jo was parroting the words DK had used at his most recent press conference, in the lead-up to the superfight. Carr said, "Anyone who thinks that is welcome to meet me in the Cube."

Nesta leaned back, switching to a solemn tone. "Speaking of unfortunate press, let's talk about what happened earlier today. There's a clip making its way around the Systemnet of you knocking a man unconscious in the middle of the street. I've heard of people taking their work home, but isn't that going a bit far?"

Carr wrapped his fingers around the armrests of the chair. He'd known Nesta would go there, but he was still having a hard time thinking about it calmly enough for an interview. "We—my girlfriend and I—got caught near a protest. People were gathering in front of this hotel on Valtego—"

"The Regency Lagrange," Nesta supplied. "Fabulous egg salad."

"The protesters, they were angry about Martians taking jobs and converting Terrans. It was getting out of hand. We tried to steer clear, but this guy started going after Risha and yelling at her. He threw a can and it hit her."

"That's when you punched him in the face."

"Yeah. I'm not sorry I did it, either." Was that a bad thing to say? Was he going off-script? He couldn't remember and he didn't care.

"Your girlfriend is Martian, is that right?"

"Half-Martian."

"Hmmm." Nesta nodded to let the idea sink in, her eyes twinkling as if she'd been digging for treasure and just felt the clang of her shovel hitting metal. "Let's talk about that. Aren't you in an awkward spot? Your fans are overwhelmingly Terran, and we all know how tense relations are between Earth and Mars right now. Trade disputes, accusations of 'scientist poaching,' the controversy over mandatory genetic modifications for Terran immigrants to Mars . . . " She tallied the issues on her fingers. "I could go on, and it just seems to be getting worse. Do you worry that being seen as sympathetic to Mars is going to cost you fans?"

The loaded question annoyed Carr. He leaned forward, elbows on knees, and shook his head. "I'm not a politician—I'm just an athlete. I was born and raised in Toronto. I'm more Terran than dirt. How does my girlfriend make me 'sympathetic to Mars,' whatever that means? She—" On a sudden impulse, Carr stood up and searched out Risha's figure standing off-stage, hugging her arms and watching. "Risha," he said, waving her over. "Risha, come out here."

He couldn't help but feel a little jolt of satisfaction at seeing her lips part in a small "o" of surprise. He waved at her again, insistently. She hesitated, then squared her shoulders and walked out in front of the cameras. A stagehand quickly set another chair beside Carr's and she sat down in it, sliding a questioning look toward him even as she put on a beautiful smile for Jo Nesta and the viewers. Carr reached out and put a hand over one of hers. He said, speaking to the host but looking at her, "Risha's face isn't on any ads. She's not followed by cameras and she doesn't have any fanfeeds. But she's my cornerman, always. When I'm in the Cube, it's like I'm fighting for both of us." He turned to Jo

Nesta, his face hardening. "For some guy to cuss at her, and hit her, just because he's mad at a whole planet... What was I supposed to do, huh? What would any guy do?"

Remarkably, Nesta appeared to be at a loss for wry or sarcastic comments.

Carr said, "As for costing me fans? My fans respect me for my performance in the Cube. All I know is, when I'm in there, I don't care what the guy looks like, or where he comes from, or what his government is. All I care about is what he can do. If he's there to fight, hard and clean, I respect that. Sports are simple that way. If people are going to judge me for something else, I can't do anything about it."

Jo Nesta nodded and smiled into the camera. "Well, if only the leaders of Earth and Mars could get in a Cube to solve their problems. That would be a diplomatic exchange worth watching."

———

On the shuttle ride home, Carr leaned his head against the side of the wall and closed his eyes. He felt tired and a headache was crawling up the base of his skull. Risha, flicking through views on her thinscreen, said, "You absolutely nailed it. Your popularity trending stats took a dip in the hours before the interview, but since then they've climbed to even higher levels than before. The poll on your feed shows that eighty-five percent of your subscribers approve of what you did, and seventy-six percent view you 'more favorably' than before."

"I just want to sleep, babe."

But he couldn't. It was late evening by the time they landed on Valtego. Standing at the corner of the docking hub's shopping plaza, Carr called for a taxi. The transportation services AI system returned a message saying there would be a five-minute wait. Simulated night had darkened the streets, but there were still plenty of people out, browsing the night markets, packing the open-air restaurants and bars, clustering around the bright lights of the casinos and theaters.

"How could DK say that about me?" he wondered out loud. "I feel like I don't even know him anymore." Maybe he didn't. It rankled him when he thought about it, but he didn't see how it could be helped. The course the two of them had once been on had diverged, spun them off on different trajectories.

"Don't let it bother you." Risha slipped a hand into the crook of his arm. "You're a champion, and champions are targets. People are always going to be coming after you now, wanting what you have."

Her words rang true, and they were not pleasant to contemplate. Last year, not a day went by when Carr didn't envision defeating Henri Manon and winning the belt for himself. Who, right now, was training with the single-minded goal of doing the same to him? Who was imagining his face at the end of a fist? Who was fantasizing about *his* championship belt? Guys he didn't even know yet, who he passed in the gym maybe. His heart started pounding just thinking about it. He knew, rationally, that few people hung on to the top spot for very long, much less forever, and that he too would one day be dethroned. But his gut cried out differently. *Never. Not me. I'm different.*

The taxi arrived, and when Risha climbed in he set the destination for her and leaned through the doorway without getting in. "I'm going to the gym for a while." When she started to protest, he said firmly, "I just need to burn off everything from today. Clear my head." She opened her mouth again, then closed it and nodded. He shut the door and watched until the vehicle had glided silently down the street.

He wanted to go to the Cube, but he didn't have his gloves or shoes with him. Half an hour on the gyroscopic trainer, then. Maybe after that he'd be able to sleep peacefully. He walked to ZGFA headquarters, moving through the crowds purposefully, with his head down, and was relieved that no one saw his face long enough to recognize him. At one point he hurried right past a large image of himself, playing on a holovid banner. It was the arms-spread, *Earth Born, Not Earthbound* ad, with the date of his next fight—against Blake "the Destroyer" Murphy—in ten weeks. Tickets now on sale.

At night, the building's translucent outer walls were lit bluish, just like the Cube under stadium spotlights. As he neared the entrance, a figure stepped forward from the shadow of the entryway. For a second, Carr thought it was Uncle Polly leaving the building, and he felt the urge to run to his coach like a little boy. He could talk to Uncle Polly and his coach would set him straight. Polly would remind him of what was important and focus him on his next fight—take him back to where things were simple and made sense.

His steps quickened, but it only took another second to see that it wasn't Uncle Polly. The man had the same height and build, but he was a stranger. He was wearing a dark coat and square-toed boots, even though there was no need for either on a climate-controlled city-station. At Carr's approach, he said, "Carr Luka?"

Carr paused. "Who are you?"

The man lifted his arm to display the identification code on the underside of his green, government-issued cuff. "My name is Detective Van," he said, just as Carr's optics matched the code and the man's face and flashed an *ID confirmed* message into the corner of his vision. "I'm from the International Commission on Genetics. Genepol."

SEVENTEEN

For a second, Carr felt as if he had taken Henri Manon's killer left fist straight to the face again. His brain bounced around inside his head, bruising itself against the inside of his skull, even as his feet stood rooted to the ground as if he were wearing magnetic shoes a hundred times more powerful than his grippers.

"What can I do for you, detective?" he heard himself say. He was surprised that he spoke calmly and without any thought at all, like raising an arm to ward off a blow.

"May we speak somewhere privately?" Detective Van's voice hinted at nothing; it was as neutral as the voice of an AI program in a car or a house. He was a lean, solid man, the detective, with an accent that sounded European and a short dark beard that made it hard to judge his age. He looked so obviously Terran it was almost caricature. His clothes were made of natural materials—cotton and leather—and his skin was rough and sun-spotted, his nails thick and blunt from working with his hands.

All these things Carr made distant note of, his mind going through the reflexive motions of sizing up an adversary. He looked toward the doors of the building. No, not in there. If there was anyone inside using the training floor, he didn't want them to see this. To see him being led away in handcuffs. He said, "There's a noodle shop across the street."

"That's fine. I won't take much of your time."

They walked over to the very same place he and Risha had first sat down together after she'd abruptly appeared in his life last year. An eternity ago. The view through the sky windows was the same, just with different ships. An invisible but searing jolt of despair raced through Carr. His worst nightmare was coming true—suddenly, without warning, like an asteroid out of nowhere. Van knew what he was. He was going to be arrested. His mom and Uncle Polly would go to jail. He would be stripped of his title. They would take his belt right off the wall of his new apartment and hand it back to Henri Manon and, in a few hours, he would be nothing.

Detective Van touched the table's menu-screen to order a soda with ice, but Carr shook his head. He felt enough like throwing up as it was. The detective asked, "Are you familiar with what Genepol does, Mr. Luka?"

Carr forced himself to shrug. "You enforce international laws on genetics. Something like that, right?"

Detective Van nodded. "Most of it is rather boring. Working with national governments to ensure uniform licensing and inspection standards for genetics service providers. Ensuring that all new chromosome packages coming to market are independently audited. That sort of dull stuff. I work on the interesting part, the investigation of genetic crimes."

Carr wondered if the man could hear his pulse, it seemed so loud. "What do you need to talk to me for?" he asked, masking his fear as impatience. He kept his hands under the table, so if they trembled Van wouldn't see.

The detective unfolded a thinscreen, similar to Risha's but a smaller model. He called an image up and set it down in front of Carr. It was a photo of Mr. R. The image was a little grainy and the man looked younger, with longer hair, but Carr knew it was him. "Have you seen this man before, Mr. Luka? Perhaps at zeroboxing matches or other ZGFA events? He may have identified himself as a prospective sponsor, or an athletic scout."

Carr's thoughts were racing wildly. He pretended to study the image carefully, as if trying to rack his memory. Would the detective be able to tell if he was lying? He'd heard or read somewhere that some police-grade optic and cochlear implants could read a suspect's facial reactions and analyze speech to detect signs of deception. Is that what was going on behind the man's cool, inquisitive gaze?

Slowly, Carr shook his head. "I meet a lot of people, detective. I'm not good at remembering all of them."

"Perhaps your optics would have captured him at some point?"

"I cycle through my transmission capacity pretty fast.

If I've seen him before, it wasn't recently enough to still be on my feed." Carr gazed steadily at the detective. Eye contact was a sign of sincerity, he thought, and he hadn't technically lied, not yet. "Who is he, anyways? You mind telling me what all this is about before you keep asking me questions?"

"He goes by several aliases, but his name is Kaan Rhys-tok. He's the leader of an international 'seed and farm' ring that's been evading prosecution for many years."

Carr swallowed. "Seed and farm?"

A service droid nudged up with Van's soda. He took it and stirred, his eyes still on Carr. "For a long time, we split genetic crimes into two categories. Discrete crimes are pretty straightforward. Like the case a few years ago, of a cult geneticist who sold a dozen people on the idea that he could design their children with wings so they'd be born as angels. You get some sad cases of really deformed kids, but the perpetrators are usually easy to identify. Organized crimes are trickier. There might be rogue governments involved—there's always a motive to enhance soldiers, or spies, or for those in political power to try to make themselves and their offspring better than everyone else. For the most part, though, we know who has the means and motive to be included on that list. Then there's the third kind of crime." The detective took a long sip of his soda.

"And that is?" Carr asked despite himself.

Van leaned back. "Do you go back to Earth much, Mr. Luka?"

"Sometimes. For meetings, publicity stuff." Carr wanted to scream. This was some kind of slow torture.

"Do you ever go out into the country, into the agricultural areas?"

"No."

"Well, you ought to. See Earth as it really is. The cities are almost as unnatural as space settlements, in my opinion. My family owns a few acres on Greenland. It's not much, but every year I plant a bunch of seeds. Carrots, sweet peas, bok choy, artichoke ... I try something new every year. The soil is wonderfully fertile, but the weather is unpredictable. I never know what will grow well and what won't, but I can always be assured that *something* will pay off for me."

"I don't have all night, detective," Carr said. "What are you getting at with this gardening story?"

"Rhystok's 'seed and farm' operation works the same way. He custom-designs enhanced embryos, usually sourced from people who can't afford a geneticist, then waits for them to develop into musical prodigies, superstar athletes, powerful politicians, wealthy businessmen ... whatever it is they're meant to be. Then, when they're far enough along in their careers, irretrievably invested in their giftedness, he extorts them. It's a unique model because instead of profiting at the time he provides enhancement, he's reaping its benefits years down the line. It's extremely difficult to prosecute him because his victims have no interest in exposing him." Van stared straight at Carr. "Many of them don't even know what they are until he pulls them into his scheme."

Carr felt as if he were watching something not real. A holovid of himself and the detective having a scripted conversation, each playing a role the other could see through. He said, "What makes you think this man is involved in zeroboxing?"

"I've been tracking him for a long time, Mr. Luka. I know he's made a number of trips to Valtego, and on this city-station, there's no bigger sport than zeroboxing."

"I told you I haven't seen him."

"Can I count on you to keep an eye out for him? To call me if you see him?" He set his drink down and sent his cuff's linkage code to Carr's.

Carr's cuff flashed a response, which he ignored. "Sure. Happy to help." Sounding indifferent, he added, "If what you say is true, then the people he … designs, what happens to them?"

The detective didn't miss a beat. "That depends on their involvement. The courts have ruled that a person who falls outside of legal genetic parameters through no fault of his own can't be prosecuted, *unless*"—and here he paused—"unless he knowingly uses his genetic enhancements in an illegal manner. Such as, say, competing in an athletic event. That's why it's extremely important that anyone contacted by Mr. Rhystok cooperates fully with the authorities."

There was long silence between them. Finally Carr said, with a very real edge of anger in his voice, "Are you suggesting something, detective? Because for the record, my genetic profile is clean."

"It does look clean, from what I can see in the public

file. I can't subpoena a full profile or request a court order for a full sequencing on a person just for being exceptionally talented." He actually smiled. It was a surprisingly warm smile. Carr imagined it was the sort of smile neighbors in Greenland exchanged. "I sincerely hope this whole conversation will never concern you, Mr. Luka. But we're getting close to catching Rhystok and putting his operation out of business. It's only a matter of time. If you ever have to choose between helping us or hindering us, I suggest you do the right thing."

Detective Van stood up, but Carr didn't move, ludicrously afraid that anything he did might crack his mask and give him away. The detective said, "I've taken enough of your evening. Good luck in your next match. You should know one other thing, though. Have you heard the story of Fillip Bryght, the champion swimmer?"

"I don't know the first thing about swimming," Carr said.

"Fillip Bryght, until a few years ago, was the most decorated competitive swimmer in recent history. He broke a dozen world records, won every competition there was to win, and racked up plenty of endorsements. Two years ago, he got into a sailcar racing accident and shattered his hip. Terrible story, it was in the news-feeds for a while. Surgeries, nanos, rehab, nothing could make him what he used to be. He became depressed, started drinking, and fell under a lot of debt. Six months ago, he died in an apparent suicide."

"Tough break."

Van nodded. "Two weeks before he died, he contacted

the police, claiming to be a victim of extortion and telling them his life was in danger. He wouldn't give details. I'm sure he couldn't stand to lose his legacy, his reputation—it was all he had left. But he was broke and had no earning potential anymore. I suspect he died because he was a loose end, a potential liability. Rhystok and his accomplices claim they're helping people, that enhancement is an extraordinary gift. But they don't think of people as people. They think of them as profit generators doing exactly what they were designed to do." Van tugged on the bottom of his jacket, straightening it. "Good night, Mr. Luka."

Carr waited until the detective had left the noodle shop and disappeared into the flow of people coming out of the gravity zone terminal and making their way down the streets, calling taxis and piling into buses. He waited until his heart rate came back down to normal and his hands steadied and the sick fear in his stomach had gone. It didn't take long, but it took longer than anything he could remember.

He walked back to the ZGFA building in a kind of fierce, defiant haze. He got on the gyroscopic trainer, then the trampoline, and the weights, trying to lose himself, to wear himself down until he was too exhausted to think. He staggered out near morning just as others were starting to arrive. He took a taxi home, crawled into bed, and slept.

He dreamed, again, that his match was about to start. The crowd was shouting, "LU-KA! LU-KA!" but he was still stranded on Earth, watching the whole thing on screen with mounting panic. He had to get back to Valtego, and, in dream logic, a fast-enough sailcar could surely escape gravity. Only now the vehicle was speeding out of control, and the AI unit wasn't responding, and the manual controls were shot to hell, and the whole contraption was starting to whine and shudder as a horrible burning smell filled the narrow cockpit. When he looked up, Mr. R was sitting next to him, impossibly, and said with a reptilian smile, "You're acting far more concerned than necessary."

EIGHTEEN

The pre-fight promotional spot opened with a high-octane series of short clips showing Blake Murphy landing brutal shots on bloodied opponents and roaring into the camera like a madman. "TONIGHT," Xeth Stone's voice promised, "the Destroyer faces the Raptor, in an epic showdown of SAVAGERY versus SKILL that you will NOT WANT TO MISS."

"He's making a big mistake taking me on, and I'm going to make him pay for it," Blake said to an off-screen interviewer. After the violent clips, the man's soft voice made him seem menacing. "I'm not worried about the Raptor. I'll fight anyone they put in front of me. When we get in that Cube, all bets are off." He looked into the camera. "You hear that Luka? All bets. Are. Off."

"The fans can love him or hate him." DK's voice spoke over shots of Blake preparing for the match—running, hitting pads, working the trampoline. "But with Blake Murphy, what you see is what you get. There's a lot of hype in this business. Some guys get a lot of attention. Others just keep doing what they have to do, getting back in the Cube, win or lose, no matter the odds, no matter what anyone thinks of them. That's the Destroyer."

Carr had shut off the screen and not seen the rest of the trailer. It was obviously meant to build his opponent up, make people think the lowmass champion wouldn't be able to handle the power he'd see at the next level. It served a different purpose for Carr. Any lingering discomfort he might have had about laying hurt on his old cornerman had vanished.

They were halfway through the second round now, and Blake was tiring. The man was tough, the toughest Carr had faced since the Reaper. In the first round, Blake had landed several clean body shots that made Carr wobbly. Once he'd sent him spinning into a wall so hard Carr felt as if he'd barely hit the surface before he was off it again, like a rubber ball bouncing off a steel plate, no time at all to set up a rebound, just his rib cage flattening and the air shooting right out of him. But even then he recovered too fast for the Destroyer to finish him with a knockout or submission, and Blake had burned himself out matching the pace Carr dictated. *Dictate the pace and you own the fight.* Just like Uncle Polly had taught him.

He'd trained with Blake often enough in the past to know that the man compensated for fatigue by getting angrier. He jabbed at Carr's head, face contorted, trying to distract him before diving low, aiming to upend Carr and plow him into the wall. Carr leaped up and back, pulling his knees out of Blake's tackle. The motion took him into a flip, his back arching in a crescent, his arms reaching. He landed hands first, feet second, in a crouch on the wall, dug his gloves into the surface, and whipped his legs around to land a kick to Blake's rib cage. The man flew into the corner and bounced before regaining his feet.

Blake shook his head like a stunned pit bull. "You're going down," he growled, then shot back at Carr.

It was hard to recognize his friend—his *former* friend—as the same soft-spoken man he'd known outside of the Cube. Inside the Cube, as the pre-fight footage had made abundantly clear, the Destroyer was an animal, as vicious as the father who'd left him with the scars now tattooed over with images of barbed wire, who watched his son's fights from the inside of a penitentiary on the Moon. Carr had to be careful; even though he'd put on a few kilograms for the fight, Blake Murphy was bigger and possibly stronger than him, and he'd never shown any compunction about sending opponents to the hospital even when he didn't have to, even if they were already losing and looking for a way out.

Anger, though, was a liability in the Cube. It clouded heads, made men careless.

"He's getting sloppy with his left," Uncle Polly's voice said in his ear, and Carr nodded in silent agreement as he evaded Blake's attack and countered to the head. He smacked the man across the ear with an open hand, as if he were a coach drilling a student about keeping his guard up. "Come on, Murphy, pick it up!" he called, his voice thickened by his mouth guard. He broke away, taking two strides up the wall. When Blake came after him, Carr put his gloved hands up around his head to defend against the blows as he waited for his opponent's slow left to drop and give him another opening. He cuffed Blake across the ear again, broke off, and climbed. "That all you got, Blake? Is that it?"

Fury and humiliation turned Blake's face a terrifying shade of scarlet. "I'm going to kill you," he said.

They might have trained together, cornered for each other, hung out swapping stories of fights and girls, but right now, Carr was sure Blake would break his skull open if he could. Through the Cube wall he was crouching on, Carr could see DK on the deck, his face bright and whitewashed by the harsh stadium lights, watching and smoldering, his lips moving as he yelled instructions into Blake's receiver.

Carr doubted Blake was listening to anything his cornerman had to say; he was all heat now—he made another wild, easily evaded grab. That was what Blake would do from this point on; he was too tired to fly hard and was counting on pinning and holding Carr long enough to submit him or beat him senseless.

"Quit playing around!" Uncle Polly's voice. "You've got ninety seconds left. Get to work!"

Ninety seconds would be enough. The fight was his now; he could always feel when the fight became his because it started to seem like something he'd already done. No need to drag this into a third round. Carr braced himself into the corner, and as Blake came for him, he slid left, as if to dodge, but let himself move too slowly. Finally seeing a chance to catch hold of him, Blake reached, over-extending his arm, and in a swift move, Carr caught it and pulled it straight as he raced his legs up and across the man's body, locking his knees around Blake's torso, pulling the trapped limb into an armbar.

Blake reacted at once, trying to escape the submission hold by kicking off the wall with all his might and jolting both of them hard. The side of Carr's head and his shoulders slammed into the Cube wall, but he shook it off and held on. He lifted his hips and pulled back with his upper body, slowly bending Blake's elbow backward. They were mostly floating now, Blake scrabbling at the wall with his feet, trying to find some angle to take the pressure off of his captured joint. His free hand tried to punch Carr in the groin, even though that was illegal, but thankfully he didn't have the right angle. Carr pulled harder.

Blake's snarl turned into a howl of pain.

Tap, you moron.

Blake screamed curses at him with every epithet in his vocabulary. But he didn't tap.

"Nine seconds," said Uncle Polly.

"Blake! Tap, goddamn it!"

"Fuck you!"

Carr gritted his teeth and arched his spine. There was a sick *snap* and the limb he held trapped against his own body went limp like a marionette's. Blake's body jerked in a violent spasm under his legs and the crowd's collective gasp seemed to suck away all the air inside the stadium.

The referee came careening toward them, thrusters firing, waving them apart and calling for a doctor. Disgusted, Carr released his hold and pushed away, pulling himself toward his hatch without looking back.

"The son of a bitch wouldn't tap," he said to Uncle Polly, who didn't answer, just nodded with lips jammed together. "He wouldn't tap." Scull put a bottle of water into his hand and toweled off his neck and chest. Carr lifted his face to watch as the referee and the doctor helped Blake out of the Cube and stabilized his arm, wrapping it tight to his body with a makeshift sling until he could get to the hospital. As the crippled Destroyer emerged unsteadily onto the deck, a deep hush fell over the packed stands. Then, slowly, a collective cheer rose up. Blake raised his head. On the screens all over the stadium, the cameras captured his expression: exhausted, in pain, but still indomitable, a tremble in his cheek as DK came up to support him, embracing him and putting Blake's good arm over his shoulder.

The crowd cheered louder. They cheered for the loser, for the fighter who'd refused to admit defeat.

Watching Blake and DK standing together on the other side of the deck, Carr felt suddenly that he'd rather have a broken elbow than this angry ache, this sense of having lost even after having won.

The referee called them to the center and Hal Greese boomed, "Winning tonight in the weltermass division for the first time, and still the undefeated, undisputed, Low-mass Champion of the Universe ... the incomparable ... the one and only ... the Raptor, CARR LUKA!"

As the referee raised Carr's arm, the cheering, which had been weighty with admiration and respect, freewheeled into something high and wild and exuberant. For the first time in his whole life, Carr didn't relish the crowd's adoration. The sweetness of victory had been stolen from him.

Suddenly, as the cameras zoomed in, Blake turned and put his good arm around Carr in an embrace. "I made you do it," he said. When he pulled back, he didn't look like the psychotic, red-faced Destroyer anymore, just plain old Blake with his lazy drawl and ice-blue eyes. It was as if having his arm broken had done something for him, lanced a boil, burnt something away. "We screwed with each other in there. But you didn't wuss out. You respected me at least that much." He squeezed his hand down on Carr's shoulder and turned slightly. "What do you say, DK? Pretty good fight. He's still the real deal in my book."

DK stood to the side, watching their exchange. You would think, looking at him, that he was the one who'd just lost. His jaw was working back and forth, sullenness lidding his large eyes. If Blake had won, would DK have taken it as a personal victory for himself as well? As proof or validation of some kind?

"Sure, Murphy," DK said, with a darker trace of his usual good humor, "if I knew you could be won over with a snapped limb, I'd have done it myself a while ago." He gave Carr a curt congratulatory nod and turned away.

"*Why?*" Carr demanded of Blake. "Your arm—what if it's messed up for good?" A pang of concern shot through him. A strange bond forms between men who've fought honestly, and Carr was suddenly worried that Blake might end up like Manon—who'd lost more than just a fight and the title, but something else too, and hadn't been the same since.

Blake shook his head. "You've never been to that place." Was it a good or bad sign that Blake was weirdly at ease, his eyes distant? "That place where you know you can't win … but you can decide not to lose."

———

At the post-fight press conference, Gant was as pleased as punch. *War of the Worlds,* the very first Terran-Martian zero-boxing championship, would happen in four months (February on Earth, Virgo on Mars) on the Martian city-station of Surya. The announcement had been perfectly timed; it had gone out on the Systemnet seventy-two hours before the Luka v. Murphy match, swelling viewership of the event by twenty percent, according to Risha's estimates. Gant stood behind the podium at the front of the room and rattled off several impressive figures—attendance, viewership, revenue, trending. "These are the highest numbers we've seen since the lowmass title match," he finished, "so I'd say we've had a very good night here, ladies and gentlemen."

A reporter in the first row asked, "Can you comment on the quality of the card tonight, and on the main event in particular? There's obviously some controversy about the way it ended, and whether the fight should have been stopped."

Gant nodded. "We had a very strong card with excellent fights all around, which just proves that the caliber of Terran fighters is the best it's ever been. Of course, whenever you have an event anchored by the Raptor, you know you're going to get big numbers, and we got that. Whether the fight should have been stopped, I'm not going to say for sure since I haven't reviewed the footage yet, but with five seconds left in the round, I think this is a case of two tough competitors giving it their all, and I'm not seeing any fault on the referee's part." He pointed to the next reporter.

"Carr," the reporter called, "this is your first time fighting in a different mass division and you won pretty convincingly. How do you feel about the fight tonight, and what's next for you?"

Carr leaned forward in his seat next to Gant's podium so the microphones could amplify his voice. "I felt good going into the fight. I wasn't thinking too much about it being a different mass division. Blake is obviously a really tough zeroboxer, so I knew I had to be at the top of my game." He looked across at Murphy's empty seat. "People get injured—that's part of our sport—but I didn't want to see the fight end the way it did. I hope he recovers and is able to get back into the Cube soon, I really do." He glanced at Gant, then back out at the packed conference room. "As for what's next, I'm happy to take on whatever challenge my boss comes up with, and he's pretty good at coming up with them. In a few months I'll be competing on Surya, which will be a huge first, so right now I'm not thinking about anything beyond doing my best there."

"Now that is a humble, respectful champion, right there," Gant said proudly.

"Speaking of *War of the Worlds*," Brock Wheeden called from his seat, "there's already a lot of hype around this event, and no lack of Systemnet discussion about whether Terran fighters are going to be able to put on a good showing on Surya, or whether Martian body design is going to be too big of an advantage to overcome."

Gant said, "I'm very excited about this event, because, coming from Mars myself many years ago, I can tell you, I think our Terran zeroboxers"—and he looked pointedly at Carr—"are up to the task. On average, are the Martians going to have an advantage in reach and endurance? Probably, and we're already thinking about that and training for it. But Martian genetic traits are strictly designed and regulated. Terrans are all over the map, and the population of Earth is so much greater. Who's to say the best fighters from our planet aren't as good, or better, than what Mars can offer?"

A riffle of eager head nodding and whispered agreement ran through the room. It was impressive, Carr thought, how deftly Gant said "our fighters" and "our planet," as if he were a Terran himself instead of the only Martian in the entire room.

Brock Wheeden's voice rose up in another question. "Carr, as the most well-known zeroboxer from Earth, do you feel any extra pressure to win against the Martians?"

Carr tried to recall the numerous scripted "talking points" that Risha had run him through, served up with the unhelpful admonition that he ought to "put it in his own words." He felt as if the fight had knocked most of it out of his head, but he recalled the general gist. "Handling pressure is something every zeroboxer has to get good at, so I don't know if I'd say I feel 'extra pressure,'" he said. He leaned forward again. "Are you asking me how motivated I am to win? Every time I get into the Cube, I have one-hundred-percent intention to win. Now, on top of that, I'm representing the ZGFA, and my home planet, and the whole Terran race. That's a huge honor and responsibility. I'll do everything I can to live up to it."

Dozens of microphones and cameras captured his words. Reporters scrambled onto their cuffs to transmit them instantaneously. At the back of the room, a face caught Carr's attention, and he froze like a rabbit in the shadow of a hawk.

Mr. R, or Rhystok—whatever he called himself—was standing by the back wall. As Carr watched in horror, he started clapping. The other people in the room didn't turn to see who'd started the applause, but they followed his lead and joined in enthusiastically, all of them nodding, showing their approval of Carr's words, of his acceptance of his role as their champion.

———

Uncle Polly paused the holovid and the two small Martian fighters froze in mid-projection. Carr swiped the scene and watched the previous ten seconds again. "Damn, he's fast with that corner reversal," he said. "Has everyone else seen this? They ought to."

"I shared it with the other trainers yesterday," Uncle Polly said. "We're already talking about it."

Carr nodded and leaned forward, studying the motionless image. All Martian fighters looked similar to him—tall, dark, fine-featured, all catlike sinew and skin that caught the light like fish scales. But this one he recognized easily now: Kye "the Samurai" Soard, the reigning Martian lowmass champion for three (long, Martian) years running and the man Carr was most likely to meet in the Cube should he make it to the finals in his division. Soard was a demigod in the Martian zeroboxing world; he owned three orbital gyms and had an engineered plant species named after him, which, on Mars, was apparently some kind of governmental honor for philanthropy. Carr wondered if people on Mars studied Terran history and if Soard's Cube name referred to the ancient Terran samurai, or if it alluded to the military corps of the Upper Valles, which had taken the name in a nod to Terran heritage some generations ago.

Carr bit his thumb knuckle, an unfamiliar anxiety crawling around his midsection. From the footage alone, it was clear that Soard was pound-for-pound faster and stronger than anyone he'd faced so far, even Henri Manon. His moves were crisp and clean. He moved on the walls the way the best zeroboxers did, like he was skimming them, and at any second he could fly into the air like a feather, or drop solid as a steel post to deliver knockout power. The man had grace, plenty of it. If only Carr could devote himself completely to training, he could break apart Soard's style, his signature moves, find his weaknesses and figure out how to beat him. And Soard was just one fighter; Carr needed to study the WCC's entire lowmass lineup and be prepared to fight any of them. That would take time.

As if on cue, his cuff vibrated a reminder. He let out a groan. "I have to meet Gant. He wants me to review the team roster."

"Again?" Uncle Polly smacked a hand to the table. "You said that domie had it finalized."

"The catch-mass format is making things messy," Carr explained. For simplicity, *War of the Worlds* was to have only three, expanded, mass divisions—low, mid, and high—so zeroboxers who normally would not face each other would be potential opponents. "He's trying to build our team lineup by figuring out who has the best chance against each of the top Martian fighters. Some guys are out on injury, some have contract renewals coming up, and he's already over budget. It's a pain in the ass."

Uncle Polly made a grumbling sound. "Why you, all the time? Can't DK handle some of this?"

"He does, but I'm the one who's going to get asked about it." Carr scrubbed a hand over his brow. Out of necessity, he and DK had fallen into a kind of stony, impersonal partnership. DK was a better captain, a better people-person, and a better all-round cheerleader for the other zeroboxers. He'd taken on the task of rallying the team and coordinating training schedules so the fighters could discuss and work together on ways to beat the Martians. But it was Carr who

Gant called into his office, Carr who the media and the fans wanted to hear from, Carr who got interviewed about everything from fight strategy to the color of the team shorts.

Uncle Polly frowned. "You need to train."

"Don't you think I know that?" Carr snapped, more shortly than he'd intended to. He sighed. "Sorry, coach."

Uncle Polly shut off the projection. He didn't look at Carr. "She told me she's worried about you."

"Risha? She's crushed with work. We've barely seen each other all week."

"That's why she's worried about you."

Carr shook his head. "Risha doesn't worry."

"That's what she'd like you to think. But she can tell something's bothering you." Uncle Polly turned toward Carr and paused. His face tightened, as if his cheekbones were hardening under the skin. He dropped his voice even though there was no need. "I saw him at the press conference, just like you did."

Carr's spine stiffened like a metal rod. His words came out flat. "His real name is Kaan Rhystok. A Genepol cop came around a few months ago and sat me down for a talk." He stifled the urge to cringe at the memory. "Genepol is hunting Rhystok. The man has a big operation going on, a whole…portfolio of investments, if you want to call it that."

His coach's Adam's apple bobbed up and down, his face turning gray to match his hair. "What did the cop…?"

"He didn't arrest me, obviously," Carr said. "He stopped just short of accusing me of being enhanced, but he didn't exactly hide his suspicions either." The anxiety in his chest seemed to be expanding, pushing against his ribs. "He wants me to cooperate, to help him nail Rhystok. He's keeping an eye on me. They both are, I'm sure of it."

Carr collapsed back into his chair. He'd told the reporter at the press conference that he knew how to handle pressure, but there was a difference, he now realized, between the sharp adrenaline of the Cube and this. *This* was not about his own expectations; it was about everyone else's. Rhystok demanding that he toe the line, keep his mouth shut, earn out his genetic potential. Detective Van corralling him to get to Rhystok, able to destroy his whole life with a simple court-ordered sequencing. Risha and Gant counting on him. Hundreds, thousands, millions of people following him on the Systemnet, watching his fights, inspired by the story of the poor, ordinary Terran boy who became a champion and rose to challenge Martian dominance on behalf of a whole planet.

He knew, with certainty, he was designed to handle the first kind of stress. The second kind was slowly corrosive, suffocating, claustrophobic. It was like forcing a greyhound to run a slow treadmill for days and days on end.

Uncle Polly knelt and took Carr's face in his hands. He used to do this when Carr was a child staring at the floor, hurting after a bad practice, a loss, or his coach's reprimands. Polly's hands were cool and dry, rough and firm with knobbly knuckles. They were comforting still.

"Don't think that I sleep well at night, knowing the fix you're in," he said.

"Second guessing yourself? It's too late for that," Carr said, his voice stiff. He wasn't sure if he was saying it to himself or Uncle Polly. Same deal, really. They'd spent the majority of his life together, wanting the same things. Money and fame—yeah, sure, sometimes. Doing right by the people they loved—yes. Deeper than that: the Promise of Greatness. The incurable need to follow the voice that whispered, *There's more. There's being better. There's being The Best.*

Now the promise wasn't just theirs. It belonged to other people too. A lot of other people.

Uncle Polly dropped his hands, as if he'd heard Carr's thoughts. "You're going to think I'm a galactic-sized hypocrite, and you'd be right. But I'm going to say it: you don't have to do this. Tell Gant you want off *War of the Worlds.* You're going to take a break, think about your career, step out of the spotlight for a little while. You're his star zeroboxer, so he'll rant and rave, but what else can he do?"

"I can't do that, coach." Carr's cuff vibrated again and flashed him an alert that he was off schedule and already supposed to be in the Martian's office. He sent a quick message in reply and stood. "I know what I can do, though." He headed for the door. "I'll grab my gear and meet you at the Cube. If Gant comes looking for me, tell him that if he wants me to win, he'll leave me alone."

NINETEEN

The send-off by media and fans was something to behold. Gant and his Merkel Media cronies had somehow negotiated with the Valtego city council to close off one whole terminal of the docking hub and set up live streaming holovid projectors connected to zeroboxing fan gatherings all over Earth. The projectors beamed in images of crowds from Toronto, New York, Moscow, New Shanghai, and a dozen other cities, so as Carr and the thirty-one other ZGFA zeroboxers boarded the jumbo-cruiser *Infinity*, it looked as if the place was packed with tens of thousands of people, all cheering and waving, some with their faces painted blue and green, others holding up signs with slogans like *WATCH OUT DOMIES* and *EARTH HAS LUKA ON ITS SIDE.*

The team made slow progress through the section filled with live spectators, hampered by reporters' questions and fan requests. Xeth Stone and Jeroan Culver, who would be making the journey with them on media passes, slowed it down further by holding on-the-spot interviews with each of the zeroboxers as they boarded.

By design, Carr was the last to get on. By the time he stepped onto the boarding ramp of the cruiser's passenger deck, he felt as though an hour inside a sensory deprivation chamber would be a nice holiday. He was accustomed to crowds and noise and media attention, but this was a bit much.

"Carr," Xeth Stone shouted over the tumult, "do you have anything you want to say to your many supporters here and on Earth?"

Carr opened his mouth and then closed it again. He could barely hear himself think. "I just want to thank them, and to ask that they watch and cheer for every man and woman on this team. Everyone has worked really hard for this, so you can expect to see some great fights," he said. Someone prompted him to turn around and punch his fist into the air for the crowd one last time. Then the airlock doors slid tightly shut behind him, cutting off the noise like a blade.

A crew member, a young Martian man with a lilting Mars Hindi accent, escorted him to the first-class suite. When he reached it, Carr dropped stomach first onto the sofa, barely bothering to take in the surroundings. "Please tell me we have nothing scheduled for the next three days," he said, voice muffled by the cushions.

"Well … barely anything." Risha came over and snuggled

in on the edge of the sofa, running a hand through his short hair, the heat of her fingers relaxing his scalp.

Carr turned over to face her. The room was large and lavish; it made him feel as though they were about to sail away on vacation without a care in the universe. There had been a time, not long ago, when he couldn't have afforded a stowage ticket to Mars on one of those plasma propulsion cargo vessels that made the trip in forty days. Now he was in the best suite aboard a fusion jumbo-cruiser that would cover the distance in just over three. Sometimes it still didn't seem real.

Risha shifted closer and, as if sharing his thoughts, said, "I can't believe I'm going back. I haven't been back in six years. Six years … It'll be so different. Mars is always growing and changing so fast." She propped her forearm casually on his chest, leaning over him. "My great-grand-parents, it took them six months to make the journey. Can you imagine what it must have been like, sailing for so long to reach such a harsh and alien land?"

"Those colonists were tough," Carr said. "They had to be." He reached up to touch the dark curtain of her hair, looping a thick strand of it around his fingers. "Does it feel strange to be going back on the other side? As part of the Terran team?"

"I'm not on the Terran team," Risha chided. "I'm on the Carr Luka team." Then she fell silent, because they both knew that it had become a meaningless distinction, at least for most people. Not for everyone though; Carr knew he was disparaged by some Terrans for literally sleeping with the enemy, and criticized by others for promoting a spirit of interplanetary animosity. He did his damned best not to read or listen to any of it, but it was hard to avoid it all the time.

Risha shook her head. "It used to be simpler, didn't it?"

Carr made the shape of a box with his hands. "Two guys go into a Cube. They fight. One of them beats the other. How much simpler can it be? People don't have to make it more than it is." They both knew he was being facetious, but he believed it too.

Risha drew a finger down his nose. "That's why you're the zeroboxer. And why you need me to think about all that other stuff."

He shook his head. "That's not the only reason I need you." Firmly, he drew her down so she lay next to him, their bodies pressed together lengthwise. Risha was like an instant energy pill. Roused, he pulled her closer, trying to squeeze away the little space between them.

The room began to vibrate as the ship lifted out of dock. Through the full-ceiling windows, they watched the stars begin to move: slowly at first, crawling across their view. The air in the room shifted, and their limbs, then their bodies, started to rise off the sofa as the *Infinity* pulled away from Valtego's gravity. An alert *ping* went off in their room and a voice reminded them to please remain stationary and harnessed during the transition to weightlessness. They ignored it. Above them, the stars turned into streaking white lines, a rushing river of light.

Carr reached for a handhold to secure them in place, floating entwined. The room was well designed: rounded furniture, tastefully textured walls, thoughtfully placed handholds and guide-rails, magnetized tabletops, drawers and closets. True, it didn't make the best use of the wall and ceiling space, but by keeping everything oriented in one direction, it ensured any planet rat could handle this place.

Taking his time, like a man about to enjoy a fine meal, Carr tugged off Risha's shirt. He released it with a flick of his wrist and it drifted off, silky lemon yellow sleeves waving a slow goodbye as it swam away from them. Risha pulled off his top and sent it chasing lazily after her own like an errant lover. The heat of her breasts pressed against him set Carr's heart churning, brought the blood to the surface of his skin. His liquid tattoo wings darkened and raced across his back and shoulders, down his biceps, inked feathers unfurling as if ruffled by a nonexistent wind. She ran her hands across them and bent her lips to his shoulder. Her fingers laced into his.

"Look at us," she said, holding up their forearms, side by side. "We're so different." His arm was hard and defined—a light, sallow, olive hue covered with thin, dark hairs. Hers was smooth and soft as a baby seal's, the color of dark tea, and iridescent.

"We're not different," Carr said. "We're alike." He kissed her neck, and the line of her jaw, and pulled her mouth to his.

Her feverish lips sent a wave of fire down his torso into his groin. He marveled that after more than a year together, she still excited him so easily. Before Risha, girls had been like key lime pie—something to be craved, and indulged in on occasion. Always somewhat alien. Risha, though, who *was* alien, down to her engineered DNA, understood him better than anyone except Uncle Polly. He would not be who he was today without her, he knew that. She had given him his wings.

It occurred to Carr, then, that if he won this tournament he would ask her to marry him.

Once they were engaged, she would move in with him and he would give her whatever she desired. They might be young, as even Uncle Polly sometimes reminded him, but that didn't matter. Carr had always been precociously single-minded about what he wanted, and he wanted Risha. He knew he always would. He would prove to her how serious he was. The idea filled him with happiness and lust and terror.

Risha read his racing heart only as arousal and smiled, pushing against him weightlessly and straddling his hips.

Carr's cuff vibrated and played its usual chime in his ear. He cursed and looked down at his arm, intending to decline it, then saw who it was from. His rising passion died like a flame doused with ice water. "It's my mother," he said.

Why was Sally calling him now, of all times? He'd messaged her dutifully to let her know he was leaving Valtego. He'd sent her more than enough money to move out of her shitty apartment and find herself a nicer place. He had even asked Enzo to check up on her and make sure she did so. He wanted to ignore the call, but Risha had already pulled away to let him take it, her warmth now frustrat-ingly absent as she drifted, topless, to the stocked mini-bar.

Carr jabbed his cuff. "Mom," he said, "I'm on a flight right now."

Her voice was so distant and tinny, time-delayed by the growing distance to Earth, that he scrolled up the receiver volume on his cuff display as high as he could just to hear her. "I don't want to bother you," she said. "I know you're busy. But Carr..."

She sounded so worried, he pulled himself back down to the ground just to have a surface under his feet. "What's wrong?"

"A man came around asking questions about you. A detective. He wanted to know who your donor was, and which geneticist I used, and how you got into zerobox-ing, and all sorts of things." Sally's voice was speeding up, climbing. "I didn't tell him anything. Well... maybe a lit-tle, but I don't think I said anything wrong. Oh, I hope not. I said that if he was going to keep questioning me, then I wanted a lawyer, but he just waved it off and left."

Carr felt as though the whoosh of blood in his head was drowning out the faint sound of his mother's voice in his receiver. "You did the right thing," he said in a mono-tone whisper, pulling further away from Risha's earshot. "All he has are suspicions. That's all."

"I looked him up afterward and found this news story from last week. Wait, I'm sending it to you right now. I

don't know what it means, but maybe..." (crackle of static)
"...prepared..." (more static) "...a lawyer..."

A crazy, desperate thought flashed through Carr's mind. He was speeding away from Earth, putting vast amounts of space between himself and Detective Van, and Rhystok, and Terran law. What if he didn't go back? What if he just kept going?

"I can *not* deal with this right now, Mom. I'm fighting in the biggest-ever zeroboxing tournament next week. We'll talk when I get back, okay?" He let out a tense breath. "I just need to get through this. We'll figure it out later. Soon. Okay?"

For a long second, he wondered if he'd lost the connection. The background interference, like a crackly wind inside his ear, made him want to claw his own receiver out of his skull. He realized he was literally bouncing off the wall in agitation, the hand wrapped around the wall grip pushing him off the surface, pulling him back, off, and back, off, and back.

Finally, Sally's voice, sounding small and vulnerable, said, "Okay. Later, then. Good luck with your fight, Carr."

"Mom..." he started, but this time the connection really was gone.

He closed his eyes and dropped his forehead against the wall just as his cuff received the news item Sally had sent. He pulled it up.

Famed Musician Sues Parents, Reveals Enhancements.

World renowned composer-performer and musical child prodigy Jaymes Wang, 16, who was admitted to the hospital last week after a botched suicide attempt, has filed a civil suit against his parents, Marissa and Austyn Wang, for intentional genetic harm. Wang claims that his parents illegally enhanced him as an embryo and squandered most of his money, which they had claimed to be saving in a trust. Wang has composed for orchestra, film, and the Olympics, and his performances regularly sell out concert halls. Wang also accuses his parents of being connected to a wider scheme of criminal enhancement, although Detective Ruart Van of Genepol declined to give further details, stating that an investigation was in progress.

"What's wrong?" Risha asked, coming up beside him. "Is your mother all right?"

Carr swiped the text off his cuff display. "It's nothing," he said. "She's just having a hard time adjusting ... to the new house ... and reporters asking her questions." He shrugged. "Nothing my brandhelm needs to worry about."

Risha regarded him silently, the space between her eyebrows wrinkling. "I know Terrans still hold the antiquated idea that their relatives might reflect badly on them. As if genes are unchangeable." She laid a hand on his chest. "I hope you know you can tell me anything."

"I know." Lying to Risha, to her open, concerned face ...

A sour wave of shame hit Carr in the back of the throat. It was the worst part of all this, of what he was and what he'd done. Just a few minutes ago he'd been imagining marrying her. Suddenly, the idea seemed light years away. How could he possibly marry Risha without telling her? He would *have* to tell her. Soon. Tell her everything.

The thought made his stomach fold in on itself. But even if he told her, he couldn't ask her for that kind of commitment, knowing what he did: that one day, maybe soon, he might break her heart, force her to watch the police lead him away or read about him as an item in the news-feeds, just like Jaymes Wang.

He didn't know how he could cope with that. But he couldn't lose her. Until then, he couldn't lose her.

"Let's go and check this place out. I've never been on a jumbo-cruiser before," he said.

————

With thirty-two zeroboxers, their coaches and cornermen, Gant and several other ZGFA corporate types, Risha and the rest of the Merkel marketing team, and the invited media, the privately chartered flight was comfortably full. The small on-board gym was always busy, and two sizable rooms had been converted into training spaces, surfaced with magnetic sheeting to create jerry-rigged Cubes. The walls and dimensions felt all wrong, but it was better than having nothing and wasting the three-day journey while their Martian opponents trained.

In the close quarters, Carr felt like just one of the guys again, for the first time in a long while. He'd gotten used to other zeroboxers going a little quiet when he entered a room, even older, bigger ones, even ones he trained with. They treated him either with a kind of wary awe or with too much cheerful backslapping and loud talk, as if to prove his stardom didn't mean anything to them. Knowing they were now all fellow Terrans competing on the same side instead of against each other changed things. He could hang out with them almost the way he used to. He hadn't realized how much he'd missed it.

"I've been wearing a cooling top all day for weeks," Adri "the Assassin" Sansky commented over a training break that had begun with a comparison of their respective supplement formulations. Carr hadn't seen Adri in months, and he was pleased to learn she was now the top-ranked Terran female midmass fighter. "That's what I've heard is the hardest thing to get used to in the domie system. The cold, and the thin air."

"It won't be that bad," Carr said. "They're bringing the oxygen in the Cube up to Terran levels, and they negotiated the temperature halfway—a little too cool for us, a little too warm for them, so they figure it's fair."

"They have home advantage," she said, picking compulsively at the edge of her glove. "Every little bit helps."

Carr couldn't blame her for being worried. The WCC had a larger and stronger pool of female zeroboxers than the ZGFA, and no one really expected the eight Terran women to win; just to not lose too spectacularly.

"I'm betting you girls will deliver an upset for the highlight reels," DK said encouragingly. "Save some glory for the guys, yeah?"

"Sure, just for you. I'll try not to steal all the thunder." Adri rolled her eyes but smiled at DK's pep talk. "Back to practicing those damn corner reversals." She grabbed her squeeze bottle of supplement shake and floated off, leaving Carr and DK alone.

An awkward moment of silence descended. DK cleared his throat. "Blake says his arm is doing okay. He might be back in the Cube in a few months."

"That's good to hear."

"Just thought you might want to know."

"Yeah. I did. Thanks." Carr searched for something else to say. A part of him wanted to extend the olive branch to his old friend; the rest of him was too proud to hear anything of it. DK looked good; he'd put on mass to compete with bigger fighters and he was carrying it well. For the first time, he and Carr would be in the same division. When the media had brought this up with him one-too-many times, DK's response had been more sarcastic than typical: "Yeah, I'll finally be in the same division as the guy you all won't stop asking me about."

Carr glanced over briefly. "So…"

They were rescued from further conversation when everyone's cuff flashed the new audio message alert at the same time. Carr picked it up and the ship's captain, sounding a shade agitated, advised them all that there would be a five

Martian-hour delay in their arrival at Surya station, due to "border issues."

"What is that supposed to mean?" DK wondered aloud.

"It means," Gant said, pulling himself into the room with a scowl on his face, "that politics are getting in the way. Listen up everyone!" He waited for the zeroboxers in the room to give him their attention. "Last night, the Martian Council of Settlements declared it would be suspending Terran mining and export licenses in retaliation for Earth withholding terraforming technology. After the news reached Earth, protests in front of Martian embassies turned violent, and now Mars is considering moving its diplomats to Luna." He made a *pah* noise of frustration and disgust. "So, in short, we're showing up at a bad time and are being held up for no good reason."

"The WCC won't cancel the tournament, will they?" someone asked.

"Are you kidding? If anything, they'll promote it even more heavily. Martian Airspace and Customs is denying us surface rights, though. We'll be allowed to land on Surya, but that's it. Anyone hoping to go to the planet to visit Olympus Mons, or the Valles—sorry, you're out of luck."

———

When they finally docked, half a day late, they were met by a welcoming committee that included the mayor of Surya, the city-station tourism director, the president of the WCC, a contingent of Martian zeroboxers, and a handful of reporters. Gant and the rest of the big shots greeted each other with Martian x-shaped handshakes: right hand to right hand over top, left to left underneath. Carr looked out across the rest of the docking hub's plaza in amazement. He had never seen so many Martians before: men, women, and children, dressed in such different clothes, many of them pausing to watch the arriving Terrans with curiosity and wariness.

Carr took a step forward and nearly lost his footing from putting too much force into it. Of course—Surya's lower artificial gravity was designed for Martians. The air was cold and dry, like the inside of Gant's office. The decorative plants adorning the public plaza were nothing like the lush, broad-leafed, bright green ones he'd grown up around, but hardy-looking things with thin needles or bulbous bodies, descendants of species from the far northern deserts of Earth. Only now did it strike him that he'd really left home altogether, traveled beyond Greater Earth orbit for the first time in his life.

In the midst of much chatter and introductions, Carr found himself shaking hands with the line of Martian zero-boxers and matching them to the video footage he'd studied for the last few months. Suddenly he was looking into the face of Kye Soard, with his fight-flattened nose and shaved, lumpy head.

For half a second, neither of them spoke. A feeling passed through the air between them—the animal recognition one good fighter has upon meeting another. It had already begun: the measuring, the flickering gaze taking note of size and stance and the way the other man moved.

"So you are Luka," Soard said. "The best of these earth-worms, yes?" He had a Southern Highlands accent that Carr couldn't place. Argyre? Hellas? His Martian geography was sketchy at best. Soard clapped a hand on Carr's shoulder with a force that straddled the line between friendly and aggressive. Carr forced himself not to tense, not to yield the mental edge. They were within a couple of kilograms of each other, Carr knew, but Soard was more stretched out. He probably had at least a fist's length advantage in reach. He looked … Carr searched for the right description. *Efficient.* His body looked efficient. "Welcome," Soard said. "We will show you a good time! Then send you back home in pieces, my friend." He grinned with a condescending, cheerful menace that suggested he was joking, and not joking.

Carr was surprised to discover that he liked and disliked the man in equal measure at once. "Or maybe I'll be taking a bit of domie hide back as a souvenir," he said with an equally threatening smile, then moved on to shake the next man's hands.

A chartered bus ferried them to the hotel where they would be staying. Even the vehicles looked different here, like the bullet-shaped skimmers capable of navigating terrain on the Red Planet. As they drove through Surya, Carr squeezed Risha's hand. "Does it feel like home at all?" he asked.

"A little," she replied, staring pensively out the windows at the rounded architecture, the people on the streets, the shops and restaurants advertising different regional specialties: *tzuka* from West Marineris, Northern Lowlands curry, Tharsian imported ale. "It's a strange feeling."

It *was* strange. Surya Station wasn't like Valtego at all. It was a real space settlement, a place where people lived. Valtego was Earth's playground, vibrant with energy and bright lights, but not the sort of place most Terrans imagined staying for more than a week unless you had reason to work there. Most Terrans did not imagine anywhere in the universe to be habitable except Earth. Why would they?

"Damn domie cold," Uncle Polly muttered, pulling on a sweater. "This place sure has gotten bigger."

"When were you last on Surya?" Carr asked.

"A long time ago. I was maybe a little older than you. Stopped over on leave for a month after two years on my first mining vessel, the *Breaker*. Even back then it was a mecca for zeroboxing. For anything zero gravity."

Risha nodded. "The Martian Space Dance Academy is headquartered here. The WCC, of course. Plenty of weightless spas in the central concourse. Recreational and competitive spacewalking is big here too—I think they have three or four major races a year."

The hotel was new and luxurious, though the rooms were small by Terran standards. Martians were used to having far less space. Carr stood beside the curved, wraparound window of his room, admiring the view. Phobos, the larger of Mars' moons and one of the busiest shipping hubs in the solar system, loomed large to one side. On the other, the Red Planet hung like a copper disk against a black canvas. He squinted hard, and his optics focused in as far as they could go until he could make out some of the features of the surface: the enormous craters and basins, the flat plains and deep canyons, the soaring mountain ranges. The great domed cities were mere dots.

Thin wisps of white, like shredded gauze, swirled over the surface of the planet. A nascent atmosphere, nothing like the dense cotton cloud cover of Earth. He couldn't see them, but he'd been told that thousands of enormous solar reflectors orbited Mars, slowly heating it. Whole tracts of the planet were already murky green with algae and plant cover, fed by the water mines that ran day and night.

"Will Mars really be like Earth someday?" he wondered. "With oceans and forests, and people walking outside?"

Risha came up beside him. Her voice held nostalgia and melancholy. "Who knows? Terraforming is enshrined in the Constitution of the Martian Settlements. Pro- and anti-terraformist politicians are constantly arguing about it. It's been going on since before my grandparents were born, and it'll probably still be going on after we're dead. But whatever Mars becomes, it won't be like Earth. It'll be its own thing."

Carr knew that Martians portrayed their ancestors as courageous and intrepid visionaries, the best and brightest of Earth, the ones who saw the necessity and potential for humankind to evolve and progress to the stars. A more Terran view was that they'd been desperate, enticed or coerced to risk their lives to escape poverty and unemployment and submerging homelands. Which was it? Were they equally true? Did it matter?

"I think," Carr said, "I can see why Mars gives Terrans the heebie-jeebies."

"Come on," Risha said, turning away from the view, "Your first press conference is in an hour."

Even though Martian days were thirty-seven minutes longer than Terran ones, the week before the start of *War of the Worlds* went fast. Uncle Polly was unrelenting, as strict about every detail as he'd been before Carr's earliest amateur tournaments. He kept Carr in thermal clothes and on a strict hydration schedule to manage the dry cold, sent him to get a radiation cleanse, kept track of what he ate and how much he slept. "Can't risk getting sick or injured now, can you?" he warned at least twice a day.

The Dr. Drew Ming Athletic Mall on Surya was even larger than Valtego's Virgin Galactic Center. Risha told him it was named after one of Mars' visionary geneticists. Martians, she said, named things after scientists the way Terrans used war heroes and politicians. Carr and the other zeroboxers spent every available minute getting acclimated to the new stadium. The Martians were there too, and the Cube was constantly occupied in hour-long practice shifts.

Adri gave voice to the generally shared sentiment: "The domies creep the hell out of me."

"Don't let them," Carr said. He looked over at the two Martian women emerging from the Cube, unfastening their gloves and toweling the sweat from their faces. The

WCC fighters looked good, all of them fit and preternaturally graceful in null gravity, their otherness highlighted by the sight of so many of them. Most of them treated the Terran visitors coolly, though they complained loudly about the extra heat.

"Dust, it's hot in here," one of the women exclaimed. "How do the earthworms stand it?" Her eyes were shaped like a cat's. The skin over her taut abs and small chest was the color of wet sand. Carr had wondered if he'd find all Martian women as alluring to him as Risha, and was surprised and mildly relieved that he didn't.

On the first day of the elimination rounds, Carr was up early in the draw and handled both his fights easily. The first ended by knockout at 4:05 in the first round. The guy was too nervous, wouldn't look at him during the staredown. Carr wondered if maybe it was the first time he'd even seen a Terran up close. The second match, two hours later, was more challenging—"the Droid" fought methodical as hell, and kept taking Carr's ample punishment like he didn't feel pain, but the judges handed Carr a unanimous victory. He figured he'd been deliberately favored in the match-ups so the organizers could be assured of their star fighters meeting in the Cube for the semifinals.

When he was done, Carr iced his bruises in the locker room, watching the other fights and waiting to find out how the rest of the Terrans did. Scull was packing up their supplies.

"Nice job today," Carr said, and the kid flushed a little, nodding. Quiet and nervous, Scull was no DK or Blake, but nevertheless he was a reliable, competent cornerman. One that Carr was confident wouldn't go sour on him because of rivalry. Scull had only three pro fights under him—one win, two losses—and he knew his job cornering the Raptor at *War of the Worlds* was to stay out of the spotlight by not screwing up.

"Where's Risha?" Carr asked Uncle Polly. She always came down to see him after his matches. He kept looking for her, but she wasn't there.

"I haven't seen her for the last hour," Polly replied.

Carr called her. Risha didn't answer. He left a message, but felt unsettled. He didn't call frivolously, and besides, she was his brandhelm; she would never ignore a call from him. What could be so important right now that she wasn't here?

After another hour, he began to get irritated and a little nervous. He wound his way through the stadium to the press box, to see if she was up there, and was immediately waylaid by Xeth Stone. "I'm here with Terran favorite Carr Luka," Xeth said into the camera, "Carr, it's no surprise that you made it to the semifinals handily. Any thoughts on your first set of matches here on Surya? You're obviously fighting in front of a less friendly crowd—does that make any difference?"

Carr looked over Stone's shoulder impatiently. He couldn't see Risha among the media people or the officials. Too many Martians; it was usually so easy to pick her out of a crowd. "No," he said, turning back to Stone, "when I'm in the Cube, I just shut out what else is going on out there. I know fans back on Earth are cheering for me, and the rest of the Terran team, and that's what matters. Being on Surya has been an incredible experience so far, and I'm looking forward to the rest of the tournament."

He hoped that would satisfy the man, but Stone pinned him down with a few more questions before the bell rang for the next fight and Carr managed to escape back to the locker room. He watched the screens for a while. So far twelve Terran men and three women were still in contention. The preliminary rounds were going to take another couple of hours at least.

He knew he ought to stay until the end. Just because Risha hadn't returned his call yet was no reason to worry. She was busy with work, maybe dealing with a demanding sponsor or a new media request, and would be back soon. He was just being needy.

On the screen in the locker room, Xeth Stone said, "Here's what I want to know, Jeroan: is it too early to be calling Carr Luka one of the best pound-for-pound fighters in the whole *history* of weightless combat?"

"You know, Xeth, people love to declare sports legends early. The question you have to ask is: can the Raptor continue to perform at such a high level into his twenties and even into his thirties? Because—"

Carr shut off the screen. He waited thirty more minutes, then threw on a warm shirt and climbed through the back halls to the stadium's loading zone. Along the way, he told Scull to let Uncle Polly know he'd gone. He took the shuttle bus back out to Surya's main ring. His cuff seemed to be responding exceedingly slowly (some compatibility issue with the Systemnet access out here, maybe?) and it took a couple of tries to summon a taxi to take him back to the hotel.

"Risha?" he called when the door to his hotel room opened. There was no answer, and at first he thought she wasn't there. Then he walked into the bedroom.

She was sitting on the edge of the bed, her thinscreen open on her lap and her head bent over it as if she was engrossed in her work. Then she raised her face to his, and he saw that her eyes were puffy and red from crying, her cheeks blotchy, and her sudden stare laser-sharp with accusation.

He walked over and took the thinscreen from her hands without a word. He saw a page with lines of information, but the first two words told him everything he needed to know: *Sequencing Results*.

Risha spoke in a whisper. "How could you?"

TWENTY

You had me sequenced." Carr felt the screen drop from his fingers, onto the bedspread. Shock and anger crawled over him in a wave of hot and cold. Had she saved a bloody towel after one of his fights? Her panties after they'd had sex? "You can't sequence someone without their permission, not without a police order. It's against privacy laws."

"You have the gall to lecture me about what's *legal*?" Risha cried. "Terran privacy laws don't apply here."

"But why? Why did you do it?"

She stared at him with parted lips, her face reddening. With a noise between a strangled cry and a bark of laughter, she flung the thinscreen at him. He didn't move; it hit him square in the chest and fell to the floor. Risha was on her feet. "Because I was serious about you! I thought we might … we might get married." Her voice stumbled over the last word as if it were a sharp stone. She blinked fiercely. "It's typical for a Martian considering marriage to check her partner's genetic profile before signing a contract. And I would have signed fifteen years with you, Carr. Twenty, even. I was that sure."

"And now?" His tongue felt numb as he formed the words.

She picked up the screen from the floor and read, in a wavering voice: "'Summary: Subject is a Terran male of mixed ethnic ancestry. Physical and mental risk factors are low. Chromosomal add-ons are present. Evidence of advanced germline modification indicates physiological and/or cognitive enhancements that fall outside of standard ranges and may preclude the subject from legal status, government benefits, and *certain areas of employment* under the Bremen Accord (consult each government's laws as appropriate).'" Her fingers shook and she dropped the screen again. "You didn't think this was something you should have told me?"

His words tumbled out in a rush. "Yes, I should have, but I didn't know. The official genetic profile filed when I was born is a fake."

"What's that supposed to mean?"

"It means a very clever splice dealer went to the trouble of designing me and hiding what I was, even from me. By the time I learned the truth, I was already fighting pro, I'd already met you ... what could I do?"

"When? When did you find out?"

"When I went to visit my mom on Earth, right after the title fight was announced."

"That was over a year ago."

"I know."

"So you've been lying to me ever since." Risha's throat moved as if she were having difficulty swallowing. "I knew there was something you weren't telling me. I thought it was some issue between you and your mom, not … anything as bad as *this* … "

He felt as though her words were carving a hole out of the center of his chest. "I'm still the same person," he said. "I always have been."

She shook her head, strands of black hair plastering to moist cheeks. "That person is a *lie*. I built the entire brand of Carr Luka around a story that isn't true. I told millions of people that you owed your success to natural talent and hard work, not to genetic enhancement. It's illegal for you to even compete." The gravity of her last words staggered her like a physical blow and she slumped back against the wall, her face ashen. In a quiet, horrified voice, she said, "I staked my whole career on you."

Hot, acid defensiveness rose and spilled out of Carr. "*Your* whole career? You might have helped tell a lie, but *I'm* the one trapped inside it. What would you have had me do? Tell me! Pull out of the title fight and go to the cops? Destroy everything you and I had worked for? The ship you set us on was flying so high, so fast, I couldn't stop it. We would have lost everything."

"We will anyways," she said, shoulders curled in dismay.

"No one will find out," he insisted, though the memory

of Detective Van and his mother's call pushed into his mind like ragged splinters. "My profile looks clean and no normal screening will pick up anything unusual. What you just did—sequencing me behind my back—isn't legal on Earth and wouldn't ever be admissible evidence."

"So you're going to keep trying to get away with it? You're *cheating*, Carr. That's what the ZGFA will decide."

"Cheating?" He wished she'd slapped him instead. He'd barely even let himself *think* of the word, much less say it out loud. It tasted all wrong in his mouth, rancid and poisonous. "*Cheating* is when someone takes shortcuts to give himself an unfair advantage. I haven't *done* that, Risha. I put in my time and blood and sweat like anyone else in the Cube. I was born what I am, same as anyone else."

"That's not how Terran law will see it."

"I know that!" He took a trembling step forward, fingernails digging into his palms. He wanted to grab and shake her. "God, I know that. But I can't rip out my DNA. How can I fight what I am?"

He couldn't. Even if he could, he wouldn't want to. That was Rhystok's brilliant criminal insight. For as much as people feared the specter of enhancement, the threat of superhumans, the terrible consequences of breeding mankind, they desired and celebrated the extraordinary. Carr understood this in the very core of his being.

Risha dropped her face into her hands. He reached for her, wanting, despite his anger, to pull her into his arms. For a moment, she seemed to soften, to lean into him, but then she set her jaw and pushed away, her face grim. "You didn't choose to be what you are, but don't tell me you're innocent. You chose to keep competing after you found out, and you chose not to tell me. You never gave *me* a choice. You trapped me, the way you were trapped, and you would never have told me. Never."

"I meant to. I did, but—" His words came out rough, as if he were choking down gravel. "I didn't want to lose you."

Risha squeezed her eyes shut, pressing the back of her hand to her mouth. "That's not your decision." She stumbled around him and toward the door.

He caught her by the wrist, his hand encircling it. "Don't. Please. There's more I need to tell you. And this tournament... we both know it's grown beyond being just about zeroboxing."

She looked down at his hand and back up to his face. Her eyes were like polished opaque mirrors, already receding from him. A small, sad voice inside of him admonished, *You knew this moment would come.* On the ship, after floating together and kissing, when she'd promised he could tell her anything, he'd known this moment would come. It was every bit as painful as he'd imagined it to be.

"Let go of me, Carr," she said.

He was much stronger than she was. She could cry and hit him until she exhausted herself, and he could hold on.

He let his fingers fall open. "Risha," he said, "I love you."

She left anyways.

TWENTY-ONE

He shattered his own rule about drinking before fights. The strongest-looking stuff from the overpriced mini-bar was a bottle of some clear green Ceresian liquor as vile as antiseptic. Carr took masochistic swallows of it, storming back and forth across the room while calling Risha unmentionable names, then sat down on the edge of the bed in a stupor of regret. A barrage of hurtful, furious thoughts raced through his mind, and he pressed his fists against his forehead as if he could drive his knuckles into his brain and silence them. *She never loved you. You were just a hot commodity, the star client that was her ticket to success. You were just business to her, the way you are to Rhystok.*

No! That wasn't true. She'd believed in him, worked tirelessly for him, been there for him after every fight. When they kissed, when they made love, he'd seen tenderness and passion in her eyes. She'd thought about marrying him.

But she left. When she found out you were useless to her, she left.

A call came in from Uncle Polly. Carr stared at his vibrating cuff in a daze. Two seconds passed, then three. He accepted the call.

"Carr, we're just about done here. We need you back. Where are you? Did you find her?"

He stood up and let his feet carry him mechanically out of the room. "I'm on my way, coach." He ended the call before Uncle Polly could say more.

On his way back to the stadium, he had the misfortune to be spotted by a group of half a dozen Terrans camped outside of the gravity zone terminal with signs that read, *NEED TICKETS TO WOTW!* They looked like they'd arrived on Surya with nothing but their bags and the clothes on their back and could all benefit tremendously from a shower. The Martians walking past on the terminal platform turned their faces away in distaste and gave them a wide berth.

"I think that's Carr Luka!" one of the girls hissed, grabbing her companion's arm and pointing.

"Really, you think so?" The boy sounded uncertain.

"What are the odds that there's another Terran on this domie station that looks *exactly* like him?"

Carr stared straight ahead, willing the shuttle bus to appear. *Please don't come here please don't come here please don't*

They came up to him, as eager and tentative as kittens to a saucer. "Hey, Carr! Mr. Luka? Is that really you?"

He turned to snap at them to leave him alone, but before he could do so, the girl, a teenager with violet-tinted optics and sandy-blond ringlets falling around her face, grabbed her friend's arm and whispered loudly, "I *knew* it was worth coming in person! Even without tickets, it was so worth it!"

Carr clenched his jaw hard, forcing a lid onto his anger. His problems weren't their fault. Risha had drilled into him over and over again the importance of "touchpoints" with his fans, and he couldn't shake her adamant voice from his head, as much as he wanted to. "You guys here to watch the fights?" he asked.

They nodded in mute awe.

"You came all the way from Earth? How long did it take you?"

"Ten days," said a skinny boy wearing a Skinnwear top in ZGFA colors. "Brenn's dad works for Virgin Galactic and got us a deal on tickets to Phobos, but we hitchhiked to Surya."

"That's ... really hard core."

They all grinned. How childlike they seemed. They were teenagers—one or two of them looked eighteen or nineteen, around Carr's own age—but to him, they all looked like Enzo, silly with enthusiasm. This was *fun* for them, traveling all the way here, sharing in the fandom, getting close to the drama of the Cube and the fighters they'd seen in holovid. Zeroboxing defined Carr's life, in every way, good and bad, ecstatic and heartbreaking. He'd given his entire childhood to the sport. It had made him and aged him. But to them, it was all entertainment.

Another girl, with dimples and short, spiky black hair, said, "We figured *some* of your fans really ought to be here in person, so even though it's mostly domies here, you'll know everyone back home is rooting for you."

The older teen the others had referred to as Brenn said, "Your story, man, your whole journey, it's like, so inspiring, you know what I mean?"

The Skinnwear logo friend nodded vigorously. "Terran pride, man, all the way."

The shuttle bus arrived, gliding into the terminal with a whoosh. "I hope I'll see you in the crowd tomorrow," Carr said. He boarded quickly. He glanced back as the vehicle began to move and caught a receding glimpse of them. They were practically jumping up and down on the platform, talking together excitedly.

Back in the stadium's locker room, he found Uncle Polly livid with annoyance. "First that domie girl, and then you, taking off in the middle of the goddamn elimination rounds," he growled. "A hell of a time to sneak off for some hanky-panky, don't you think? What's wrong with you? And where is she, anyways?"

"She's not here."

"Why not?" Polly leaned in close to Carr and his eyes lit with astonished fury. "Have you been drinking?"

"Coach," Carr said. His pained look brought even Uncle Polly to silence. "I can't talk about this right now."

"Luka!" Gant bellowed from somewhere down the hall. "Someone seen Luka? We're bringing all the semi-finalists up on deck!"

Carr stripped down to his fight shorts, jammed his feet into his grippers, and tugged his gloves on with his teeth as he launched himself up to the stadium entrance. The president of the WCC, a heavyset man by Martian standards, with thick fingers and thin eyes, was saying, "And last but not least, the final four combatants in the expanded low-mass division ... "

Carr grabbed the guide-rail and swung himself onto the deck next to DK. His teammate had a torn ear that had been hastily patched, but he flashed a triumphant, high-wattage smile and raised his hands to the crowd as the two of them stepped forward alongside Kye Soard and the other Martian semifinalist, Yugo Macha.

Carr didn't hear much of what was said. His head felt stuffed with cotton. He scanned the rest of the deck, noting how the other divisions had shaken out. The final four in the men's midmass had two Terrans in contention, the highmass had one Terran to three Martians. Adri, looking battered and a little shocked, had made it to the woman's midmass semifinals. Six Terrans on stage, out of the thirty-two who'd made the journey.

"Tomorrow then, earthworms," said Soard cheerfully as they shook hands.

Yugo Macha held onto Carr's hands too tightly and leaned in with his voice lowered. He had a bony face, all jutting angles as if he had a metal cyborg skull under his dark glistening skin. "The feeds, they call you 'a Terran treasure.'" He sneered. "You worms, your time is over. You just don't realize it yet. You don't stand a chance. When you turn out be a disappointment to a whole planet, you'll wish you were never born."

Carr felt his lips twist in a rictus of irony. *I don't need you for that.* He wished, suddenly, that the semifinal fight was right now, this very instant, so he could hit Macha in his smug domie kisser, and keep hitting him, and keep hitting him. It didn't have to be Macha. It could be Soard. It could be anyone.

Get a fucking grip. He was off-kilter, he knew. Bringing personal crap into the Cube—that was a mistake for amateurs. "Save your breath for the fight, domie," he said, and turned his back.

Gant gathered all of the Terran fighters together in the locker room. "It's been a hell of a day," he said. "I saw some good, hard fights, some of the best I've ever seen. Whether you won or lost, every single one of you ought to be proud just to be competing at this level." He paused, his eyes drifting over the group. There were a lot of bruised and tired faces, and Carr could tell that despite the upbeat tone of Gant's speech, everyone in the room was disappointed that at least a couple more Terrans hadn't made it to the semifinals. "Tomorrow is going to be a big day, a big crowd. Those of you fighting, get enough rest tonight. We're rooting for each and every one of you."

There was smattering of applause and people dispersed to change, get their gear, and, for most of them, to nurse injuries and the pain of loss. There was chatter about going out to one of the few Terran bars on Surya. Carr made his way over to Gant.

"We did all right, Luka," the Martian said when he saw Carr approach. "Could've been better, could've been worse."

Carr nodded. "Could I get some extra tickets?"

"I haven't got that many more, but for you, sure. What do you need? Three, four?"

"Six ought to do it."

Gant grunted. "Some family or friends of yours decided to unexpectedly show up?"

"Sort of like that."

———————

Uncle Polly got so angry at Risha that Carr got angry too and told him to shut up and not call her the things that he'd been calling her himself a few hours ago. Then he said he didn't want to talk about it anymore and asked Polly what he thought of Macha and Soard's qualifying fights earlier in the day. They sat around the small table in Carr's hotel room, studying the videos. Carr was hydrating like mad, trying to clear his head and flush the nasty green Ceresian antifreeze from his veins. He had to get up every fifteen minutes to piss blue electrolyte solution. Tournaments were hard; there was no time for repair nanos between rounds. They would get picked up in pre-fight screening.

"Soard had easy fights," Carr said. "He's not even trying yet. But he's striking a lot more than he's grabbing."

"Martian joints and bones aren't as solid as Terran ones, even if they do self-remineralize," Uncle Polly said. "Might be why he's avoiding joint locks." He paused, rubbing one of his leathery hands across his forehead. "You already know all this. You're better off getting some extra sleep."

Carr was silent for a minute. "Okay."

Polly stood up and looked down at him for a long moment. "You'll be all right?"

"You're asking if I can fight tomorrow? Yeah, I'll be fine."

"That wasn't what I was asking."

Carr swiped the holovid off the table and raised his eyes to his coach. He was surprised to see an aching softness in the old man's eyes. Uncle Polly had been married once, though it had ended before Carr had known him. He didn't have any kids of his own, and besides his brother Morrie, he didn't talk about his family. Carr realized, a little painfully, that most of the time *he* was Uncle Polly's family. His coach's life was as linked to his as Risha's had been. Had he long ago trapped Polly in the same way he'd more knowingly trapped Risha? Was Uncle Polly angry at Risha for his sake, Carr wondered, or just resentful that she'd escaped— done the right thing—when he had not?

"I don't blame her." Looking at his hands, Carr didn't realize at first that he'd spoken out loud. "I just didn't think it would happen this way. I thought I had time. I meant to tell her. I just...couldn't."

Uncle Polly looked away from him for a moment. "I know how that feels."

"Do you think she'll come back?" Carr asked quietly.

"I don't know," Uncle Polly said. Honest. Carr could appreciate that. "What I do know," Polly said, and he cleared his throat, "is that I couldn't give you up. I almost did, when I learned what I going to be a part of. But I couldn't. Not when I thought I should, and not anytime since. I don't see how anyone else could either. Doesn't matter who designed you and why."

Carr's eyes stung. He dropped his gaze and managed to mutter, "Thanks, coach."

"See you tomorrow, champ." Uncle Polly hadn't called him that since he was a kid.

When he was alone, Carr got into bed and lay with his head turned so he could look out into space. Against the backdrop of pinprick stars, Mars looked dark and dusky, like a dull copper coin he'd once seen at an antique store on Jarvis Street near his mom's apartment. His cuff told him that it was late evening, but he wasn't sure what part of Mars the station kept time with. And he had no idea what time it was back on Valtego, or in Toronto. Was his mom awake? Was Enzo madly posting to his feed?

His bed felt large and empty, like an ancient ghost ship from the earliest days of spacefaring, long ago flung out of orbit, destined to travel beyond the reaches of civilization, into nothingness. He slept.

When the rising tone of an incoming call played in the middle of the night, he jerked awake at once, slapping at his cuff to accept the call even before he'd opened his eyes to the dark room. "Risha?"

Two beats of heavy silence came from the other end. Carr blinked, managed to focus on his cuff's display, and realized his mistake.

"Mr. Luka," said Detective Van. "Meet me in the lobby. I need to speak to you."

TWENTY-TWO

Carr was silent for so long that Detective Van said, "Mr. Luka, did you hear me?"

"What are you doing here?" It was all Carr could think to say. His voice sounded like sandpaper.

"I will explain if you meet me in person."

"Now?"

"Yes."

"It's the middle of the night. I have..." Carr stopped himself. Was Van here to arrest him? Was that why he was being awakened, to be dragged off before he could fight in tomorrow's match? He sat up fast, his mind sprinting in all directions, considering ludicrous options for escape.

"The timing could be better," the detective conceded, "but I just arrived." As if reading Carr's racing thoughts, he added, "I'm here to talk, nothing more. But it's important that you meet me."

Carr hesitated. "Do I have a choice?"

"I can use my police identification to have the security system give me access to your room, so I would say, no, you don't."

Carr cursed under his breath. "Okay," he said. "Okay … just wait."

He threw on his clothes and made his way through the halls to the lobby of the hotel. It was brightly lit, austere and functional, having more in common with the entrance of a docking hub or a laboratory than with the opulent foyers of Valtego's ritziest hotels. The walls were the color of red clay and all the furniture was matte steel. Very Martian. Detective Van was standing in the middle of it, looking utterly out of place in his sun-faded leather jacket and scuffed black boots. He was alone; that must be a good sign, Carr thought. Surely, if he were being taken into custody there would be more people, wouldn't there? Detective Van motioned him over to one of the small workspace/meeting booths on the far side of the lobby. "Have a seat."

Carr sat. Van sat down across from him. The man leaned his forearms on the table and pulled a small tin from his pocket. "Mint?"

"What do you want from me?" Carr asked.

Van popped a mint into his mouth and stowed the tin. His beard looked as if it could use a trim, and his eyes had the brightness of someone who'd been running on caffeine instead of sleep for a long time. "Kaan Rhystok has fled Earth. He's charged with numerous violations of genetics laws, as well as fraud and extortion. We have enough evidence now, from all the years his 'seed and farm' ring has been operating, to make the case against him stick for good."

"Congratulations," Carr said.

The detective snorted. "Congratulate me after we've caught him. He's left Terran space, and getting the Martian authorities to cooperate with us on anything right now is difficult given the political situation. Fortunately, I'm sure he's here. On Surya."

Carr's mouth went uncomfortably dry. "Why would he be here?"

"To watch you fight in *War of the Worlds*. I would put money on him being at the semifinals tomorrow."

He wished he hadn't agreed to meet Van after all. When he managed to speak, each word came out flat. "What makes you so certain?"

Detective Van let out a long sigh that smelled of spearmint. "Come now, Mr. Luka, we both know what you are."

When Carr didn't answer, Van shifted forward and fixed him with a no-bullshit gaze. "Last month, a teenage music prodigy came clean on being enhanced, told us everything he knew about the scheme his parents were part of, which wasn't all that much we didn't suspect already. He volunteered for a full sequencing, which proved that his official genetic profile was fake. We traced the geneticist's license number on the fake profile and discovered that it doesn't exist; it's on a list that Genepol has now compiled of expired and rescinded license numbers that were cleverly and fraudulently used during a five-year period, right around the time you were born. I pulled up your public profile and sure enough, your geneticist's license number is one of the ones on our blacklist. Your genetic profile is as fake as wood on Mars." Van tapped his green government cuff. "In the hour it takes to get a message to Earth and back, I could have a court order for you to be sequenced."

Carr felt vaguely ill. He was watching his future evaporate with every word out of Van's mouth. How was it possible, he wondered, to lose everything in such a short period of time?

Quietly, he said, "Why do we have these chats, detective?" He was amazed at how calm he sounded. "If you're here to arrest me, why don't you just do it?"

"I'm not going to arrest you. You need to fight tomorrow as if nothing is different."

Carr choked back a laugh. "So you can ruin me more publicly afterward?"

The skin around the detective's eyes wrinkled, his expression incredulous, impatient, and slightly pitying all at once. "This isn't all about *you*, Mr. Luka, though it may seem that way, to someone with the ego of a celebrity athlete. My first priority is bringing Kaan Rhystok to justice. My second is not setting off a political and media firestorm to get it done. The story of a Genepol manhunt is barely a blip on the news-feeds, but half of Earth is watching you fight. You think I'm going to spook Rhystok and throw the entire carefully conducted investigation into the public eye on the eve of a huge Terran-Martian sporting event?" Van shook his head. "My two boys, they're ten and twelve years old. They have no idea what I do, but they sure as heck know what you do. They've watched all your fights, and all three parts of that cheesy documentary. They have your posters on their walls and your Skinnwear line in their closets. Illegally enhanced or not, you're on our side, you're one of us, you're Terran. You may be alone in that Cube, but combat has always been tribal. You have to finish this tournament."

Carr was silent.

"I'm sending you an authorized police alert code. Fight your match. Rhystok will show himself to you at some point tomorrow. When he does, try to get close to him, speak to him, delay him if you can, and send the coded alert from your cuff-link. It will go straight to me, and to the Surya station police."

"He might not show up," Carr said.

"He'll show. He's an extremely meticulous and careful man, but he has a weakness, a kind of pathological interest in the people he's designed. He thinks of them as his creations. His children, in a way. He attends their performances, follows their feeds, keeps tabs on them. I think he's particularly fond of you."

A shudder of distaste ran through Carr, along with a strange and immense fatigue. Why was all this happening to him? There was a time, not that long ago, when things were a lot simpler. When he knew who he was, and what he wanted, and the world seemed like the sort of place that would reward him if he worked hard enough, and each step he took went forward, toward something better.

He studied his hands. They were slightly curled, permanently so, from countless hours spent climbing the Cube.

A couple knuckles were misshapen. The skin was pale and soft from being marinated in sweat under gauze and gloves. What good were these hands for, if not zeroboxing?

"If I do what you ask," he said, slowly raising his eyes to the detective's, "is there anything you can do for me? Or am I done? Is this tournament the last time I'll fight?"

The detective's chin tilted; he'd expected the question. His brown eyes were not without sympathy. "I can't make you any promises. The law isn't clear about how to handle a case like yours. And Genepol has no say in how the ZGFA decides to deal with you." He paused, tugging his beard. "I *can* keep the nature of your involvement under wraps until well after the tournament. It'll give you time to come to grips with what you are before the rest of the world has to."

"My coach," Carr said. "And my mom?"

Van gazed at him, solemn. "Help us tomorrow, and I can make sure they get off quietly."

Slowly, Carr nodded. That was the important thing now. His heart felt as heavy as a lump of ore in the center of his chest. He wanted to hate the man, this country farmer cop who was ruining his life, but he was too numb.

A group of people staggered through the hotel lobby, bantering loudly. The booth shielded them from view, but Carr recognized the voices. His fellow zeroboxers, the ones who'd lost in the elimination rounds earlier today—or was it yesterday, now?—were returning from a night of revelry, having drowned their defeat in drink and camaraderie. One of them exclaimed, "Shitty domie food, what does it take to find a cheeseburger around here?" and the others laughed.

Burning envy skewered him. Those guys didn't know how good they had it. They'd lost today, but there would be other days, other matches, whole careers still ahead for them. He was nineteen years old and staring at what felt like the end of his world.

Detective Van rose from his seat. "I'm sorry to have to do this right before your big match. It couldn't be avoided. You understand why." He truly did look sorry. Unmovable as rock, but still sorry. "Even knowing what you are, maybe even because of it … I'll be cheering for you tomorrow."

TWENTY-THREE

Only sheer emotional exhaustion enabled Carr to catch a couple more hours of fitful sleep before he was on his way back to the Dr. Drew Ming Athletic Mall. Normally, the morning of a fight day brought with it a crystalline mental focus. Not so this morning. As he stared out the window of the private car, Carr's thoughts were sluggish and jumbled; whenever he started to dwell on any one of them, it threatened to swell to psychologically unmanageable dimensions.

The vehicle drove them past the mass of people waiting in line for the shuttle buses that ran a doubled schedule to the stadium. Mixed in with the sea of tall Martians were rowdy clusters of die-hard Terran fans, their faces painted, carrying signs, shouting, and jostling for space. They were jostled back, and not in a friendly way. Heavy lines of security droids enforced orderly entry onto the loading platform, and watchful Surya policemen were everywhere.

They made it to the athletes' lounge without incident, where they waited for the draw to be determined. Scull kept patting down his drifting hair and checking and rechecking all their supplies, which, Carr wanted to tell him, did nothing to ease anyone's nerves. Uncle Polly was a lot quieter than he usually was on a fight day and kept stealing concerned glances over at Carr, who did his best to act as if nothing was out of the ordinary. If his coach thought what had happened with Risha yesterday would compromise his ability in the Cube, the man certainly did not need a whole additional level of worry.

Risha. She hadn't come back at all last night. She hadn't called or messaged, and she'd blocked her cuff signal so he couldn't track it. Was she even still on Surya? Was she watching?

The WCC official came in and had each of the four low-mass semifinalists reach into a metal container and pull out a small magnetic ball. "Blue goes first, red second," he said. The two Martians chose first; Soard wiggled his fingers dramatically as if choosing a piece of candy from a jar. He reached in and pulled out a blue metal sphere. Macha drew red.

The marbles were replaced. Carr put his hand through the cut-out rubber lid and his fingers touched the cold round marbles stuck to the bottom of the box. He pulled one off and it floated free before he closed his hand around it and brought it out. It was red. Macha nodded, fixing Carr with a pleased, predatory expression.

"Soard and Kabitain, you're up," the official said.

DK started for the locker room. Carr called after him. "Hey, DK… good luck." He pulled himself over so they were face to face. He had no anger left for DK, not with everything else that had happened yesterday. He regretted losing their friendship, for ignoring him and leaving him behind, and he couldn't even fault the man's jealousy and resentment. "Let's make it a Terran final."

The corners of DK's mouth twitched up. He was older and more jaded than the DK of a few years ago, but his voice held a touch of familiar good humor. "I never figured I'd have to get through the Martians for a shot at you." He kicked off down the hall.

It was hard to pinpoint how a man could swagger without gravity, but Yugo Macha pulled it off. He nodded after DK. "I know how it feels to always be in another man's shadow. I get sick of Soard taking all the glory." His mouth curved in a smirk. "But today, *I* get to be the one to break Terran hearts." He turned and made his way in the opposite direction, toward the locker room on the other side of the stadium.

"I don't like him," Uncle Polly muttered. "He's got a desperate look." Carr frowned after Macha in silent agreement. A man like that, all sharp edges and bitterness, could be wild and illogical in the Cube.

The entire zero gravity center seemed to be vibrating with energy. Above them, through the thick floors and walls, he could hear the throbbing noise of the crowd as the bell rang, ending the midmass semifinal. On the nearest wallscreen,

Danyo "Fear Factor" Fukiyama swayed in stunned relief as the referee raised his arm, announcing a split decision victory that advanced him to the final. The Terrans in the stands screamed in excitement. The cameras zoomed in to capture one of them unhooking his tether in clear violation of the posted signs. His friends threw him clear and he went soaring upward, cycling his arms all the way to the clear netting above the seats. A couple of security guards with minithrusters retrieved him and pulled him from the stadium.

A few minutes later, the interlude of hypnotically deep bass Martian trench music faded out. Over the hubbub of the crowd, a taller, skinnier, Martian version of Hal Greese announced the first lowmass semifinal match.

"What are you waiting for?" Uncle Polly snapped Carr back to himself. "Go get dressed and warmed up!"

They made it to the locker room in time to see the opening launch of the fight. On the screen, DK propelled himself up and around the corner like a shot, punching his heels toward Soard in a signature double kick. Soard twisted his long body nimbly and let DK's momentum carry him past, then landed a well-braced body blow that sent the shorter man spinning. Captain Pain tucked and found the wall, rebounded, and came back at the Martian without a hitch.

"Come on, DK," Carr found himself urging under his breath as he changed into his shorts. He kept an eye on the screen while Scull taped his hands and helped him pull on his grippers. "You've got to cut angles around his reach," he muttered.

After the first round, the camera cut to Xeth Stone and Jeroan Culver, their heads bent close together to hear each other. Xeth's animated voice filled the locker room. "I'm impressed! Kabitain put on several kilos expressly for *War of the Worlds,* but it hasn't slowed him down. He looked strong in this first round, against a very tough opponent." The camera shifted to focus on a knot of about twenty Terrans in the stands, all of them with DK's big ears and bronze skin, waving signs: *WE LOVE OUR CAPTAIN!* "There's Kabitain's cheering section," Xeth exclaimed. "Quite a family turnout!"

"You've heard me say this before," said Jeroan Culver, scolding, "but Danilo Kabitain is one of the most under-rated zeroboxers in the ZGFA, and at age twenty-three, he still has a promising career ahead of him. In fact, people forget that he was an up-and-coming star in the feathermass division before Carr Luka became a household name."

"Wouldn't that be something, to see him versus Luka in the final here on Surya station!" Xeth exclaimed. "There's a match-up that would make Terran fans in this crowd and back on Earth very, very happy."

The first half of the second round went well for DK. He landed plenty of technical blows, bracing and climbing well and attacking from all angles, minimizing Soard's advantage of reach.

Carr stretched and jogged the walls of the warm-up area. It was bigger and brighter than the one back home, but he was careful to start out more slowly. The cool air stung as he drew it in, warmed it with his lungs, pushed it back out.

He knew he ought to be concentrating on his own upcoming match, but he kept drifting over to the wallscreen.

The third time he did so, Uncle Polly threatened, "I'm going to turn this off."

Carr motioned for him not to. "I want him to win. He deserves it." *Terran fans should have a champion. One that won't let them down.*

With a minute left in the second round, Kye Soard shifted into high gear. From a crouch, he spun up into a kick that sent DK into an airborne head-over-heels spin. DK tried to stop his dizzying rotation, but as soon as his reaching fingers found traction, Soard's power-launch plowed him in the other direction and sent the side of his head into the wall with a smack that made the entire stadium suck in a collective breath. For the rest of the excruciatingly long Martian minute, DK fought just to hold off Soard until the bell. When it rang, the cameras zoomed in for a shot of the competitors' faces. DK looked dazed as he went to his corner. Soard drifted through his hatch lazily, took some water, and bounced on the balls of his grippers.

"What happened?" moaned Xeth. "Captain Pain was doing so well, but Soard just clobbered him in the final minute."

"Unfortunately, Xeth, this is where you see Martian physique become an advantage," Jeroan mused. "Soard relied on his endurance. He waited until he saw Kabitain start to tire, then just closed in and swarmed him."

As the two commentators kept talking, the camera panned across the stands, zooming in on sections of the crowd. Carr picked up his pace but kept watching the screen with a queasy apprehension. Every time he saw a Terran man, he half expected it to be Rhystok. Whenever the camera settled on a Martian woman, he felt the sting of it not being Risha.

Thirty seconds into the final round, Carr could see DK was outgunned. Soard keep pummeling his lower body, his thighs and shins, which didn't end the fight but wore DK down and crippled his ability to launch or climb, or do anything, really.

Carr sliced his hand across the front of the screen angrily, shutting it off. "Time me."

"Three minutes," said Polly. "No more than that."

Carr ripped across the training space, ping-ponging from wall to corner, up, down, and around, throwing himself into fast launches that gave him only a second to execute full turns and changes of direction as he pummeled each of the suspended targets. When Uncle Polly called time, he'd started to break a comfortable sweat and the warmth had reached his fingertips. As he pulled himself over to the bench, he heard the muffled roar of the mostly Martian crowd and knew that DK had lost.

Uncle Polly helped him out of his thermal top, then checked his gloves and grippers, refastening them more out of habit than necessity. "What do you remember from watching Macha in the videos?"

"He runs his mouth off in the Cube, tries to mess with people's heads, gets them to make stupid mistakes."

Polly nodded. "Are you going to let him do that to you?"

294

"I'm not, coach."

"No matter what he says or does. Don't let him get to you, don't get drawn into his game. What else?"

"He takes risks, opens himself up to try and land big moves."

"That's right. Stay steady and patient in there; sooner or later, he'll get twitchy or cocky and leave himself open."

The same official who'd done the drawing thrust his upper body into the locker room. "Luka, you're on in five."

"Things could get crazy out there," Uncle Polly said. "This crowd, it won't be like on Valtego. They won't be on your side. You're going to have to block all that out. Stay focused."

"I'll be fine, coach."

Uncle Polly clapped his fists down over Carr's, but there was still a worried set to his mouth. Carr wondered at what point in the last year the shift had happened between them. Before every fight in his childhood, Uncle Polly had been the one pumped up with boundless energy and optimism, completely confident of winning. Was it that he'd never worried back then, or that Carr had never noticed?

Before he reached the entrance to the deck, DK came through, his coach and cornerman supporting him on either side. He saw Carr but looked away quickly, his expression shattered. Carr swallowed whatever lame words of sympathy had started to form in his mouth. A loss this bad and this fresh was something a zeroboxer needed to be alone with for a while. It would take months, maybe a year or more, to find out if Danilo Kabitain could come back from it.

"And now … the second semifinal match of the expanded lowmass division," boomed the announcer's voice. "In the blue corner, at seventy-four kilograms, hailing from New Nanjing, Elysium Minor, and representing the WCC … YUGO 'THE MANIAC' MAACHAAA!"

Macha landed on the deck in a dramatic crouch, then stood and thrust his arms up, screaming something unintelligible as he exhorted the crowd to get crazy. The Maniac, Carr had heard it said, lived for three things: fighting, fucking, and fame. He'd once offered up, as a stunt, a zero gravity combat match between himself and two Elysian Rottweilers. His antics on the deck now were met with a wild cacophony of cheering and booing. Even in a mostly Martian crowd, it seemed he had about equal numbers of fans and haters.

"In the red corner, at seventy-three and a half kilograms, all the way from Valtego station, and hailing from Toronto, Earth, representing the ZGFA … CARR 'THE RAPTOR' LUUKAAA!

As Carr flew out onto the deck, sections of the stadium erupted in wild cheering and others with deep boos, so the two sounds melded together into an indistinguishable slurry of noise. He saw the multiple screens cut between him and the crowd, landing on a cluster of enthusiastic Terrans in the stands. It was the group of teens he'd met on the terminal platform yesterday. Had it really been just yesterday? They'd nearly had seizures when he'd returned to the terminal platform that evening with tickets for them. The girl with the curly hair in ringlets held up a sign: *VIDA TERRA, VIDA LUKA.*

Risha, are you out there?

The first round went pretty much as Carr had expected. Macha was a lot of bluster and dangerous energy, like a piece of sharp machinery set on too high a setting, jittering and spitting bits of shrapnel. "Come on, earthworm," he shouted. "Hit me. Come on, try to hit me, wormie!" When this didn't get a rise out of Carr, Macha got creative. "Hey, wormie, I hear you have a Martian girlfriend. You like to be fucked by Martians? I'll fuck you! Come on, then!"

I can't believe this guy, Carr thought. *I'm going to beat the piss out of him.* He held his ground while Macha bounced around, daring him. When the man slipped into range, Carr feinted a strike, then dove in close to clinch. Macha leaped and sprawled his limbs in defense, but Carr adjusted and went for Macha's leg instead. He threw it hard, forcing his opponent into an uncontrolled spin. Carr sank his hands into the wall and shot both legs out, punching the man in the back with his heels and sending him flying to the other side of the Cube.

After that, Macha talked less and fought more, though he still spat profanities and insults whenever they weren't trading blows. As much of an asshole as he was, the man was a strong zeroboxer, frustratingly good at defending against Carr's grabbing, and wicked fast. He gave a lot of deliberate openings that Carr quickly learned to recognize as traps that led to being hit. At the bell, it was still anyone's fight, though Carr thought he'd probably won the first round, narrowly.

"You're doing everything right," Uncle Polly said into his ear, and again in person back on the deck. "Stay cool, pick him apart, just like you're doing."

In the middle of the second round, Carr landed a punishing series of blows and a flying knee that started Macha's nose bleeding. The blood oozed onto his face like a giant, nasty red blister, but some of it floated free, half a dozen small dark bubbles drifting in front of the man's angry snarl.

Carr couldn't help himself. "A little harder to talk now, domie?"

Macha's face went scary dark. He started going for big hits, launching from weird angles, anything he could to land something on Carr. And he was relentless. Carr felt his heart rate skyrocket. But his mind grew calm. It hummed, found the pattern of the fight. He saw Macha's exuberant moves coming and threw himself into answering them. He still couldn't manage to grab and submit the man, but he was picking his places, landing strikes and the occasional throw. By the time the bell rang, he was pulling for air as hard as he ever had in a fight but confident he'd dominated the round.

Uncle Polly worked his hands over Carr's shoulders. "Breathe for me, Carr. Take it all the way in, let it *drop* out. That's it."

Carr looked past his coach's head, out across the crowd. It was unruly; people shouting, throwing their squeeze bottles, or releasing big floating globs of beer into the air. An announcement came over the speakers, sternly reminding everyone that untethering from their seats was strictly prohibited and would result in expulsion from the stadium.

Someone on or near the deck yelled, "Macha, you SUCK! Quit fooling and knock the earthworm out already!"

Scull toweled Carr off and took the ice pack from his neck so he didn't cool too much. "You've got this one," Uncle Polly whispered, fast and excited. "One more round just like that last one, and you've got it. Don't do anything crazy, don't get distracted, just keep the pressure on. Keep it on and keep scoring the way you have."

Carr nodded. His heart rate and breathing recovered. He unhooked his feet from the bar, stood up, and dove back through the flashing hatch.

There was a kind of frantic, darting hatred in Macha's eyes now, and a grim madness in the set of his lips. His skin, slippery with sweat, rippled with light when he moved, like that of a dark, wet eel. He stalked toward Carr murderously. His nose had stopped bleeding and his face had been cleaned off, but he sounded nasal when he spoke. "No Terran is going to win in this Cube."

"Is that so." Carr launched up and around a right angle, his cocked fist flying down at Macha's face.

The man barely slid his head out of the way, but Carr had the follow-up knee strike ready. They collided, grabbing for each other in a tangle of limbs, and as Carr's knee went into the man's stomach, Macha's right fist connected with his ribs.

He knew right away something was wrong. The left side of his body erupted with unusual pain, as if a metal tool had been driven into his flesh. Macha hit him again and he jerked, tried to kick the man away. The Maniac—so aptly named—held on and punched him a third time, the impact landing like a hammer on a slab of meat, then nearly took forward control. Carr drove his knees up and his hips back with all his strength and the two of them flew apart.

Carr swiveled to get into position for a rebound, but his torso screamed at the movement and didn't complete the turn. He wondered if his ribs were cracked. He caught the wall with his stretched hands, his shoulders and arms straining to check his momentum, and the rest of him hit the wall flat. He pulled his feet back up under him before the impact could throw him off the surface, but Macha was coming at him again, like a comet. Carr brought his arms up to defend his face and the blow came down across his forehead, like the lash of a steel rod. He reeled in confusion, saw Macha still advancing, and dove out of the way, throwing himself into free space.

The Cube blurred and spun. He stretched his feet to the nearest incoming wall and bent his legs to stick the landing. Warmth was spreading across his brow, and when he put his hand up to his forehead, the fingers of his gloves came away dark and wet. He wiped again and a stream of blood came off into the air, a wobbly red worm breaking into segments.

"Carr!" Uncle Polly was saying, "What's going on in there?"

"His gloves," Carr said, although without his cuff, his coach couldn't hear him. "He's wrapped something in his gloves." Weighted them with something sharp and heavy. Easy enough to do. Completely illegal. "You domie prick." Carr held up his hands, trying to signal to the dour Martian referee, but all he managed to do was shout, "Hey, stop the—" before Yugo Macha flew at him with a barrage of strikes.

Carr grabbed for his opponent, tried to pull him close to jam up his attack, but the man's momentum was too great; he slammed into Carr and threw both of them free of the surface. Instead of trying to work his way into a proper submission hold, Macha held on to Carr's neck with one hand and swung deliriously with the other, hitting any part of Carr he could.

"Are you crazy?" Carr screamed at him. He'd lost track of the hits. Couldn't anyone see what was going on? Why weren't they stopping the fight?

"No … worm … beats … me," Macha ground out between blows.

Carr's brain fired hot with rage. Macha wasn't out to win, just to maim. Even if he lost, or got disqualified and thrown out, he'd consider it a job well done to send Carr to the hospital. End his tournament run, one way or another.

He pushed past the pain lighting up all over his body and slammed his hands down on Macha's shoulders, heaving himself in the other direction. It didn't separate them, but it got his face away from the man's fists and Macha's head down to the level of Carr's chest. He landed an uppercut before they both collided with the wall. Carr got his feet in place first and planted his grippers hard, throwing his body into a blow that connected with Macha's kidney right before the Martian's fist opened another cut above Carr's eye.

Blood and sparks of light clouded his vision. He shook his head to clear it, saw bright globs of his own blood break free. He didn't feel pain anymore, just a kind of singular telescopic focus. He was going to kill this low domie cheat. He felt himself move before he knew what he was doing; he pulled Macha forward onto him as he threw his body backward. His back slammed into the wall and, as the rebound carried them both off the surface, Carr strained his torso to throw his legs around Macha's hips. His ribs screamed in protest, but he had forward control now, *finally*, and they were spinning. Injured and bleeding, he'd never felt so strong or fast. Every sight, sound, and sensation felt as sharp as cut ice. He slammed his fist into the man's cheek, then his mouth. He kept hitting, and hitting, just as he'd once told Enzo to do, even after the referee's whistle blew for the second time and the man came shooting up, waving his arms and halting the fight.

"*Now* you stop the fight!" Carr shouted in disgust. "Where were you when he was cutting me?"

"Let me at him," Macha gurgled, wild-eyed and drooling blood. The air in the Cube was filthy pink.

"Get back to your corners!" The referee shoved them apart. "Now!"

Carr climbed back to his hatch and out onto the deck.

Scull's face blanched. "Jesus." He pulled Carr to his seat. Uncle Polly must have switched off his connection to Carr's receiver because Carr hadn't heard him yelling and cursing, as he was still doing now. The WCC official who was bearing the brunt of this assault said, "We'll review it, I said! Now get back before I have you and your fighter thrown out!"

"He's the one who should be thrown out." Uncle Polly's finger shook with rage as he pointed in Macha's direction. "He cut my fighter! You saw it, and didn't stop the fight. What kind of warped gig are you domies running here?"

"I said get back!" the official shouted.

"Coach," Carr called, and Polly broke off at last. He came over and got to work, helping Scull press towels to Carr's face. They came away red. The doctor came over to stitch him. Carr saw himself on the screens. He looked ghastly. Even worse than he'd expected. "He weighted his gloves, coach," Carr said.

Bax Gant appeared on the deck. He bent down next to Carr, one hand on the railing. "You're sure, Luka? If you're going to make an accusation like that, you'd better be sure."

"I'm sure."

Gant went to speak to the officials. The cameras showed him and the president of the WCC gesturing and holding a low, intense conversation that couldn't be overheard. The noise from the stands churned like storm waves crashing against rocks. Furious Terran fans were shouting and throwing things. Two fights had broken out and security guards with thrusters were dragging people off.

Gant came back. "They're reviewing the fight." He didn't hide the disgust in his voice. "Macha's people deny it. They showed the referee his gloves, said you were lying."

"That's bullshit," Carr said. "He has another pair. Or the domies are covering for each other." He winced as the stitches went in. "Macha's a headcase and a cheat. He knew he was losing."

"We can file a formal complaint and call for an investigation," said Gant. "But that's not going to solve anything right now. The match will go to the judges."

The officials didn't even bother to bring the fighters back out to the center of the deck. Maybe they thought the two men would go after each other again, or that the sight of them would send the crowd into a full-on riot. "By judges' decision," the announcer said, then hesitated, "the lowmass semifinal match between Yugo Macha and Carr Luka is declared a draw."

"A *draw*?" Uncle Polly was apoplectic.

Everyone was shouting. There were too many people on the deck, and not all of them were tethered. A few pushes and shoves sent some of them flying free, colliding into others. The crowd was going nuts. Hundreds were out of their seats now, and every fight caused a chain reaction of people spinning into each other, unable to stop their own momentum, grabbing onto or hitting their neighbors.

"What does that mean?" Carr asked. "How can it be a draw?" Now that he was out of the Cube and no longer fighting, his body was cooling fast and he was feeling all the places Macha had injured him. His chest, his sides, his face—everything hurt.

"Two judges went in his favor, two in yours, and the fifth declared a tie." Gant shook his head. "This is ugly. Really ugly."

"I beat him," Carr shouted. "I had the second round for sure, and he cheated in the third! How is that a draw?"

"Get those fighters back to the locker room!" a security guard yelled at them.

"Go," Gant said. "I'm going to sort this mess out."

Carr was ushered toward the hall. The entrance was jammed with reporters and cameramen, everyone talking and shouting questions at once. Scull and Uncle Polly went ahead of him, trying to clear the way and keep people back. Carr pulled himself along the guide-rails in a daze. How was it possible to feel so slow and heavy in weightlessness?

Out of the corner of his eye: a pale Terran face, calm and watchful in the midst of all the excitement. A blond specter. Rhystok.

Carr swiveled his head to try and catch another glimpse of the man as he was tugged along into the bowels of the stadium. Rhystok was standing still, magnetized shoes firmly planted, hands on the rails. His gaze followed Carr before his receding figure was lost behind the media and security people that pressed ahead of him.

Shit. What was he supposed to do now? He certainly couldn't do what Detective Van had asked of him. He couldn't escape this crowd of people, he couldn't get close to Rhystok. Carr looked down at his bare left forearm. He couldn't send the police alert either; Scull still had his cuff. The detective had been right—Rhystok had come all the way to Surya to see him fight, and having done so, perhaps he would now escape. What would happen if he did? Would Van rescind his promise?

I tried, he imagined himself saying to the detective.

I tried, to millions of disappointed Terran fans.

They would reply, *Trying isn't good enough for us.*

In the locker room, there was relative quiet at least. Several of his fellow zeroboxers who'd seen what happened gathered around, grim-faced and muttering. Scull grabbed more towels and wiped him down. Uncle Polly kept ice on his face, then helped him into a thermal top. Carr winced as he lifted his arms to pull it on, but the garment's heating cells were a relief from the cool air goose-pimpling his skin. Polly was silent as he checked Carr's stitches. His thin lips were set in a deep downward curve that carved his face like a canyon. He was seething, with anger and something else, like guilt or pain. Like his heart was breaking on his face.

"Goddamn domies," Adri said, scowling, her arms crossed. "They hate us. As much as we hate them."

"I don't hate domies," Carr said quietly, replacing the ice pack on his face with a new one that Scull offered him. He could almost hate Risha for not being there, but he didn't. "I wish I'd had another minute with Macha, though."

"Macha can rot," Adri agreed. "But that ref looked the other way. The officials, did they really check his gloves? What about the judges, calling it a draw? What a joke."

She smacked the side of a locker with the flat of her hand. The sound rang through the room. "The domies think they're better than all of us from the old planet. They're all engineered, full of 'new world leading humanity into the future' crap. They agreed to this tournament just to show us up, and they can't stand to see a Terran win in the Cube. Half the crowd was on Macha's side, yelling 'cut him!' and 'bleed, worm.'"

The locker room riffled with angry agreement. Carr was surprised to hear Scull speak up. "Wait until the broadcast reaches Earth," he said. "When people see what happened, a whole planet is going to come down on your side."

That was the last thing Carr wanted, but he left the thought unsaid.

The room shushed as Gant came back in. "Okay," he said. "There's going to be an investigation into whether Macha did anything illegal, but in the meantime, the draw stands." Gant held up his hands to silence the outburst. "Normally, that would mean a rematch."

"Carr isn't going back into the Cube with that domie psycho," Uncle Polly said.

"There's no time for that anyways," Gant said, "and it would turn this place into a war zone. Security is having a hard enough time getting all the spectators out without more fights or property damage. But someone has to go up against Soard tomorrow, and that's been determined by record. Including this fight, Macha's pro record is 11-6-1, and Carr's is 13-1-1." Gant brought a hand down on Carr's shoulder. "Congratulations, Luka. You're in the finals."

He gave Carr's shoulder a squeeze, though to Carr it felt more like sympathy than celebration. There was a round of muted applause from his teammates, but he sensed and shared their uncertainty. The Martians weren't doing him any favors with this verdict. Fight tomorrow? He wasn't sure he could *walk* tomorrow. After today's fiasco, he might be a wronged hero; after getting pummeled by Soard tomorrow, he would be a disappointment and a loser. Was that the plan all along? For Macha to tenderize him so Soard could take an easy victory?

Uncle Polly peeled Carr's sweat-drenched gloves from his hands. "Carr," he said, "There's not a person on any planet that could fault you if we decide not—"

"There's a clinic not far from the hotel," Carr said. He pushed off the bench and grabbed his clothes off the magnetic pegs.

———

He took in a little food and a lot of liquids on the way there. The vehicle's AI kept taking them in strange directions to avoid the disorder streaming from the gravity zone terminal. Several streets were blocked by drunk and infuriated fans. Carr saw a pack of Terrans vandalizing a zero-boxing fan shop, smashing the fixtures, tearing apart the WCC-badged clothes and merchandise and dumping it in the street. They were set upon by a mob of angry Martians. Security droids appeared and both sides recklessly attacked them, too, until a dozen people lay on the ground, stunned into paralysis.

Disbelief layered onto Carr's injuries. "Is this really because of my fight?"

Uncle Polly turned away from the window with a swift jerk of his head. "Not a chance. But you're the excuse they've been waiting for."

His coach was right, of course, but Carr didn't feel reassured. He of all people had reasons to feel enraged, to want to scream and destroy things. Part of him did. But it was one thing to own that feeling, selfishly, and quite another to watch others lay claim to it, ostensibly on his behalf. It was grotesque, obscene, he thought, like watching someone else impersonate you naked with your girlfriend.

There his traitorous mind went again. Risha was somewhere safely away from this mess, he hoped.

At the clinic, the medics sealed up his gashes and brought the swelling and bruising down. Carr agreed to have nano quick-repair patches placed over his ribs after being assured that the topical stuff didn't stay in his bloodstream and was legal before competition. He couldn't believe he was worried about something like that. "Wouldn't want any rules to get broken now, would we?" He laughed. It hurt. Uncle Polly didn't laugh with him.

He'd retrieved his cuff from Scull before sending the kid back to the hotel, and as he waited at the clinic, the display lit up with a deluge of activity. Thousands of people were pouring onto his feed and other zeroboxing feeds. His name was popping up all over the Systemnet. He'd been messaged so many times by so many fans that he pictured his cuff overloading, bursting into flames on his arm. The only ones he bothered to pick up were from Enzo. There were three of them.

"Holy shit, Carr, I just saw the whole thing," the boy's breathless voice said in his receiver. "I can't believe it. Everyone here is *pissed pissed pissed*. God, I hope you're okay?"

Enzo's next call had been sixteen Terran minutes later. "I just posted this on my feed and it's already been reposted twenty-five thousand times." Carr's cuff pulled up the embedded image: a profile shot of him right after the fight with Macha. He barely recognized himself. His head was slightly bowed. Blood clung to his skin like rainwater on leaves. Perhaps he'd just heard the judges' decision, because his lips were slightly parted, his eyes lifted and burning with intensity. In thick white letters underneath, Enzo had added the word *UNBROKEN*.

Enzo's third and final message, thirty-eight minutes afterward, was two short sentences. "Just heard you're going to the final. Check this out." He'd sent Carr a short clip from his optic feed. Enzo was standing on a street in Toronto. The corner of Queen and Jarvis, Carr guessed. The light was muted; it was either early morning or early evening. There was a lot of city noise in the background along with people shouting. On the sides of buildings, holovid banners were blinking out, then coming back to life all with the same image. *UNBROKEN*. Enzo turned in a circle. It was all around him, from small storefront banners to the enormous ones gracing the tallest towers. *UNBROKEN. UNBROKEN. UNBROKEN.*

Carr swiped the video off his cuff and leaned his head into his hands, his stomach clenching with humility, gratitude, dismay, and dread.

Two long Martian hours later they were back at the hotel. There were security droids outside. The rest of the team was sitting or standing in the lobby, watching one of the wallscreens. The footage was cutting between scenes of arrests being made as Martian and Terran fans clashed on Surya, and snippets of news from Earth, where angry crowds had taken to the streets, attacking Martian businesses. A commentator was saying "political ramifications" a lot, while images played of unconscious figures being dragged away from the three blackened, smoking security droids that had been lit on fire outside Toronto's Martian consulate.

Adri whispered, "Things are going to hell."

"Turn this shit off," Danyo said, though he made no move to do so.

Carr felt the shift as he came up to them, faces and bodies moving fractionally so that the weight of many gazes pooled around him as he looked at the screen. A spokesperson for the Martian Council was making a televised statement from Ares City: For the safety of their staffs, all Martian embassies were officially on lockdown. All Martian citizens were advised to stay inside the secured expat sectors or leave the planet.

Carr turned away from the talking head. "Nice fight

today, Adri. Good luck tomorrow," he said. "You too, Danyo." He walked away, silent stares following him. He heard, after a moment, the rest of them begin to disperse back to their rooms.

Uncle Polly walked with him, but he paused at the hallway junction where one corridor led to his room, the other to Carr's. "Tell me the truth." His grizzled face was long and solemn, his eyes scanning Carr's with interrogative ferocity. "Forget what anyone else wants or thinks of you. Screw the fans, the press, Gant, the team, screw *me* most of all. Do you really want to fight tomorrow? Tell me the truth. Because if the answer is no, I will go to bat with whoever I have to for you on this. What you want matters. You're not a martyr. You don't have to be."

Carr didn't know what to say. Did his coach know what an impossible question he'd asked? Maybe there had once been a time when he would have been able to do what Uncle Polly suggested—separate himself from all the expectations that surrounded him. But they had long since fused together, grown into each other; it was hard to tell where one ended and the other began. He'd had aspirations attached to him since the moment his genes had been so fatefully spliced. What defined him, if not that? He didn't want this weight he carried, but he couldn't bear to lose it either. He didn't want to go into the fight with Soard feeling the way he did now—wounded, anxious, and hurt—but pulling out was unthinkable.

"I want to do it, coach."

Uncle Polly's face slackened. Carr read acceptance, resignation, even pride. His coach let out a soft breath. "Get some sleep."

Carr watched Polly walk down the hall and into his room. He went to his own room, setting his cuff against the entry reader and pushing the door open. Before he stepped through, he felt a second of ridiculous optimism that Risha would be there, sitting on the bed, working on her thinscreen and waiting for him.

She wasn't. Instead, sitting in the armchair next to the bed, was Mr. R.

"Hello, Carr," he said. "It's nice to see you."

TWENTY-FOUR

The door shut behind Carr. He stared without speaking. Finally, he said, "How did you get in here?"

Rhystok made a dismissive, *no matter* motion with his fingers. His other hand held a scotch on the rocks that he'd helped himself to from the mini-bar. The small bottle was sitting on the table along with another glass of ice. Rhystok poured liquor into the glass and set it down on the edge of the table nearest to Carr. "Sit down. Have a drink with me."

Carr sat down slowly. Rhystok seemed a little different. His voice and movements were quicker, harsher, stripped of their practiced languidness. Despite the cool air, a thin sheen of sweat glistened on his taut brow. He was a hunted man now. Carr fingered the edge of his cuff under the table, thinking of the alert code Van had given him. Rhystok raised his glass and held it in place expectantly. Warily,

Carr picked up the one he'd been offered. "What are we drinking to?"

"To victory."

Carr's lip curled. "Yours or mine?"

Rhystok drank and set his glass down. "They're the same thing. They always have been."

Carr's grip tightened around his glass. He set it back down. "I don't drink before fights."

"Just as well. Martian whiskey is made from corn-barley hybrids. Tastes all wrong." Rhystok leaned back in the chair. His face looked stark and weirdly ageless, deeply shadowed under the room's orange-hued light. "I take it you've seen the latest news-feeds from Earth. Quite something, isn't it?"

Carr shook his head. "I didn't want anything like this to happen."

"You're a hero, Carr. Millions of people are watching you. Remember that." His words hung in the air, threaded through with an undercurrent of warning. "You've been speaking to a detective from Genepol."

The man's flat, matter-of-fact affect made Carr flinch inside. "As if I wanted to," he said shortly. "He tracked me down. He knows all about you, and about me."

"I suppose he asked you to cooperate with him, in exchange for leniency for your mother and your coach."

"Something like that." Carr's eyes flicked down for a split second, then returned. He wondered if could find and send the code without Rhystok noticing. "I know you're on the run. Some music prodigy of yours ratted you out. Others too, maybe."

The man's nostrils flared in a sigh of disappointment. "The genetic constellation for artistic genius can be so emotionally unstable. Not resilient like yours." A cold smile cracked his sculpted face in an expression of paternal knowing. "You were something to behold today. Fierce and indomitable. *You* wouldn't be intimidated into throwing yourself on the mercy of the authorities."

Carr had his face slightly lowered, as if accepting his creator's praise. He found the police code on his cuff. His finger hovered over it as he raised his eyes. "I didn't win today. I beat Macha, but I didn't win. You can keep fighting all you want, but you can't win if they've got your number. Genepol will hunt you down and have me sequenced sooner or later."

Rhystok *tsked*. "Ah, Carr, Carr, Carr." Each use of his name jabbed Carr's ears like a toothpick. "You have nothing to worry about from Detective Ruart Van." The splice dealer reached into an inside pocket of his jacket and pulled out a crumpled, palm-size object. He held it up, then dropped it onto the table between them.

Carr froze. The display and components were smashed, so that nothing could be sent or retrieved from it, but he still recognized it. It must have been how Rhystok got the security system to grant him access to the hotel room: a green, government-issued cuff with an ID stamp on the underside.

Carr's blood chilled to the roots of his teeth. A personal

cuff could only be removed by its owner. "What ... what did you do to him?"

"I imagine he's making his way through Surya station's dematerializing system by now."

"You killed a cop."

"Lives can be bought or sold just like anything else. Especially off-planet, where a Terran government ID doesn't mean anything. Stupid of him to leave Earth's airspace, but he simply couldn't resist coming after me himself." Rhystok's lips twitched into a smug shape. "You know, it was almost as if we were trapped in a box together. Only one of us could emerge in the end. You understand how that works."

Carr felt welded to his seat, horrified, fascinated, and morbidly impressed by the man's cavalier tone. Did he think of himself as some sort of god? Capable of designing, granting, and taking life with impunity?

Rhystok's papery eyelids hooded. "You didn't think I would let him ruin you, did you? It's a shame you even had to put up with his threats. Well, no matter now. Delete that silly code he gave you and put it all behind you."

Involuntarily, Carr's hand drew away from his cuff. "You're completely vaccked if you think this will end it." His voice sounded too fast. "You're a wanted man. Genepol will still come after you. And me."

"I suppose I'll have to disappear for a while," Rhystok conceded. "But as for you ... I suspect that Detective Van kept his knowledge of you to himself." He finished his drink and set down his glass with an appreciative smack of his thin lips. He picked up the ruined green cuff and pocketed it.

Carr wasn't sure if he imagined the dark stains on its surface. "Go back to doing what you're good at, what you're meant to do. I'm watching out for you. You and I will always be on the same side."

Sudden, fierce hope climbed into Carr's throat. It tasted sickeningly sweet, like rotten fruit. If Rhystok was right, if Van had been the only one who'd known … and he was now dead … then Carr was safe. *He was safe.* He recoiled from his own guilty relief.

"Good luck tomorrow. Show everyone just what Terrans are capable of." Rhystok stood. He tilted his head just a bit, pitching his voice conspiratorially. "You know, Carr, you're one of my favorites." He turned toward the door.

Carr knew he ought to do something—press his finger down to send the alert, move to stop the man—but he felt paralyzed by his own awful, racing optimism. In three seconds, Rhystok would be gone. At worst, he would fade back into haunting the periphery of Carr's existence. At best, he'd disappear to some far-flung space outpost. Tomorrow … tomorrow Carr would go up against Kye Soard. If he won, he'd be a hero. A legend. He'd find Risha and convince her to return. Life would continue, upward and onward, as it was meant to.

As he walked past, Rhystok paused as if a thought had just occurred to him. He set a hand on Carr's shoulder. "By the way, I take it you had a falling-out with your Martian girlfriend?"

Carr stiffened, his flesh prickling under the man's touch. "What makes you say that?"

"Your personal feed. It's normally very well maintained. Hardly a day goes by without a fan or media engagement of some sort. The last two days have been unusual. Where is Ms. Risha Ponn?"

Carr was abruptly thankful he could answer this question honestly. "I don't know."

"A shame. She was an excellent brandhelm. Replacing a girlfriend is easy, but good brandhelms ... " He made a clucking noise. "Those are truly valuable." Another pause. "She knows everything, doesn't she?"

The man's voice didn't change, but a finger of frost crept down Carr's neck. He turned his head slowly, looking at the man's white fingers on his shoulder and the deceptively placid inquisitiveness of his face. Something told him Rhystok would see right through a lie. "She won't tell anyone."

"You're too young to appreciate that there is nothing more unpredictable than a disappointed woman." Rhystok leaned down and put his face near Carr's, his voice taking on the quality of a neighbor offering friendly advice. "I'm going to do you a second favor tonight. She's at the Solstice Hotel, in the beta quadrant of the inner ring. You ought to pay her a visit after your match tomorrow. Try to patch things up. If you can't, I'm counting on you to make sure she knows to keep quiet. For her own good." The hand on Carr's shoulder gave a final, firm pat, and was gone.

Carr closed his eyes. A thousand thoughts hurricaned through his mind, but only one rose clearly over the others. This murderer knew where Risha was. Had known, all this time Carr hadn't.

His hands gripped the edge of the table so hard they shook. Then he turned and rose from his seat in one motion.

Rhystok had just started to open the door when Carr slammed into him. There was no rebound like in the Cube; they crashed into the door together and fell against it like a sack of rocks. Carr rolled on top of the man, pinning him, seeing Rhystok's eyes fly wide with disbelief as he coiled his fist and swung it into the man's jaw.

A knockout blow, right on the button. Rhystok's head lolled back on the floor, mouth slack, body limp under Carr's legs.

Carr stood up. His heart was hammering, but he felt, oddly enough, shaky relief and mild disappointment. Sprawled unconscious on the ground, Rhystok had lost his strange, weighty presence. He was not an architect of fate. He was just a man like any other. Carr had beaten men before.

He found the alert code, still called up on the display of his cuff. He sent it. Then he made a call.

"Luka," said Gant, irate, as soon as he picked up. "Is this about Risha? Because I can't reach her. Sure picked a fine time for a lover's spat, I tell you! If you weren't fighting tomorrow, I'd have called to give you hell."

Carr breathed in, then out. "In a few minutes, Martian police will be at my hotel room door," he said. "We need to talk."

TWENTY-FIVE

The police lieutenant identified herself as Officer Jin. A no-nonsense, middle-aged Martian woman who towered a head taller than Carr, she ushered him into one of the hotel's small conference rooms while the other two Surya cops handcuffed and carried Rhystok, still unconscious, out to the waiting police car.

The lieutenant tapped her cuff. "I have to make you aware that your responses are being recorded. Do you understand?"

Carr nodded.

"I need you to say yes," she said.

"Yes."

"You testify that the man who entered your hotel room this evening confessed to killing a government agent?"

"Detective Van," said Carr. "He worked for Genepol. His cuff is in the man's jacket pocket."

Jin looked disturbed. "The detective was last heard from nineteen hours ago. He informed us he had a civilian agent on Surya with an authorized police alert code. I assume that was you."

"Yes."

"The man we just arrested—did you know him?"

"Kaan Rhystok. Yes."

"Did you know he's a fugitive? The Terrans want him on charges of genetic crimes, fraud, and extortion."

"I know."

Jin tilted her chin, eyebrows rising under the fringe of her short, severely cut hair. "Why would Genepol involve *you*—a celebrity zeroboxer—as a civilian agent?"

Carr ignored the whiff of condescension. "Rhystok is a…fan of mine. He comes to a lot of my fights. The detective was sure he'd be here on Surya to watch the tournament."

Jin kept looking at Carr in a way that made him suspect she'd seen his face on a promotional holovid banner and was comparing him unfavorably to a more idealized image, one without the puffy bruises, shadow of stubble, or dark circles under the eyes. "What is the nature of your relationship to Kaan Rhystok, Mr. Luka?" she asked. "Why would he put himself at risk by using a police cuff to enter your room and confess his crimes?"

"I think," Carr said slowly, "that anything else I say should be to Genepol, with a lawyer in the room."

The lieutenant's expression grew tight. "I'll remind you that you are under Martian jurisdiction right now,

Mr. Luka. If a foreign policeman was killed on Surya, it is entirely *our* concern, and we expect your full cooperation."

The door opened and Bax Gant strode in with Uncle Polly. Carr's insides contorted, heart leaping and stomach dropping. Uncle Polly had the look of a man jolted from sleep by the apocalypse—wild-eyed and blank-faced as he tried to decide if what was happening was real. Seeing Carr gave him his answer; he stopped as if he'd walked into a wall. His cheeks and shoulders sagged as if air had been let out of them.

Gant planted his fists and leaned his weight on the top of the small table. He turned his head from the policewoman to Carr and back again. "Is one of my athletes under arrest?"

Officer Jin stiffened at the accusatory tone. "No, but—"

"Then that's all the questioning you're going to be doing tonight, officer."

"Under what authority—" The policewoman drew herself up and said something sharp and affronted to Gant in a Tharsian regional dialect. To Carr, it sounded like a pidgin of two or three Terran languages, and he guessed, from the way Gant's eyes narrowed, that it wasn't flattering.

"Check with your superiors," Gant said, unmoved. "Everyone from the ZGFA is here under special visiting-athlete status. If you intend to question Carr Luka in connection to a crime—which you haven't established yet, by the way—you'll need to clear it with the Terran embassy on Mars, and he has the right to a consular lawyer."

Jin glared. "None of you are permitted to leave Surya Station in the meantime."

"Wouldn't dream of it."

The lieutenant jabbed her cuff's recording off, turned sharply, and left the room.

Gant made sure the door was firmly closed before he rounded on Carr, thrusting an accusing finger. "Of all the guys on the team, you were the last one I expected to have to bail from the cops. What sort of mess have you gotten yourself into, Luka?"

"Bax," Uncle Polly said at once, stepping forward, "this isn't his fault."

"It's all right, coach," Carr said, putting a hand on Uncle Polly's shoulder and tugging him back. He faced Gant, not allowing himself to hesitate. "The man the cops took is named Kaan Rhystok. He's a criminal on the run from Terran law, and he killed the Genepol detective who followed him here. When I got to my room this evening, he was waiting inside to tell me about it."

Gant grimaced. "A crazy stalker fan?"

"Kind of. He's a splice dealer. Not the tabloid kind; he's got a high-end, organized gig that's been going on for a while. I'm a custom job of his, and as payout, he's been taking a cut of my winnings."

Carr had not dared to look at Uncle Polly, afraid doing so would make him lose his nerve completely, but now he heard his coach's soft, hissing intake of breath. It took a couple of additional seconds for Bax Gant's face to pale with understanding.

"You're enhanced." The Martian's throat bulged. He gripped the back of a chair. "In what way?"

"Reflexes, stamina, temperament, a little of this, a little of that," Carr said. "Nothing so crazy that it'd be suspicious."

"Just a notch better in everything," said Gant. "A perfect athlete."

Carr felt as though his words were falling from him like pebbles into a deep, dark crevasse. "When he told me, I was already on contract. You and Risha had sent me to Earth on tour. I was a title contender. I couldn't bring myself to throw everything away, and he knew it." He paused. "It's not an excuse, but it is what it is."

A long, silent minute passed. Then, voice shaded with irony and wonder, Gant said, "Earth's favorite athlete, the hero of Terran zeroboxing, is a custom splice job." A low chuckle escaped his lips. He tilted his head back and began to laugh, mirthlessly. Carr stood silent and stoic, but he felt hot and ill, his toes curling in shame. The Martian only shook his head and laughed louder.

"Are you out of your warped domie mind?" Uncle Polly's rough voice trembled. "How can you laugh at this?"

Gant wiped his eyes with the knuckles of his thumbs. "Warped? I'll tell you what's warped. If that crook had come to me with whatever gene recipe he used to make you"—he pointed at Carr—"I'd have ordered up another four or five zeroboxers from him. If it wasn't so goddamn *illegal*."

Carr risked a glance at his coach. A muscle in Uncle Polly's cheek was twitching. "I knew, Bax. I've known for a long time. If you're going to pin the blame for this on someone, pin it on me. It's ten times more my fault than it is Carr's."

"I don't give a rat's ass in space about your guilt right

now, Polly." Gant spun and started pacing across the small room. "I've got millions of people, dozens of sponsors, and an ungodly amount of money hanging on a tournament that's supposed to finish tomorrow. The media is already going to town over the Macha fight. I've got politicians on both Earth and Mars calling me. People are rioting. *Rioting*." Flecks of white spittle gathered at the corners of his mouth. "Can you imagine what's going to happen when you don't show up to fight tomorrow, and *this* comes to light instead? Can you?"

A nauseating weight sank into Carr's gut. Come morning, on the heels of the semifinal fiasco, Gant would announce that the ZGFA's star zeroboxer and *War of the Worlds* finalist had been suspended pending an investigation into his genetic legitimacy.

Everything would go absolutely fusion. Terrans would scream Martian conspiracy. Martians would seize upon Carr to prove the hypocrisy and underhandedness of Earth. Everyone in the solar system would be cheated out of the most highly anticipated tournament final in the history of zeroboxing, and pissed-off enough to make the previous twenty-four hours seem like a polite garden party.

Gant's eyes were wide and bright with the same awful premonitions. He stopped pacing and leaned his hands back on the table, his frame slumping. "This won't just ruin us, it'll ruin the ZGFA. Ruin the sport."

Carr opened his mouth, not even sure what he was going to say. Something about how he would do what he could to help, take all the blame and punishment needed, cooperate with Genepol and the Surya police. Before he could choke out the miserable words, the door slid open and all three of them turned toward it. Risha stepped into the room.

Something inside of Carr broke, melted into a relief so great he felt as though the room tilted.

"I'm sorry," she said quietly, as if apologizing for being late to a business meeting, but with a somberness that let the two words encompass far more. She shut the door behind her. She was in the clothes he'd last seen her in, and her beautiful face was tired and grave. For a second their eyes met, and he read in them something raw and tentative, enough to make his insides writhe with ache and his heart skip with hope.

Risha turned to Gant and Polly. "I found out myself yesterday. I got upset, and didn't think…" Her voice wavered and steadied. "Well, I'm here now."

"Fantastic," said Gant, with an unsympathetic glance. "You can help us figure out what to do about this disaster."

Risha pulled in a deep breath. "Nothing."

"Nothing?" Uncle Polly's sharp tone made it clear he was not about to forgive her so quickly. "That's a strategy?"

Risha's lips were pressed tightly together, but the gaze she turned on Gant was strong and certain. "Don't say anything. In fact, you don't *know* anything."

Gant's mouth twisted. "Nice try, but I won't get away with *that* line. This story is coming out, one way or another. A Terran cop was killed in Martian airspace, by a renegade gene splicer, who was just carried unconscious from Carr Luka's hotel room. You don't think Genepol, the

Martian authorities, and the media are going to descend like a Category Seven dust storm?"

Risha's face went still. She listened in quiet, growing dismay as they gave her the details. Then, shaking her head, she spoke. "It'll take time. At least a day for the Surya police to get in touch with the Terran embassy on Mars and to communicate with Genepol. Even more for the Martians and Terrans to sort out the full story between them. In the meantime, *War of the Worlds* has to go on."

Carr was nodding even before Risha finished; it had taken only a few minutes for her to strike the vein of truth, to steel his resolve. "I have to fight tomorrow. Doesn't matter if I win or lose—I have to show up."

Uncle Polly said, stern and sad, "You'll only make it worse for yourself."

Carr looked around the small room, at the people to whom he owed so much. "I need to go in there. I made a promise. I told a whole planet that I was fighting for them, representing them, that I would do everything I could to live up to that honor and responsibility." He swallowed, feeling as stripped as a naked wire, his soul laid bare and vulnerable. "Even if I can't ever do that... I can do this. I can give them what they want."

Gant's incredulity was sharp. "You've been fighting illegally all this time, and now you're asking me to let you do it again?"

"Yeah. I guess I am."

"Bax," Risha said, "we're in Martian airspace."

Gant went silent. Grim calculation spun in his eyes. "Huh," he said. "You're right about that."

"Why does it matter?" Uncle Polly asked.

"On Mars, there's strict control and oversight of genetic design, to ensure consistent adaptive traits," Risha explained. "Genetic enhancement is not explicitly banned under athletic rules because it's a non-issue. On Surya, there are no laws keeping Carr out of the Cube tomorrow."

Carr could almost hear the gears in Gant's head whirring. He looked at Carr the way he had once before, deciding whether to place a bet. This time: Fold or double down? Abandon course or stay at the helm?

"Great stars," the Martian finally murmured, half in disbelief, half in dark excitement. "We're actually going to ride this ship into the sun together, aren't we?"

Stay, then. For now.

Risha's gaze reached for Carr like a physical touch across the space between them. With a wrenching pang, he forgave her everything, even without wondering if she could do the same for him. Her voice changed, dropped. "I saw the semi-final fight … and then the news-feeds, and the riots … you were right, this is bigger than us. We set out to strike a chord with people, and we did. Now we have to own what we made. We have to finish the story we promised to tell."

"And afterward?" Uncle Polly asked quietly.

Inside of Carr, the sealed box had finally fallen open, spilling contents that were no longer sharp and poisonous, but dull and molten, mixing with the rest of him in a cloudy alloy. His smile was leaden. "One fight at a time, coach."

TWENTY-SIX

Risha commandeered the hotel conference room and set up an interplanetary link. By midday Surya time, Carr had released statements on his personal feed and the ZGFA official feed and done an exclusive interview with Enzo. Within minutes of being posted, the interview was picked up by *Cube Talk With Brock*, and from there it sped through the Systemnet like a nuclear reaction.

They'd crafted the message carefully. Carr talked about the semifinal fight; he stood by his conviction that Macha had cheated in the third round, but stated that he placed no blame on the WCC, and while he was going to file a complaint against Macha, he wasn't going to fight the judges' ruling. He thanked his fans for their outpouring of support, but strongly denounced the violence that had occurred and urged it to stop. He promised to do his best in the finals, expressed his respect for Kye Soard, and told everyone that win or lose, this would be his last fight for the indefinite future.

"Everything else can wait," Risha said. They were alone, finally. Uncle Polly had gone to check on the progress of the tournament and bring them both something to eat. Carr looked down at the last message on his cuff, sent by Enzo a few minutes ago: *Thanks for the interview. Good luck!! Your first and biggest fan, forever and no matter what.*

He dared to bring his hand up to Risha's face, then around her neck. When she didn't resist his touch, he pulled her to him, fiercely, and closed his mouth over hers with the desperate relief of a drowning man surfacing for air. She gave in, folding herself against him, and he closed his eyes, moving his hands through her hair and down her shoulder blades and waist, drawing comfort from her warm and familiar contours. He felt wetness on her cheeks and drew back, wiping away her tears with the pads of his thumbs.

"I'm sorry. And I'll understand if you don't stay," he said, though he wasn't certain he could keep such a promise. "Once we go back to Valtego, you have your own decisions to make."

Her chin quivered. "I almost left Surya, you know. For Mars, or Phobos, or Ceres—it didn't matter where. I thought I'd lost my career, the future I'd pictured with us together, everything. Then, even though I didn't want to, I watched your fight with Macha..." Anger lit her face as she touched the sealed gashes across his forehead with her fingertips. "And all I wanted was to be there. I should have been there."

"No," he said, putting a hand over her mouth. "You had every right not to be."

She drew his fingers away from her lips. "I called you a *lie*." Water gathered in the corners of her eyes. "You've been lied to. You lied in turn, to me and to others. But *you're* not a lie. You're the truest thing in my life. Even if I have to thank an unscrupulous splice dealer for what you are. You're still all the things I believed in and asked other people to believe in." She closed her eyes again for a moment, and when she opened them, they were steady. "I'm here because I love you, not because I forgive you. But I do—love you. Walking away … *that* would be the lie."

She leaned her head on his shoulder. Carr's throat was too clogged for him to reply, so he just held her, and kissed her on the eyes and lips and neck, and felt, for the first time, that maybe, just maybe, he could handle anything, even losing the tournament and being stripped of his titles and falling from the highest high to the lowest low, if Risha was there to hold him up.

They stepped away from each other when they heard the door opening. Uncle Polly came in. He looked away from their flushed faces and busied himself setting down a foil-wrapped vegetarian burrito for Risha and a pre-fight snack for Carr: a small bowl of whole-wheat pasta, a cup of yogurt, an apple. "That's all you're getting," he said. "It won't be long now."

"How's it going in the other divisions?"

"Story of the day is Adri. She pulled off the upset of the tournament and won the women's midmass."

"That's fantastic," said Carr, grinning widely for the first time in two days and being reminded of his facial bruises as he did so.

"That's the only bright spot, I'm afraid. Danyo put up a hell of a fight but ended up losing the final on points. Brut got knocked out in the semi, so it's two highmass Martians heading into the Cube now." He glanced at Carr and they shared the same thought. There wouldn't be another Terran men's champion to deflect any of the attention or pressure off Carr's fight. "Once they're done, there'll be a break. And then you're up."

Gant had worked some scheduling miracle to push the lowmass final to the end of the day, to give Carr and Risha enough time to do what they had to without sacrificing the few, badly needed hours of sleep Carr had snuck in earlier. Even so, Carr felt as though his body could use three weeks of rehab and daily nano injections. He'd always appreciated his ability to heal quickly, but one night was not enough, not even for him. Twisting his torso to the right brought on a painfully tight hitch in his left side. His face was still swollen, and he suspected a hard blow would open up his gashes again. When a WCC-appointed doctor had come by a few hours earlier to check up on him, he'd smiled through the whole range of movements and the doctor's prodding. "Feels fine," he'd lied. Uncle Polly grimaced behind the doctor's back but kept his mouth shut.

They ate in silence. Carr's jaw hurt; he chewed slowly.

The belly of a Martian passenger ship was gliding across the ceiling window of the hotel's conference room, cutting through their view of the Red Planet. He wondered if the cruiser carried new immigrants—Terrans who'd given up the natural bounty of Earth, who'd consented to permanently altering their genes and those of their descendants, all to start fresh on a frontier world. "We're so close to Mars," he mused. "Seems a shame I don't get to see it."

Risha put a hand on his arm. "Maybe you will. I've already gotten half a dozen interview requests from Martian media."

"You're kidding me."

A private car arrived to take them to the stadium. Security droids marked their progress all the way along the route to the gravity zone terminal, and when they'd passed the last set of them and were shooting through the freeway tube, Carr looked out and saw the enormous holovid figure of Kye Soard posed along one whole side of the exterior stadium wall. His receiver picked up the audio tag and Soard's cheerful, accented voice started up in his ear. "I'm Kye 'the Samurai' Soard, ready to defend Martian zeroboxing against all invaders!"

Carr grimaced, stabbing his cuff to mute the ad. The familiar transition to zero gravity tugged on his insides in a way that had not bothered him since he was a boy flying up to Xtreme Xero for the first time, watching his home recede into miniature, feeling terrified and exhilarated to be leaving the security of solid ground for a future anchored to nothing. "Talk to me, coach," he said.

"You know it all, Carr. You don't need me to yammer at you."

"Yeah, I do."

"All right," said Uncle Polly. "How are you going to stop Soard from pulverizing your legs, like he did to DK?"

"Keep moving, keep my legs under me, and crawl tight. Work my flying game and stay light on the walls."

"When you close, close *fast* and get deep into his range. How about his reversals?"

"Push him out into the center as much as I can, where he's slower. Cut the corners before he does."

Uncle Polly nodded. "You can run a corner as fast as he can. He's not going to be expecting that. He's going to be waiting for you to fade in the third round, and you're not going to do that either."

That was optimistic, Carr decided, since he was going into the match wounded and tired in a way he'd never gone into any fight before. But he kept talking, and answering everything Uncle Polly asked him, and the familiar high-octane verbal back-and-forth of their pre-fight drive was like a tether that a space walker might hang on to, and Risha's warm hand in his was his oxygen supply.

There were half a dozen security guards holding back a crowd that had gathered at the athletes' entrance for his arrival. As soon as he emerged, people started cheering and shouting questions all at once, and Carr found himself unable to even reach the guide-rails. In order to move himself forward he had to push off the crowd itself, as if it were a single amoeba-like organism covering the walls. When they got into the hallway, the guards blocked it off and he breathed easier as they made their way toward the locker room. Where the hall split, Risha leaned in to kiss him, briefly and softly, her hair drifting around both their faces like a breeze. "See you after," she whispered.

"See you after."

She drew away, the warmth of her fingers lingering on his jaw. He tried to memorize everything about her face, the sadness and the tenderness, her beauty and her strength. Then she turned toward the stadium, and he pulled himself through the entrance of the locker room.

Scull was waiting for him, with all his gear. Next to him, toes jammed under the stabilizing bar, was DK. When he saw Carr, he pushed himself up and the two of them regarded each other in silence. DK looked nearly as bad as Carr did, his face bruised, moving gingerly after yesterday. "Big fight," he said. "I wondered if you could use a second cornerman."

A thin smile crawled across Carr's face. "Yeah, I sure could."

He changed into his shorts, leaving his thermal top on. He drank a little water and took a long piss, nerves acting up in a way he almost welcomed. Scull wrapped his hands; DK helped him into his gripper shoes and gloves. As he warmed up, people began to arrive, and soon the locker room was full of his fellow zeroboxers: from the ones who hadn't made it through the first round of preliminaries to Adri, aglow with victory, and Danyo, his eyes dull from losing a hard-fought battle just a few hours ago. None of them said anything; they just gathered around as he got ready, heating the dry, motionless air of the locker room with his breaths. When the five-minute warning came down the hall, Carr pulled himself over to the bench and let his heart rate come down as Uncle Polly helped him out of his top and did a final check on his gloves and shoes.

He'd never been in a locker room that was so quiet before a fight. He remembered, all of a sudden, his first fights on Valtego, being ushered out to the Cube with a lot of pep talk and backslapping: *You're so ready, kid* and *Go get 'em* and *Make him float.* Rookie zeroboxers needed that kind of thing. That's how you pumped a guy up, sent a youngster out to battle. Had it really only been a few years ago for him? It felt like a lifetime. Now, with the camaraderie of old soldiers, there was a solemn, expectant respect in the nods and the whispered "good lucks" that piled around him as he pulled himself out toward the bright lights of the stadium.

He didn't shoot through the air and somersault to the deck in a flashy entrance. When he heard his name announced, he drifted out and caught the deck lightly, like a bird alighting. The stands were dark and full, the lights white and harsh, the air thick with the smell of ozone, beer, and the sweat of many bodies. Carr straightened and walked steadily on his grippers, straight to the center of the deck, where he motioned for the surprised announcer to hand him the microphone. He held up a hand to the crowd.

"I have something to say," he said, then repeated himself, more loudly. The roiling cheers and boos fell silent. The shadowy crowd rippled forward expectantly. "I have something to say to everyone here, and to everyone else who's watching, whether you're on Earth or Mars, or a Moon settlement or a city-station." He heard his voice magnified and echoing back to him disembodied, not sounding like his own at all. He turned in a slow circle, looking out across the tiers of seating, recognizing sections as unmistakably Terran by the huge waving placards of his own bloodied, resolute image. *UNBROKEN*. So many of them.

"I've always said that I'm proud to be Terran. But yesterday, a lot of people were hurt and a lot of things were destroyed because people are looking for something in this tournament that has nothing to do with zeroboxing. I'm one man, here to compete against another ... not because I think I'm better than him, but because we're both trying to be the best we can be, and the other person can make us better. That's how you find out if you have the guts to give everything, to respect the other guy and come back to fight another day."

They were listening; Carr could even hear the Cube fans whirring. "The real spirit of the Cube isn't about winning against an opponent," he continued, "but winning against yourself. Whether you're Terran or Martian, cheering for me or for Kye, just please ... remember that."

He handed the microphone back to the announcer. There was a lingering moment of collective silence, and then the noise started up: a wave of murmuring conversation, turning into applause, climbing into alternating, blending chants of "LU-KA! LU-KA!" and "SO-ARD! SO-ARD!" Across the deck, Kye Soard was regarding Carr with a baffled but grudgingly respectful expression. At the referee's call, he came up and they stood before each other.

"Yesterday," Soard said, "what Macha did. It was a disgrace to Martian zeroboxers. I am sorry for it. I will beat you, how do you say on Earth? Fair and square."

Carr extended his glove and the Samurai touched it with his own. He sauntered away, lean and graceful as a panther. He looked healthy and rested and confident. He looked like a champion.

Carr went back to his side. The technician checked his optics and receiver. Scull put in his mouth guard. DK spread gel on his face. Carr said, "Thanks," and hoped they both understood he meant it to mean more.

DK put his battered face up to Carr's. "Just so you're clear," he said, "this doesn't mean I like you. As much as I hate to admit it, behind the pretty face and the marketing machine, you really are the best of us. You're the only one who can beat him." A spark danced in his round brown eyes and his teeth flashed in a wide, cheerfully vengeful smile that made Carr think, *the Captain is going to be just fine*. DK clapped Carr on the back. "Now go to it."

The hatch flashed red and Carr dove through. The Cube swallowed him, abruptly cutting his perception of everything outside to a distant, blurry presence. He closed his eyes for a second and free-floated, knowing exactly where he was, bounded by the six clear sides that defined his world. Without conscious thought, he reached above his head and landed lightly on the nearest wall. His senses were sharp, his body coiled, but he felt as calm as a deep, still lake.

He had only one thing left to prove. He might have been designed and conceived to serve another man's ambition, raised and trained under a lie, marketed and attached to causes beyond reason, but here, in this prism, he was only himself. There was truth to him—for three rounds of six Martian minutes each, there was nothing else.

Kye Soard came at him with shocking speed. Carr leapt, striking Soard in the air like his namesake, a bird of prey dropping onto a rival, feet and fists hailing down damage like talons and beating wings. Soard braced one leg and one arm to the first surface he reached, and, with the other arm, hurled Carr like a sack of flour. Carr felt his ribs jolt painfully as he struck the Cube, but he tucked his legs in time to use the rebound, powering off the wall and toward the spot where Soard was supposed to be but was no longer. A whip-like sweep to his legs nearly sent him spinning, but he grabbed the Martian fighter's arm, dragging him into the rotation and preventing him from racing up and around the corner.

Mere seconds into the first round, and Carr knew the idea of pacing himself was moot. Soard was too fast, too good, too instinctive. They fought, back and forth, up and down, in the air and on the walls and across the corners. For everything that Carr did, the Samurai had a response. Each strike was answered by a faster strike, each movement by an opposing movement, each change of direction matched and raised. The air sang with the fight. Time and space carved around it. They were escalating, both of them striving to outmaneuver the other with greater strength, speed, and agility. It would look, to a spectator, like a video being sped up.

Soard kicked him with so much force that his body flew backward, and he lost his grip on the surface completely. The breath went out of him as his torso lit with pain, but he grabbed for the wall with both hands and skidded along like a falling climber dragging at the sheer surface of a cliff. With only the strength of his arms and shoulders, he checked his momentum and hurled himself back before Soard could get out of the way. They clinched and landed close-in blows.

"Lock him up! Don't let him go!" Was that Uncle Polly's voice or his own thought? Too late; Soard spun out of his grasp before he could secure a hold and nailed him hard in the side. The man's shin crunched into him like a long, blunt iron blade; Carr felt his insides take the shock like a bowl of jelly. Under gravity, he would have crumpled to his knees. He could barely feel or move anything below his sternum, but he dug in his feet and swung anyways, slipping a fist through Soard's guard and cracking him solidly across the cheek. The bell sounded.

Carr pulled himself back out to the deck. "He's really good," he conceded, holding his sides.

DK dug out his mouth guard and gave him a squeeze of water. Scull pressed ice to his face and neck. The two of them exchanged a glance of mute astonishment. Scull said, "That was the hardest-fought first round I've ever seen. Coaches are going to make future zeroboxers study it."

Carr was slicked with sweat and sucking hard breaths

that made his head throb. He couldn't remember ever feeling like this after a first round. He could hear the ventilation fans in the Cube working like mad to move out the air heated by their exertion. Uncle Polly bent in front of him and cupped his hands behind Carr's head, pacing several long, deep inhalations until Carr's breaths followed his.

Polly nodded. "You've got his attention all right." His rapid-fire voice was low and serious. "The two of you are burning like hyper-charged atoms in there. Don't get fired up so hot that you get shoddy with defense, you hear? If he decides he can't wear you down, he'll start taking bigger risks to try to end it quickly. Pare it back, start looking for openings."

Carr paused just before entering the Cube. Something seemed strange. The mostly Martian crowd, which had been chanting Soard's name nonstop, was nearly silent. It was as if these people, who'd paid good money for the pleasure of watching men fight, had come to some collective realization that they were witnessing something extraordinary. The pinnacle of zeroboxing, the very frontier of what human beings could physically accomplish in a weightless chamber.

The bell rang on the opening of the second round. Carr dove through the hatch and Soard was on him again, right from the start. For all his jovial arrogance outside the Cube, the man was a silent, focused machine inside. He didn't waste time; he didn't waste movement. He started attacking Carr's legs as he'd done with DK. It was a sound strategy—striking required bracing, and that meant legs were often planted, immobile and vulnerable. Soard's own legs were long and bony, the shins tempered to steel, and he could whip them around with astounding swiftness. Carr found himself fighting like a mongoose on a snake, crouching tight to walls, striking, leaping out of the way of the taller man's range, cutting angles, all the time moving and seeking chances to close in.

Something in the first round—probably many things, come to think of it—had made the painful tightness in his left side worse. Every time he twisted his shoulders toward the right, he felt a sharp stab. It was impossible to fight without rotating his torso, so he didn't even bother trying, resolving to ignore the pain outright. Soard, however, sensed the weakness like a shark scenting a single drop of blood. He started aiming for the left side of Carr's rib cage. Gasping, Carr let his arms drift up, opening his bruised body as an irresistible target. Soard went for the ribs again. This time, Carr slid forward, captured the incoming blow, and drove his shoulder forward. His screaming body slammed hard into Soard's chest, stunning him long enough for Carr to wrap arms and legs around his opponent's limbs as they both spun in a free-fall grapple.

He was impressed and dismayed that the man was as swift and competent in his grappling as he was on the walls and in the air. He went for a choke and Soard neutralized it, flowing straight into an armbar attempt. Carr distracted him by punching him in the liver, then tried the choke again, but Soard worked one knee free of Carr's restraining leg and drove it up into his side. Carr felt his grip give but he held on, trying to get his legs up and around the man's waist to take forward control.

He didn't make it. They hit the wall, its magnetics tugging at both their waists. Soard was better positioned to capitalize on the direction of their spin; he rolled along the surface and, in a seamless reversal, trapped Carr's left leg in a submission hold. He began levering the knee at an unnatural angle.

Carr would have to tap out or watch the joint pop from its socket. In a desperate move, he slammed his body back against the wall and the rebound jolted Soard's grip and Carr's spine. Pressure shot up his thigh as he used the split-second of slack to twist his hips hard and force his leg free. He kicked back with the other, catching Soard in the clavicle. They climbed away from each other, both grimacing, and that was how the second round ended.

Out on the deck, Uncle Polly probed his knee and Carr jerked, wincing. Then a chuckle bubbled from his lips and he started grinning like a maniac.

"What's so damn funny?" Uncle Polly asked.

"Nothing." It was just that, in some truly messed-up way, he was grateful to Kye Soard. He'd finally found an opponent he didn't think he could beat. Every fight he'd ever fought—including his one loss to Jackson, his match against Henri Manon for the title, and the bout against that cheat Macha—he'd known, deep down, that he could beat them. Whether he actually would or not might have been in question, but he'd always felt that the fight was his to lose. Soard, he didn't think he could beat. The Samurai was an outlier even in an engineered race. Carr doubted any Terran could defeat him.

But Carr was not any Terran.

He was pushing against the envelope of his enhancement. His heart rate and breathing were actually slowing, kicking into some hyper-efficient state. He could see the movement of every mote of dust in the spotlight-drenched air. He could hear someone in one of the cubeside seats going *tap-tap* on their cuff. The pain in his side and his knee were receding fast, as if the injuries were being compartmentalized and shunted away.

The doctor came and examined his leg. "Hmmm," he said, "not good."

Carr noticed, all of a sudden, that there were police officers on the deck. Not the stadium security guards, but uniformed Surya cops, three of them, standing near the entrance and holding themselves stiffly upright on magnetic-soled boots. He recognized the lieutenant from last night, Jin. She looked across the deck at him, her gaze cold and curious.

"If you can pull him, I'd say do it," the doctor was telling Uncle Polly. "If that knee blows out, it could end his career."

Carr shook his head vehemently and tugged his coach down by the front of his shirt. "I don't have a career."

Uncle Polly's glare was pained and fierce. "No fight is worth seeing you crippled. You can't ask me to do what no trainer—"

Carr cut him off. "What are those cops doing here?"

Polly made a face, like he hadn't wanted Carr to notice.

He dropped his voice. "They showed up a few minutes ago. They've found the detective's body. Or what was left of it. Gant says there's a tug-of-war going on now between Gene- pol, who wants Rhystok extradited to face Terran criminal charges, and the Surya authorities, who've charged him with murder in Martian airspace. You're a key witness, and I think they suspect you're more than that too. They're not taking any chances on you rabbiting out of here after the tournament."

A WCC official came up to them. "I need a decision here."

Carr stood. He wasn't sure his leg would hold up his weight if gravity were involved. "This can't be the way it ends, coach. Pulling out can't be the last thing I do in the Cube." DK and Scull were staring, bewildered, between him and Polly, but Carr plowed on. "Like Blake said: sometimes you can't win, but you can decide not to lose."

He went back into the Cube.

Soard was not smiling now. His mouth was set in hard resolve, and his eyes held a hint of uncertainty. Carr real- ized, with some irritation, that the Martian champion had never, not for one second, not until now, seriously enter- tained the idea that he might lose to an earth-born Terran.

"All right, have it your way," Uncle Polly said softly in his ear. "You want to fight, then *fight*. Take it to him. Make it *your* fight."

Carr sent himself into the air in a tight somersault and uncoiled, springing across the right angle of the Cube with his good leg, and down on Soard from behind and above.

The man dropped to the wall and shot out a kick from a crouch, connecting with Carr while he was still in the air and sending him flying. Carr launched off the rebound, but his injured leg altered the angle of his flight and he went sailing past his intended target. The Samurai made a grab for him; Carr swiveled his body away narrowly and landed in a crouch.

Soard flung himself across a steep angle, attacking Carr from the left. Carr felt time elongate. He had to decide: which would it be? He shifted his stance to protect the knee; Soard dropped a blow onto the body. As the punch connected, Carr pushed up onto the toe of his good leg; the impact buckled his midsection and knocked him into the air, but that was better than absorbing the full force with his battered rib cage. As it was, one side of his torso had gone completely numb. He reoriented and found his footing. Soard came after him again and they clinched. He felt the other man's breath, his sweat, the straining of his body. They jammed up each other's attacks, then flung apart again.

They faced each other across a corner. Soard relaxed a little. Carr sensed it in the set of his shoulders, the way they came down just a fraction. It was obvious that Carr couldn't move the way he used to, couldn't rely on his left leg to strike or climb, couldn't get full range of motion from his body. All Soard needed to do was pick him apart for the rest of the round and count on a win from the judges.

Carr's mouth was dry. The fight seemed infinite, yet he was running out of time. His knee throbbed, not with pain but with a kind of frantic, pulsing heat, as if it were trying to repair itself, but not fast enough. With his mobility down, he needed to fight from close in. Minimize the handicap of his slow leg. Grab his opponent and hold him. There was no way Soard would let him do that, not if he was being smart.

His opponent flowed toward and around him like a riptide. They clashed again, and Carr, his breath roaring in his ears, began to feel that it wasn't enough; what he had wasn't enough.

Soard relied on his endurance. He waited until he saw Kabitain start to tire, then just closed in and swarmed him. That's what Jeroan Culver had said.

Carr let himself sag a little. It wasn't hard, he wasn't even feigning. He steadied himself and went after Soard with a few heavy-handed punches. Soard hit him in the side and he let out a very real grunt of pain, putting his hands up in weak defense. The man clocked him across the ear. Carr's head rang like a bell and he swayed on his grippers. Two more unanswered blows to the head, and Soard eased into his final victory stretch. His face slackened with confidence, his long limbs loosened, and he went to work, backing Carr into a corner and punishing him steadily.

"Carr!" Uncle Polly shouted. "DEFENSE! Get the hell out!"

No. I know what I'm doing; this is the only way.

A stinging sensation spread across his forehead. His gashes had split back open. Wet warmth jellied over his brow, red droplets scattering into the air and across his eyes. The crowd had started to roar, sensing finality. Carr saw the next blow fly toward him in slow motion and slipped it. There. There was his opening. He dug in his feet and slammed a fist into the spot where Soard's chest and arm connected, sending the man's upper body into a rotation. Carr saw his opponent's back come into view and threw himself across the broad shoulders, right arm wrapping around the neck, left arm locking it into place.

He almost got it, the perfect chokehold. Almost. Soard managed to turn his head and slide a hand in next to his throat. Carr squeezed anyways; it was the best hold he'd gotten so far, and he was out of time. Soard's eyes bulged, but he tucked his free left arm into a chicken wing and drove the elbow into Carr's injured side.

Carr's rib cage contracted with concussive red pain. His grip started to wilt and he fought off the weakness, redoubling his effort and squeezing down harder on his choke. He didn't have the windpipe, but he could still cut off blood to the man's brain, make him pass out. The Martian fighter hit him again and Carr heard his own sucking gasp. A third blow. A fourth.

Desperation and urgency coursed through both of them. They were locked together in some primal stalemate, like two prehistoric beasts rending each other even as they sank together into the tar pit. The edges of Carr's vision blurred; the Cube walls seemed to be shrinking and receding at the same time. He imagined he was tightening a screw, and every bit of his own hurt was another notch. He wouldn't stop. His ribs would turn to powder and he would pass out before he stopped.

Kye Soard tapped.

He tapped, again, frantically, before the signal reached Carr's brain.

Carr let go. He fell away, oblivious to which direction he drifted, unaware of where the walls were. His shoulder bumped against a surface and he pawed at it weakly. In his ear, he could hear Uncle Polly shouting as if from a very vast distance, but it was unintelligible. He put his hands and feet on the wall and laid his cheek against the Cube. It was cool and bumpy against his skin, humming with fans and magnetics, its microgravity tug like a gentle and welcome embrace. Like putting his ear up to a seashell. He felt transported.

In a corner of his brain, Carr knew he'd won. He didn't want to get up and shout his victory to the heavens. He didn't want to do a triumphant lap around the Cube, or raise his arms to the crowd, or somersault through the air in jubilation. He wanted to lie here with his face against the wall and feel relief. And joy. And sadness.

The referee came up to him and said, "Can you get up? Do you need a doctor?" He let himself be pulled off the wall and toward the hatch. Everyone was there, crowded on the deck. Uncle Polly, Bax Gant, DK, Scull, Adri and the rest of the team, and Risha. Poor Risha, crying. They stared at him in silent awe, no one moving. Then they surrounded him, all at once, and lifted him. In the crush, he said, "Risha," and held out his hand, and the warmth of her fingers slipped into his.

He started shivering, and they put towels on him, and a heated top, and wiped the blood from his face and gave him water, and through it all, the crowd, the immense crowd of thousands, was silent.

Finally, they helped him to the center of the deck, where the referee and Kye Soard stood. The Martian put a hand to his bruised neck and looked at Carr as if seeing him for the first time. "The old planet delivers surprises, after all," he said. Shock and bitter admiration crawled up his sweat-slicked face. "You're wasting your time on Valtego. You should be fighting in the Martian system, my friend, though I hope you never do."

Carr extended his hands, right crossed over left, and they shook. The referee raised Carr's arm, and the Terran sections of the stadium lit up with delirious screams of elation. Then, slowly, the rest of the stadium began clapping. Grudgingly at first, then louder, then cheering and standing up and drifting out of their seats. Over by the entrance, even Officer Jin and the cops were applauding.

Carr didn't cry, though his heart ached, for he knew that what he'd once dreamed to be his future had already come and gone. He had no dreams for tomorrow, not yet. The truth of him would emerge, slowly, in the days and months to come, and he couldn't imagine what would become of him, what would be said about him, and what he would mean, in the end, to everyone who'd ever looked to him for meaning. But he knew he would always remember and be remembered, for this moment, and for others like it, raw and honest.

He felt free.

Acknowledgments

The fighter climbs into the ring alone, but it takes many people to get him or her to that moment, and an entire team is working just behind the ropes. So it is with authors.

Thank you to the team at Flux for getting behind *Zeroboxer* and shepherding it into the world. My editor, Brian Farrey-Latz, loved the story immediately, even though, as he admitted to me, he never thought he'd be "bouncing up and down in his chair over an MMA book." Brian, thank you for backing me and Carr all the way, and for your consistently insightful editorial guidance. Thank you to Kevin Brown for designing a stunning cover, and to Alisha Bjorklund, Mallory Hayes, Steffani Sawyer, and Sandy Sullivan for taking care of *Zeroboxer* every step of the way.

My seemingly unflappable agent, Jim McCarthy, is a source of encouragement and humor, a prompt answerer of endless questions, and a hell of a man for an author to have in her corner. Thank you Jim.

Thank you to early readers Vanessa MacLellan, Holly Westlund, Sarah Wong, Eloise Doubleday, Mukund Raguram, Marie Fernandez, Kyle Schiller, Susan DeFreitas, Linda Epstein, and Jessica Morrell for helping me to hone this story. The Fearless Fifteeners, the Class of 2K15, the community of young adult and speculative fiction writers in Portland, and my martial arts friends have been invaluable sources of support and encouragement. There are too many people to name here, but thank you all.

Thank you to my husband, Nathan, and my two children,

for being understanding of all the hours I spent ensconced in front of my computer, my mind off in orbit. Remarkably, my family, in particular my parents and in-laws, never questioned my decision to turn from a perfectly respectable and well-paying career in corporate strategy to writing science fiction and fantasy novels. Regardless of my own bouts of doubt and angst, their faith and enthusiasm never faltered. For that, I am profoundly grateful.

About the Author

Fonda Lee was born and raised in Canada, spent years as a corporate strategist for Fortune 500 companies, and is now a writer and black belt martial artist living in Portland, Oregon. Visit www.fondalee.com or follow Fonda on Twitter @fondajlee.